BENEDICT

XVI

Paul Wiebe

KOMOS BOOKS
UPLAND, CA

A Komos Book
Copyright © 2002 by Paul Wiebe

An earlier edition was published by Writers Club Press, 2000.
ISBN: 0-595-09513-5

Printed in the United States of America on acid-free paper.

Publisher's Cataloging-in-Publication
(Provided by Quality Books, Inc.)

Wiebe, Paul, 1938-
    Benedict XVI / Paul Wiebe.
    p. cm.
    LCCN 2002091238
    ISBN 0-9718599-0-6 (Paper)

    1.   Popes—Fiction. 2. Amish—Fiction. I. Title.

PS3623.I433B46 2002   813'.6
                              QBI33-876

Cover art and design by Stan Waling.

KƆ
Komos Books
991 Saint Andrews Drive, Ste. 138
Upland, CA 91784
komosbooks.com

This is for Charlotte and Erika,
delights both,
who make me wonder how such different peas
could come from the same
marvelous pod.

And if I laugh at any mortal thing,
'Tis that I may not weep.

—Lord Byron, *Don Juan*

Contents

BENEDICT

XVI

1

Enter Benny, Stage Left

AT THE VATICAN, the pope was sound asleep, having four hours earlier mumbled the simple benediction he had learned as a child. In New York City, the anchors at the major networks were preparing to sign off after reading the news of the most ingenious and entertaining samples of human depravity that had appeared in the last twenty-four hours. In Las Vegas, thousands of American parents were busy initiating their offspring into the deepest mysteries of the nation's folklore. At a race track in Southern California, eight sleek thoroughbreds were pounding the turf and coming down the home stretch as the spectators either clutched their tickets in anxiously sweating hands or, resigned to their temporary fate, began to destroy those tokens of hope.

And in the Kansas metropolis of Kirkland, not its real name, two men were preparing for a meeting that would launch a chain of events that was destined to have profound consequences both for America and for the largest and most powerful ecclesiastical organization in all Christendom. Unaware as yet of his significance in the grand scheme of things, the older of the two ambled down a nondescript hall toward an unexceptional office at the rear of an unimposing tan cinder block building standing at the foot of an ordinary radio transmitter at the outskirts of this typical Middle-American city.

"Sit down," said Dennis Bright as large, unkempt Benny Good sauntered into his office.

Benny squeezed himself into the chair across the desk from his smallish, kempt boss, who was dressed in a new Sears suit, a new Sears shirt, and a new Sears tie, a uniform designed to highlight a generic male managerial face still on the pleasant side of forty.

Bright strummed his fingers on the desk. He adjusted his glasses. He cleared his throat. He inserted an index finger under the collar of his new Sears shirt and straightened his new Sears tie. He took a deep breath. He exhaled, slowly but audibly. "Benny," he began. "This is not working out."

"It's only been a month," said Benny.

Bright wagged his head sadly. "The numbers just aren't there."

"One. Incredible. Month," said Benny.

Bright sighed. "'Benny's Begonias' is not the blockbuster we projected."

"One month of lively discussion of the delights of indoor gardening!" said Benny, growing eloquent.

Dennis Bright frowned as he tilted back in his chair and placed five pairs of interlocking digits behind his head. "Listen, Benny," he said to the older man, "I hate to tell you this, but."

Benny carefully placed a foot on Bright's desktop. That foot was fitted with a sandal. Between the sandal and a pair of wrinkled shorts stretched an expanse of hairy, well-fed leg. Between the shorts and a soiled T-shirt stretched an expanse of equally hairy, equally well-fed abdomen. The T-shirt bore the insignia of KKKS ("First in Alternative Programming for the Kirkland Listening Area") and a pocketful of cigars (Swisher Sweets). Above this T-shirt rose a head that had frequently invited comparisons to the head of Larry Flynt—it had the same broad features, the same rugged handsomeness, the same wavy hair; some of

Benny's old colleagues used to take pleasure in observing that the glint in his eye also bore an uncanny similarity to that of the king of porn, though others took equal pleasure in protesting that Benny was cut from somewhat nobler cloth.

"I had five call-ins today," said Benny in an attempt to shift the conversation in a more promising direction.

"Two were from your regular listener," Bright pointed out.

"She's very knowledgeable about plants," countered Benny.

"Why shouldn't she be? She runs a nursery."

"Actually, she's retired from the business. The stress got to her. Probably from watching the plants grow."

Dennis Bright smiled in spite of himself. But then he remembered his responsibilities as the KKKS program director and recovered his dignity. "One was from Shannon," he pointed out.

"She asks very intelligent questions."

"That's because you tell her what to ask."

"It's not just *what* she asks, it's how she asks it. Her phrasing is impeccable."

"Her phrasing may be great, or whatever, but the woman doesn't know a tulip from a cactus. I oughtta know. Ten years I've lived with her."

"Aha!" said Benny as he placed a second foot on the desk. "So *that's* where she picked up her impeccable phrasing."

Bright ignored this remark, but not the foot, which was dangerously near his coffee cup. He stared at the encroaching sandal. "One was a wrong number," he pointed out with a warning frown.

Benny carefully relocated his sandal to a site several millimeters away from the cup. "Did you notice how curious she became about begonias? I think we can expect to hear a lot more from that young woman."

"One was from an Alzheimer," Bright pointed out. He could be hardnosed. That was part of his job. He liked his job. It allowed him to show the ruthless side of his personality. It also paid reasonably well. It kept the wolf from the door, his wife

Shannon in the less expensive varieties of French wine, and the Sears men's wear department in business.

"Did I or did I not have fun with her?" asked Benny.

"You had fun with her," admitted Bright. "But," he added, "you gotta wonder how well it went over with your regular listener. I don't think we can expect to hear a lot more from that old lady."

"She must like my act or she wouldn't keep calling."

Bright removed his coffee cup from the danger zone and took a long sip. "Listen, Benny," he finally said. "The issue is not whether you got the gift. That's not what I'm trying to say."

"What *are* you trying to say, Dennis? Speak up, lad. Don't be shy."

Bright prepared his reply by emitting another sigh. "What I'm trying to tell you is, the numbers are not there. That's the bottom line. The numbers. Are simply. Not. There."

Benny tilted his head back. He closed his eyes as if in deep thought. He eventually broke the silence. "Maybe if we came up with a new format."

"A new format."

"Impeccable phrasing, Dennis. 'A new format.'" Benny paused long enough to unwrap a cigar and plant one end between his teeth. The other end began to describe circles in the air as he plunged into virgin territory. "Here's how we do it. I call numbers at random, ask them if they can define the word *begonia*, send them scampering to their dictionaries, arouse their curiosity about the wonders of nature, suggest that they call several of their closest friends and start an indoor gardening club, invite this expanding network of plant-lovers down to the station, show them around the premises, take them over to meet our sponsor, and in no time at all 'Benny's Begonias' is the talk of Kirkland and the bottom line is decorated with the color black and the Kingdom of God has been reconstituted on a capitalist basis."

"Numbers do not like being called at random," observed Bright. He was busy scribbling on his writing pad.

"You scored a point, Dennis." Benny gestured toward the pad with his unlit cigar. "What's the score by now?"

Bright consulted his pad. "The score is five to one in favor of management, who's sitting here checking the numbers, which at this point in time are simply not there." He glanced up at Benny, who had returned the cigar to its natural position between his teeth. "The one thing in your favor is the fact that you got the gift." He looked back down at his pad and frowned and began to sketch the outline of what appeared to be an evergreen. "The question is, finding the tree to put it under."

Benny consulted his fingernails. He might have been thinking, That's a very good question. Or, That's the story of my life. Or perhaps, When was the last time I cleaned my nails? Possibly even, Would this be a good time to light the cigar? The one thing certain is that he wasn't just being modest.

Bright's chair became untilted. "Come back tomorrow with an idea," he said. "A halfway decent idea wins you a one-hour slot and maybe a little extra pocket money." He placed his elbows on the desk and cupped his chin within his two sets of knuckles and gazed at his employee, following the instructions on page 127 of *The Personnel Manager's Manual.*

Benny removed his feet from the desk, following his instincts. "What about two ideas?"

"Sure. Give me a choice."

Benny removed the cigar from between his teeth and gazed at it thoughtfully. "Think you could handle a dozen?"

Dennis Bright consulted his appointment calendar. "My schedule only allows for a lunch hour." He looked up. "Tell you what, Benny. Hold it to two ideas and everybody goes home happy. Okay?" He flashed a facsimile of a smile.

Benny stood up and stretched. "Great," he agreed with a yawn. Then he saluted, clicked his heels, did an abrupt about-face, and ambled out of Bright's office.

§

Benny Good had enjoyed a long and distinguished career as a truck driver. He had roamed the interstate highway system of America, transported a wide selection of its products from east to west and back again, eaten in a high percentage of its better truck stops, made the acquaintance of many of its friendliest truck stop waitresses, and talked his way out of more than his share of speeding tickets.

If, a short month ago, he had been asked to reflect on his life, Benny would have said that he had found happiness in his chosen profession. There were times when he missed Lucy, of course, but in his view the bliss of married life was overestimated by a small but vocal minority of the American public. Besides, he enjoyed the camaraderie of the other truckers, and the truck stop waitresses more than made up for the slight hole he felt in what may or may not have been a heart. As for the long hours he spent in the cab, they were not always solitary. There was of course the radio, with the country music and the talk shows that provide a trucker's main source of entertainment. But there were also the occasional waifs who would accept his invitation to use his cab as a temporary home away from home.

The single drawback to this life was the fear faced by all male truckers, the fear that month after month of bouncing across America in a sitting position might lead to impotence. This fear had played some part in his decision to start a new chapter in his life, a larger part being played by the loss of his Peterbilt on a bet during his last run across Kansas. Fortunately, he happened to hear KKKS advertise for a qualified voice to host a radio talk show devoted to indoor gardening. He stopped in at a used Kirkland bookstore, rummaged through the stacks, strolled out the door with a book on the art of indoor gardening tucked away in his shorts, became an overnight expert, and called the station next morning to set up an interview.

Dennis Bright hired him on the spot. "You got the gift," said Bright, shaking his head in amazement and relieved that somebody had finally answered his ad.

§

"I'll have what he's having," Benny informed the waitress.

The waitress cast a gaze in Dennis Bright's direction and quizzically lifted a well-penciled eyebrow and wondered aloud what he was having. Bright, after some reflection, said he was having the small shrimp salad with French dressing and a cup of decaf.

Benny frowned and announced that he was reconsidering. He would begin with the large turkey salad (Italian dressing), accompanied by a milk shake (chocolate). From there he would move on to the large sirloin (rare). He would finish with the apple pie, topped off with a generous portion of ice cream (tutti frutti, if possible; if not, strawberry). He also suggested that the waitress put a bottle of bubbles on ice, explaining that he and his friend were there to celebrate a great moment.

"We're not allowed to serve alcoholic beverages," said the waitress, as if repeating a mantra. "Kansas law."

Benny feigned disbelief. "What? The State of Kansas discourages the celebration of great moments?"

The waitress ignored this question, glumly plucked the menus from their hands, and shuffled off with their orders.

Bright got right to the point. "Idea number one," he began.

"Idea number one. Benny does the news."

Bright shook his head. "John already does the news."

Benny crossed his arms and assumed a Buddha-like calm. "The news, as John delivers it, produces insight and knowledge, and tends to calm, wisdom, enlightenment, and Nirvana." Then he went into a manic frenzy: "The news, as Benny delivers it, produces smiles and laughter, and tends to delight, folly, skepticism, and riotous living."

Bright stared at his employee. "God, Benny, where do you come up with that stuff?"

"You're forgetting, Dennis, that I am an educated man. I know a thing or two about wisdom and enlightenment and Nirvana. I once took a course in World Religions."

This was true, up to a point. At one time early in his adult life, when he was between employment opportunities, Benny had enrolled in an institution of higher learning, where he had signed up for an evening class in World Religions. He had stayed the course until the first machine-graded exam, after which he concluded that he could do a better job of improving his mind than any community college in the State of Arkansas. So he returned to the trucking life, borrowing books from libraries and bookstores and supermarkets and devouring them during those moments when he wasn't driving or eating or entertaining waitresses and waifs.

Bright took a quick peek at his watch. "And that's idea number one?" he asked, referring to Benny's offer to do the news.

"That's idea number one. Would you like a sample?"

"We're going with number two."

"What's wrong with number one?"

"I just told you. John already does the news."

"So? We switch shows. I do the news, our young, handsome friend does 'John's Jonquils.' The ratings for the evening news skyrocket, the ratings for the gardening show remain at their present modest level. A net gain."

"You're forgetting one thing."

Benny nodded wisely. "Ah yes. John is allergic to plants."

"That's probably true, but it's beside the point."

"Which is?"

"Which is, John's father-in-law owns the damn station. The old man wants his son-in-law in that particular slot."

"Because he can read."

"That's part of it."

"The other part being, reading's about the only thing he can do."

"You said it. I didn't."

Benny thought for a moment. Then, "Are John and What's-her-name happily married?"

"Forget it. She's a bitch. Idea number two."

Benny groaned, either because his heart had been set on doing the news or because his literate colleague's wife, though attractive, was a bitch. "Idea number two. 'Truck Talk.'"

"'Truck Talk'?" Bright was drawing a blank.

Benny explained. "There's this radio program called 'Car Talk.' Maybe you've heard of it."

"Can't say that I have. What's the hook?"

"A couple of crazies field questions from motorists who want to know why their vehicles make strange sounds."

"Yeah?" Bright's curiosity was aroused. "You know, my Infiniti has been—"

"Unfortunately," Benny interrupted, "they never get around to explaining the strange sounds."

"You mean those guys don't answer the questions?"

"Right. We the people, who have a sacred right to know, are never informed."

"So what's the point?"

"The point is to produce smiles and laughter, which tend to delight, folly, cynicism, and riotous driving."

A dim light went on in Bright's eyes. "Now, why does that sound familiar?"

"Because I took this course called 'World Religions,'" Benny reminded him.

"So we're back to World Religions."

"These things go in cycles. Did you ever notice, Dennis—may I call you by your Christian name? no?—did you ever notice, Mr. Bright, that these things tend to go in cycles? The correct answer is Yes."

"Yes," said Mr. Bright.

"An excellent answer. And have you ever wondered why these things go in cycles?"

"Listen, Benny, I haven't got all day."

The waitress came and distributed food. She removed a greasy tab from her apron pocket and placed it midway between her two customers. She left. The two customers eyed the tab warily. Benny chose this moment to resume their conversation.

"These things go in cycles because the universe itself goes in cycles. If I remember correctly, that was the main point of the course. The professor explained that the universe, vast though it is, occupies a limited amount of space. So if it wishes to move around, it has no other option than to go in cycles. Being restless by nature, the universe is always on the go. Therefore, cycles. In case you're wondering, I believe he got that bit of information from a book."

"All I can say is, he must've read a lot."

"He was a major-league reader," agreed Benny as his fork attacked a large chunk of turkey. "I believe he had a degree in Hinduism." Benny transferred the turkey to his mouth. "Or maybe it was Buddhism." Benny chewed thoughtfully. "I could never quite figure out the difference."

Bright toyed with his salad. "Those are religions, right?"

Benny swallowed. "I'd have to look that one up, Dennis, but I believe you're correct. If not, we should probably alert the publishing industry."

Bright took a sip of his coffee. His eyes narrowed. He appeared rapt in thought. "Idea number three," he suddenly announced. "'Religion Talk.'"

"What's wrong with number two?" asked Benny, continuing his assault on the turkey salad.

"I see a problem with our sponsors. They wouldn't want the public to notice that their trucks make funny sounds."

"Good point," said Benny with a full mouth.

"I'm glad you noticed. 'Religion Talk.'"

"An excellent idea, Mr. Bright," agreed Benny with a gesture of his fork. "However, there's one problem."

"Yeah? What's that?"

"I don't know a damn thing about religion."

"So what? You also don't know a damn thing about begonias."

"I know they require water."

"My point is this," explained Bright. "In this business you don't need to actually *know* anything about a subject to talk about it."

"Congratulations, Dennis, and my apologies. I had no idea you were so perceptive. I thought you were like the rest of your tired, your poor, your huddled masses, yearning for a tax cut."

"So what about it? 'Religion Talk.'"

"'With your host, Benny Good, who in the distant past took a course dealing with Hinduism and Buddhism—though he can't seem to remember the difference—and who for the following hour will answer questions from puzzled believers who are eager to know why their ministers, priests, rabbis, and mullahs make strange sounds.'"

Bright leaned forward. "Benny, you can do it!" he said with sudden enthusiasm. "You got the gift!"

Benny shook his head slowly and sadly. "I don't think we've found the tree to put it under."

Bright frowned. His fork began to make quick, furtive forays into his salad, separating the shrimp from the non-shrimp. He captured the shrimp and guided them, two by two, into his mouth. "What *do* you know about religion, Benny?"

"I was brought up Amish."

§

This time Benny was telling the whole truth.

Approximately forty-three years ago, while old Eli Good was attending an evening worship service, an unknown person or persons had left a tiny infant in the back seat of his black buggy.

Instead of seeking help with this active bundle of joy, as both the church elders and his sisters urged, Mr. Good, an honest but simple Amish bachelor and raiser of rabbits, chose to rear the child himself. He started by christening him Kaninchen (the German word for Bunny), a name the lad later shortened to Benny.

With his sunny disposition and verbal gifts, Kaninchen quickly worked his way into the hearts of the Amish community. But as he grew in wisdom and stature, his playful curiosity occasionally got him into trouble. By the age of four years, he knew the location of every cookie jar within a two-mile radius. By the age of six, he had composed irreverent versions of over half the songs in the Amish hymnbook and taught them to the other children. By the time he was eight, the young prodigy had moved from music to literature and was entertaining his little friends with bawdy paraphrases of the Bible stories that were their daily fare. When he was ten, Eli Good found him at the rabbit hutches, amusing himself by placing a love-starved buck in the hutch of three does and cheering the results. At twelve, he was caught peering into the bedroom window of a neighboring couple. At fourteen, it was reported that he had attempted to break into the bedroom of a young Amish woman. Then, at sixteen, his adoptive father died of a heart attack. Because the elders could find no one to volunteer a spare bedroom, they took Kaninchen aside, gave him a hundred dollars and a shoo-fly pie, advised him to make his own way in the outside world, and, with fervent but desperate hope in their hearts, said a parting prayer.

§

"I'll be damned," said an intrigued Dennis Bright. "Amish, huh? Who said you didn't know anything about religion?"

"I'm afraid," warned Benny, "that I'd be the one held responsible for that statement."

"Listen, Benny. You got the perfect background for doing a show on religion." A broad smile made its way across Bright's face. "Amish," he repeated. "Perfect!"

"That's a common misconception. They have their faults."

"Yeah?"

"Your typical Amishman deprives himself of the pleasure of the radio talk show. Your typical Amishman distrusts the American way of life. Your typical Amishman is a kindly, gentle person and when he finds himself under enemy attack he loves nothing better than to turn the other cheek. Your typical Amishman"—here Benny caught sight of the tab floating in a pool of water near his former milk shake—"much like the rest of us, occasionally needs to purge himself of nasty fluids."

He left for the men's room.

Bright rescued the tab from drowning and went to the register and paid.

Benny returned. Checking for eyewitnesses and finding none, he swept a scattering of coins from the top of an unattended table and then sauntered over to his former booth and distributed them among the empty plates and cups. After completing this exchange, he joined his boss at the door.

"I got the tip," he announced, lighting a Swisher Sweet.

§

Dennis Bright, Benny Good, and Swisher Sweet were back in Bright's office, where Bright and Good continued their discussion while Sweet described circles in the air.

"Okay, Benny, it's 'Religion Talk' or it's nothing."

"Could you explain the difference?"

"Listen, you got the gift. You can take it back on the road, or you can put it under this tree called 'Religion Talk.'"

"I move we go with 'Truck Talk,'" said Benny. "Do I hear a second? Second. The motion has been seconded. Discussion? Question. The question has been called for. All those in favor, say Aye. Aye. Those opposed, speak up or forever hold your peace. A moment of silence. The motion passes. 'Truck Talk' it is, with Benny Good as your host."

Bright stared hard at his employee. "What've you got against religion, Benny?"

"I'm afraid we're running out of time, Dennis. I'd like to thank you for being my guest." Benny leaned over and offered his boss a hand in a mock gesture of parting.

Bright ignored the hand. "What've you got against religion?"

Benny removed a large handkerchief from the pocket of his shorts and dabbed insincerely at his eyes. "I had an unfortunate experience as a child."

"Yeah?"

"The Amish made me eat shoo-fly pie till I escaped and converted to a religion based on apple pie."

"You're kidding. What religion was that?"

"The name escapes me. All I remember is spending evenings in a church, rolling around on the floor."

"You were a Holy Roller?"

"Is that what they're called?"

"Did you speak in tongues?"

"Mostly English. But I scattered a few German phrases here and there, just to show my solidarity with the cause."

"Seriously, Benny. You left the Amish and joined the Holy Rollers?"

"Only because of my love of apple pie."

§

This was all true, though a good lawyer would have quibbled.

After Kaninchen's excommunication by the Amish, he had hiked to the nearest town, where he dumped the shoo-fly pie into the first trash can he could find, bought a new set of non-black clothes, and changed his name to Benny. He then wandered the streets, looking for food and companionship. He found them in a corner café, where he met a kindly minister of the Gospel, who introduced himself as Reverend Barnabas and invited him to sit down and share an apple pie. Within thirteen minutes, Benny had embraced the tenets of foursquare Christianity and had promised to give his life to the ministry of the Church, in exchange for room and board and a small allowance.

It happened that Reverend Barnabas, who was nearing sixty, had a young wife whom he had saved from the life of the street. Lucy spent several evenings a week in the church sanctuary communing with God, openly petitioning Him to relieve her of her childless state. Listening from behind a pew one evening, Benny learned of her plight and came forth to offer his sympathy. Touched by his concern, she pressed his hand to her heart. Touched by her grief, he asked her what he could do to relieve it. She put her head to one side and smiled at him through her tears. "Oh Benny," she exclaimed, "you are an answer to my prayers!" *"Ja,"* he replied in a good German accent, "I vas up brought to halp vun anodder," and on the floor of that sanctuary, Benny Good did as he had been brought up.

§

"Well I'll be damned! A Holy Roller!" marveled Bright. "Any bad experiences?"

"Several," said Benny. Though he did not volunteer any further information, he may have been thinking of the twins God had sent to relieve Lucy of her barren state.

"What about good experiences? Have any of those?"

Benny considered this question carefully. "Well—I got the chance to do the work of the Lord."

"Yeah? I guess that's gotta count for something."

"It made me what I am today," declared Benny, snuffing out his cigar.

"Host of 'Religion Talk.'"

"Trucker," said Benny, standing up.

"Sit down, Benny."

Benny headed for the door.

Bright beat him there and turned around and confronted him. "Hold it right there, Benny," he said. "Let's just stop and think about this for a minute. One, you got the gift. Why waste it on the road, listening to crap like country music and talk shows? Why not have your own talk show? Face it. You got the gift, point one. Add to that this fantastic background. Two religions, Amish and Holy Roller! *Plus* a course in World Religions! My God! Perfect for something like 'Religion Talk.' So you had a few bad experiences. Who hasn't? That's why people would wanna tune in. They could identify. This business is built around the concept of identification. That'll be the whole point of 'Religion Talk.' Identification. You show me somebody with a religious background and I'll show you somebody who can identify."

"Blessed are those who identify," observed Benny.

"Exactly!" agreed Bright, pounding his slight fist on the desk. "I couldn't have said it better myself."

"That's because Benny's the guy with the gift."

Bright chose to ignore this remark. "Two religions," he went on. "You're making my case for me."

Benny paused to retrieve another cigar from his shirt pocket. He eyed his boss shrewdly. "Frankly," he said, "I'd feel a helluva lot better with half a dozen under my belt."

"So, visit a few churches. Then in, say, six weeks we're in business."

"I'll stay on the payroll?"

It was Bright's turn to pause. "Yyyyes—let's make that three weeks. One church, synagogue, and mosque per week. Isn't that what they're called? Synagogues and mosques?"

"I believe you're right, Dennis. But I sense you may be misspelling them."

"The place Jews and what-do-you-call-'em meet every week? On Saturdays?"

"Since Day Seven."

"So, come back in three weeks and we're in business."

Benny rolled the cigar between his fingers. "Travel expenses?"

Bright balked. "You weren't thinking of somewhere like Rome?"

"I assure you, my lord and master," said Benny, bowing as low as his well-fed abdomen would permit, "Rome is the farthest thing from my mind."

Bright hesitated. The abacus hidden in the spongy portion of his skull was busy having its beads shuttled hither and yon. "Okay," he finally agreed. "Travel expenses."

"I was thinking of somewhere," said Benny, lighting up, "more like," aiming a perfect smoke ring at the ceiling, "say," then gazing directly and cunningly at Bright, "Beverly Hills."

2

On the Road Again

"HELLO, DOLLY!" announced Benny as he planted his magnificence on a stool and slapped a hairy paw on the counter.

"Benny!" sang a chorus of baritones who were perched along the counter like birds along a telephone wire.

"Norm!" sang an off-key tenor.

"Well, speak of the devil," said Dolly from the far end of the counter.

"Somebody has seen behind my façade of childlike innocence," protested Benny.

Dolly, not her real name, wiggled a seasoned hourglass shape over to her new customer. She handed him a menu and planted her palms on her hips, a gesture designed to exhibit ten long audaciously-red fingernails. He handed the menu right back to her and winked.

"Make it a barrel of oats, three bushels of corn, a sack of potatoes, a small truckload of your best quality sorghum, and a bale of hay. And to wash it all down, a six-pack of Bud Light."

"Benny's on a diet," observed a chorus member.

"For dessert," Benny went on, "let's have an apple pie to go and a world-class waitress to enjoy it with when she gets off work. And when does she get off work? I'm glad you asked that question. She gets off work in half an hour. Has she had dessert tonight? No, she hasn't yet run across a world-class customer to enjoy it with."

Dolly shook her audaciously-red head and shrugged helplessly. "Sorry, Benny. My old man picks me up in forty-five minutes."

"What? Married? Is this true?" Benny looked around at his former comrades for confirmation.

The chorus nodded sadly.

Benny turned to Dolly. "How long has it been, what's his name, how old is he, what's his social security number, how much can he bench press, and why wasn't I consulted? That's six questions. Start from the top. Think each question over carefully before you answer. You have one minute. Ready? You may begin."

"It's been three months, Juan, he's seventeen, he's an illegal, and he bench presses me."

"He could even bench press you, Benny," warned a far stool.

"Sorry, young lady, your time is up," said Benny.

"Let's hear why she didn't consult him," sang the tenor.

Dolly reminded the jury of her constitutional right to remain silent. Then she turned to Benny, exhaled a pink bubble, tapped her pencil on her pad, and asked him what it would be.

"You have a special? Good. I'll take it. You have two specials? Better. I'll take them. Three, you say? Best. Keep the cook busy. It is written, busy hands make happy faces. Where's your phone?"

Dolly aimed her pencil at a niche near the restrooms and left with his order.

Benny hoisted himself off his stool and headed for the phone. On arrival, he punched a number of its keys and fed it with the loose change he had just rescued from the coin return.

"Lucy here," said a voice. "I can't come to the phone right now, but at the tone please leave your message and I'll try to get back to you in the morning, unless you want a wake-up call in the wee hours."

"Damn," said Benny under his breath.

The tone sounded.

"Lucy. How the hell are you? This is your ex, Benny Good, King of the Open Road, Knight of the Admirable Tongue, and Protector of Defenseless Women. I'm in Amarillo, on my way to California. I've got a new job. Would you believe they're paying me for talking? Care to hear the details? Great. I'll be passing through Reno in about two weeks. Keep your ears peeled to this phone."

Benny hung up and returned to the counter to reclaim his stool.

Talk centered on the merits of the competing brands of trucks.

A newcomer arrived at the counter and called for Dolly. The chorus glanced over at him and grunted a collective welcome. The off-key tenor sang a half-hearted "Norm!" and returned to his drink. Dolly wandered over to the newcomer and exchanged banter.

Talk of trucks resumed. At stake was the matter of male pride.

"My Peterbilt," boasted Benny, "can accelerate up a hill with a full load. Zoom, just like that," and he demonstrated with his hand, forgetting to replace the word *can* with the more accurate *used to.*

"Which hill are we talking about?"

"Dolly! Benny's been telling stories about you!"

Dolly sashayed over to her admirers and winked. "I can tell stories about Benny."

The newcomer wanted to know who belonged to the Infiniti outside.

"Guilty," said Benny, raising a hand. "Has cook rested from his labors?" he asked Dolly. "Yes? No? I won't take No for an answer."

"Really?" said Dolly.

"Take a look at these lips. Do they look like the lips of a liar? I stand by my original question. Has cook rested from his labors?

Ich Hunger habe. I'm hungry. Sorry, I don't know any other way to say it. Latin wasn't taught in Amish schools. I have no idea why. If you're curious about this matter, I can make discreet inquiries."

"I mean, really, you're driving an Infiniti?"

Benny placed a hand over the spot on his chest over where one would presume a beating heart to exist. "I stand before you today as a guilty man, Your Honor, and throw myself at the mercy of the court. Keep in mind those who would be hurt most by my incarceration—my children, my ex, my ladies, my creditors."

Dolly smiled, either at Benny's exhibition or at the thought of riding in an Infiniti, and headed for the kitchen.

"You left the road for another woman?" someone asked Benny.

"Only because of my pioneering spirit, the birthright of every patriotic, red-blooded American."

"What happened to your Peterbilt?" someone else asked.

"It is in safe storage, my friend, waiting for another day, another chance, another defenseless woman."

Dolly came back with Benny's order and placed the three specials before him.

"How about the apple pie?" he asked softly. He began to undress her with his eyes, which conveyed the impression that his hands were willing to finish the job.

She cocked her head to one side and looked at him. She bit her lip. She fluffed her apron and took a deep breath and let it out slowly. She checked around for curious ears. She leaned forward. "Half an hour," she whispered, and headed for the phone.

§

At seven-thirty next morning, Benny left Dolly in Amarillo and headed for California.

As Benny had already learned, Dennis Bright's Infiniti was capable of triple-digit speeds. It was also equipped with a Fuzzbuster, which appeared to be in impeccable working order. He reached Gallup just before noon.

His regular truck stop was only half full. He discovered that his regular Dolly was on maternity leave. She had been replaced by an older woman, who complained of sore feet. Benny did not greet this replacement with his customary "Hello, Dolly!" He did not engage her in his customary banter. He did not bother to order his customary apple pie. Instead he crossed the street to a liquor store to purchase his dessert, which he chose to drink en route.

In Arizona he was greeted by a siren. He glanced in his rearview mirror and observed a flashing red light. He removed his foot from the gas pedal, pushed a button that caused his right front window to roll down, hurled the bottle of dessert from the moving vehicle, and punished the unfaithful Fuzzbuster with the back of his hand.

Dennis Bright's Infiniti came rolling to a stop while its driver reached into his shirt pocket and extracted a package of breath mints. He unwrapped the package and threw a handful of mints into his mouth and began to chew rapidly. He pushed another button. Down slid the left front window. Out peered Benny through the mirror. He watched as an apparition approached.

The twenty-something apparition was soon at his side.

She leaned down. "Sir," she said nervously, "my radar had you clocked at 113."

Benny looked skeptical. "Have you had your gun checked lately?"

"Sir?"

"I find it's always a good idea to check your gun regularly. I try to do it on a daily basis, or once a day, sometimes both. Night is also an acceptable time. In fact, many prefer it then. For those with no strong preference, a healthy combination is an option."

She looked bewildered. "Sir, I'd like you to step outside."

"In this weather?" It was 72 degrees Fahrenheit.

"Please don't argue."

"Not argue? What would life be without an occasional disagreement? One need not resort to barbarities."

"Sir," she said in a more decisive tone.

Benny Good opened his door and stepped outside. He moved to the side of the Infiniti. He placed his hands on the hood and leaned over. "Frisk away," he invited her.

"That won't be necessary, sir."

He maintained this position.

"Sir."

"I want to be frisked. I have a constitutional right to be frisked. If I'm going to pay the State of Arizona for the brisk use of its highways, I expect the full treatment. Nothing less is acceptable."

The officer shifted her weight from one foot to the other.

"I took a shower this morning," he volunteered. "If that's the problem."

She shifted her weight back to the first foot.

"Or are you bothered by my reference to a gun? I was speaking metaphorically."

While she tried to decide which foot to rest her weight on, he frisked himself.

"There. Was that so bad? No. Find any concealed weapons? No. Any illegal substances? No. Pulse rate? Rapid, but out of the danger zone. Any disgusting odors? As you said, sir, a recent shower. Is the prisoner free to go? Not yet, sir, if you'll just walk along this white line and then come back with me to the squad car for a friendly visit."

Benny stood up straight, turned around, and raised his hands above his head.

The officer involuntarily flashed a set of milk-white teeth.

Benny hopped on one foot along the white line toward the squad car. He got in on the passenger side.

She watched him. Then she came over and climbed into the driver's seat. She picked up her clipboard and prepared to write. She paused and sniffed. "Do I smell breath mints?"

Benny leaned over to her and returned the sniff. He inspected her closely. "Great noses smell alike."

"Was it my imagination, or did I see you throw something out of your car?"

"It was your imagination. If not, the item in question was the rest of my dessert. It's biodegradable."

She stared at her clipboard.

"Maybe *I* should make this out," he said, taking the clipboard from her. "Now, young lady. My radar had you clocked back there at 113. It also showed you thinking evil thoughts. As for the speeding, I'm going to let you off with a warning. As for the evil thoughts. . . ."

He turned to her and winked.

She blushed.

He lowered his voice. "When do you get off work?"

She stared straight ahead.

"Make it Flagstaff, Motel 6. Nine o'clock. Ask for Benny Good."

She bit her lip. "Benny Good," she murmured.

Benny tore an unmarked sheet from the clipboard, folded it, and put it in his shirt pocket. He got out of the squad car and hopped over to the Infiniti. He turned around and smiled and blew her a kiss. He stood for a moment to light a cigar. Then he waved and got in the car and drove off.

§

Early next morning Benny awoke, stretched, yawned, sat up, and took a piece of motel stationary and wrote:

Denny—

Running a wee bit behind schedule—hoped to get to California last night—only got to Flagstaff—flat tire kept me in Amarillo the first day—enclosed find motel receipt—was cruising along this a.m. drinking lemonade—spilled some on my lap—accidentally hit gas pedal—Arizona employee pulled me over to discuss ins and outs of traffic laws—assumed he'd be a guy—not so—didn't realize Arizona was an Equal Opportunity Employer—my ex always used tears to get off hook—claimed they work best with persons of opposite sex—tried this method—no success—sorry—in future I'll keep an onion in your glove compartment—enclosed please find traffic ticket ($129, or $3 per extra MPH)—already paid for, as per advice of employee of State of Arizona —please deposit reimbursement in my account—

Faithfully,
Benny G.

After scrawling this note, Benny lit a cigar and reached for the motel phone. His right index finger negotiated a series of familiar numbers.

"'lo," said a youthful male hungover voice.

"Hello?" said Benny. "Is this the residence of Lucinda Good?"

"Who?" said the voice.

"Lucinda. L-U-C-I-N—"

"Like in Lucy?"

"Right. Lucy Good."

"Nobody here by that name."

"Are you sure? Last time I called this number, her sweet voice left me a message. She invited me to call back. As you can see, I'm taking her advice."

"Ain't no good here."

"But there's a Lucinda? A Lucy?"

"Who wantsta know?"

"This is Benny Good. Benny as in Benny, Good as in somewhere on a scale between average and excellent."

"So?"

"I'm her second husband. Her favorite—she keeps going back to the name of Good. Seems to think it fits her. Is she there?"

A pause.

"She ain't here."

"Could I ask when she'll be back?"

"Sure."

Another pause.

"Well?" said Benny.

"I mean sure, you could *ask* me when she'll be back. But that don't mean I'll tell ya."

"Where is she? You could at least tell me that."

And another pause. Then, "She's out dealin'."

"Dealing?"

"That's what I said, dealin'. You deef or somethin'?"

"I thought she worked at night."

Benny heard a voice in the background. Then the sounds of what appeared to be disagreement.

"Hello," said a dreamy female voice.

"Hello, Lucy?"

"Yes? Who is this?"

"Don't you recognize your ex?"

"Hans?"

"Nein, ist nicht Hans."

"Dmitri?"

"Nyet."

"Luciano?"

"Sorry, my Italian is temporarily kaput. Guess again."

"Benny!" A pause. The voice woke up. "Where the hell are you?"

"I'm in Rome. At the Holiday Inn. Did you get my message?"

"Message? What message?"

"I left a message on your machine. I said, and I quote, 'Dearest Lucy. I love you. I miss you. Please come back to me. All is forgiven. Sincerely yours, Mr. Benjamin Good, Esquire. P.S.

How are the twins these days? Why do they never write?' Who was that kid, anyway?"

"Sal."

"Sal who?"

"It's not important."

"Sounded important to me."

"Well . . . I guess so. We got married, uh, last week?"

"Is that your best guess?"

"Maybe it was two weeks ago."

"Congratulations. What is this, disciple number twelve?"

"Don't exaggerate, Benny."

"If I don't see you at least once a year, I risk missing one of your husbands."

"Now I remember why I left you. Or was it the other way around?"

"I forget. It's probably written down someplace."

"I doubt if it's in the Lamb's Book of Life. More likely in some D.A.'s office in a folder called 'Child Support.'"

A pause. Then, "Where did you meet this guy? At the twins' birthday party?"

"At work."

"You're still teaching Sunday School!"

"Knock it off, Benny. I have a new job."

"Well? The world is waiting to hear. What's Lucy doing these days?"

"Something I happen to be very good at."

"Getting people to marry you?"

"I'm a blackjack dealer. At a major casino in town."

"So you finally found a job that fits your skills."

"And what's Benny up to these days? Making license plates?"

"I just quit my lucrative job rearranging America's freight and have become a major, major host for a major, major radio talk show."

"Let me guess. 'You and the IRS.'"

"Close. 'Religion Talk.'"

"I'll bite. What's that all about?"

"I haven't decided. That's why I'm headed for California, where for three weeks I'll be staying at the Beverly Hills Hilton in gorgeous surroundings, lounging at the poolside, playing tennis, rubbing shoulders with the rich and the powerful, quizzing them about their profoundest religious convictions, asking them what it's like to be saved and was it worth the effort."

"You mean you don't remember?"

"I just want to compare notes. Say, I was just wondering if you've got room in your bed for a warm body in about two weeks."

"I sure do, and his name is Sal."

"For old times' sake?"

"You'll have to get written permission from the kid."

"What are my chances?"

"Oh, I'd say about the same as winning the Utah jackpot."

"I never could figure out why they put Utah and Nevada side by side. Saints and sinners so close together. Ever wonder who did the place settings for our fair nation?"

"Listen, Benny, I'd love to riff all day, but."

"Listen, Lucy, I'd love to achieve closure, no buts."

"We just did—"

Benny stared at the silent receiver and frowned. He gave it a punishing blow and snuffed out his cigar. He stood up and went into the bathroom, where he prepared himself for his last day on the road. Finally, he left his motel room and headed for the mail box, being careful to close the door softly so as not to disturb a sleeping employee of the State of Arizona.

3

The Church for Those
Who Hate Religion

The next Sunday evening, Benny Good found himself creeping along a Southern California freeway in Dennis Bright's Infiniti, dressed in a new suit and tie and looking for the exit leading to the church of his choice.

Benny's schedule for his three-week all-expenses-paid vacation had called for five days at Santa Anita cheering the horses of his choice, one week in Reno mending fences while enjoying the best of what that city has to offer, and of course one week coming and going. This left a full weekend to check out one or two religions and to browse around a used bookstore seeking information about several of the others.

He was approximately on schedule. It had taken him three days to get from Kirkland to Pasadena. His five days at the track had been rewarding. Yesterday he had bought the suit and visited a bookstore and then gone back to the motel and written Bright a letter enclosing more receipts testifying to his expenditures and reporting that his week had been spent visiting a synagogue, a cathedral, a charismatic church, a mosque, and a Buddhist monastery, as well as attending a spiritualist séance in which he had been put in touch with the mother he had never known.

He found his exit and inched his way along in stop-and-go traffic, tailgating a Jag being nursed along by a gorgeous head of blonde hair that he judged to be in his preferred age range. During the stops he forgot the Jag and thumbed through one of the books he had lifted from the bookstore, an excellent piece of writing entitled *Religion for Dolts.*

He followed the Jag and a long line of cars into the church parking lot, which was only slightly smaller than that of the Rose Bowl. Obeying the directions of half a dozen men and women in reflective orange jackets, he found a place for his Infiniti among the Beemers and Lexuses and Mercedes Benzes and Jaguars and Jeep Cherokees.

That morning, after consulting the Yellow Pages, Benny had decided to attend the Church of the Wide Open Door. "A Full-Service, State-of-the-Art Church," said the full-page ad. "One Stop Shopping," it said, listing over a dozen of its chief enterprises. "Open Seven Days a Week, 6 A.M. to Midnight," it said, and "Twelve Sunday Services, running from 9 A.M. to 9 P.M.," which meant he could spend the afternoon at the beach. But the clincher for him was the church's motto: "The Church for Those Who Hate Religion."

He climbed out of Bright's Infiniti and adjusted his suit and straightened his tie. He glanced around. The building several hundred yards away did not look like a church; it had no stained-glass windows, no belfry, no steeple topped off with a crucifix. It looked like a cross between the Kirkland Shopping Center and the corporate headquarters for Unisys.

He joined the growing stream of religion-haters, including the Jaguar-driving blonde fifty yards ahead of him, and began trotting toward the wide open door.

Benny had not seen the inside of a church in twenty-six years. In fact, during his entire life he had been inside only two churches: the Amish meetinghouse of his youth and the modest missionary church with the floor on which he and Lucy had rolled in seeking an answer to her prayer. Neither of those ordeals had prepared him for this new experience.

Once he was inside the door, a charming young woman sporting a name tag that identified her only as "Diana" approached him and grasped his hand. "Hi," said Diana with a bright smile. "I'm Diana."

"And you'll be my waitress tonight," he said, trying to start a conversation. But Diana didn't answer. She was already exercising her charm on the couple behind him.

Benny's eyes searched for the blonde. She had disappeared. He made a firm resolution to lose fifty pounds. Perhaps, he thought, he should inquire into the distasteful regimen of jogging? He quickly decided against taking such an extreme measure and turned his attention to the business at hand.

Benny looked around at the other worshipers and noticed that he was the only one wearing a suit and tie. Almost everyone else was dressed in Levi's Dockers. A few even wore shorts and a T-shirt proclaiming the wearer a FDFX, a "Fully Devoted Follower of Christ." He could have come directly from the beach, he thought with regret, except that the only T-shirt he had brought along proclaimed him BTSC, "Born To Smoke Cigars."

He had some extra time before the eight o'clock service, so he wandered around the lobby.

He came across a pedestal featuring a map of the terrain. "You are here," said an arrow, pointed to where he was. From this spot one could locate the various enterprises operated by the Church of the Wide Open Door. These included a baptismal pool, a wedding chapel, a marriage mediation room, a divorce recovery room, a funeral chapel, a bookstore, three basketball courts, five racquetball courts, a weight room, a matching pair of shower rooms, a salon, a miniature golf course, a virtual driving range, a dance hall, an Olympic-sized swimming pool, several restaurants, three bars, and a casino.

He strolled over to the nearest bar and ordered a whiskey sour. A couple of fiftyish women wrapped in chinchilla were sitting on bar stools, blowing smoke through thin nostrils and devouring Bloody Marys and discussing the Spirit-filled life. One of them was contemplating whether the Holy Spirit was leading her to a tan Lexus or a light blue Jaguar. The other was pondering whether the Holy Spirit was leading her to Jack or Darryl. Several other patrons were watching Sunday Night Football, cheering every time the Lions blitzed the Saints. The bartender brought him his whiskey sour with a swizzle stick in the shape of a cross. He downed the drink and went next door to check out the casino.

A sign at the casino door announced that all proceeds from the operation were earmarked for the planting of similar churches and were therefore tax-deductible. Benny stopped to consider the odds. But a voice over a loudspeaker interrupted his calculations, reminding him that the service started in five minutes.

He left the casino and passed the bookstore. The merchandise in the window display included two books on God, seven on angels, a dozen or so on coping with the various forms of grief, and hundreds of scientifically-authenticated splinters of the Cross at fifty percent off.

He followed the crowd and found himself on an escalator going up.

Just outside the sanctuary stood a large clear plastic box into which worshipers were depositing penance for their sins. A sign recommended ten dollars. He longingly eyed the mounting pile of donations and passed.

At the door he was greeted with a choice: smoking or non-smoking? He headed for the smoking section and was faced by another choice: cigarettes, cigars, or pipes? He chose cigars and joined a substantial contingent of young-executive types in a glassed-in area, where invisible ceiling fans quietly wafted their burnt offerings safely heavenward.

Benny stopped to scan the sanctuary. It looked like an all-purpose arena—similar to the old Chicago Stadium. Rearrange the floor below, he thought as he lit a Swisher Sweet, and you could play hockey. Place a basket at each end, invite a rejuvenated Michael Jordan and several dozen of his imitators, and you'd be set for the NBA finals. Decorate the stage with red white and blue banners, drop a few million balloons from the ceiling, seat a row of heroic ordinary Americans in the gallery, and you'd have yourself a political convention. Bring on the clowns and acrobats and a small zoo and bingo, a circus. And you wouldn't even have to worry about the three rings. They were already in place. The stage was divided into three sections, one with a pulpit, the second with a platform on which rested a king-sized bed, the third occupied by a puppet theater.

He found a seat in the rear of the convention-hall-turned-sanctuary and sat down. He noticed a set of earphones dangling from the pocket behind the seat in front of him. He clamped them over his ears and heard a choir singing a song about Jesus, with occasional references to God. This reminded him that he was in church. It also reminded him that the Church of the Wide Open Door had advertised itself as a church for those who hate religion. "Bait and switch," he muttered, tearing off the earphones.

He looked around at his co-religionists to see if he could spot any potential co-plaintiffs for a class-action suit. Everyone was wearing earphones, but all seemed pleased with what they heard. Several were nodding and mumbling "Praise the Lord." Some had their eyes closed and were swaying gently back and forth. A substantial number were excitedly snapping their fingers and jerking their bodies around.

The neighbor on his left was a finger-snapping body-jerker. Benny strained to hear what the excitement was about. He heard rock music seeping through the earphones. He tapped the young man on the shoulder. "How do I get hold of that?" he whispered.

The young man pointed at a giant overhead screen and continued to snap his fingers.

"Thanks," whispered Benny.

The screen gave instructions for selecting your own personal musical prelude. There is a dial on the side of your seat, it explained, showing an icon of a seat and a dial. Each setting of the dial delivers a different musical experience, it explained. There were channels for gospel music, for traditional Christian hymns, for Christian mood music, for Christian country and western, for the sound of waves lapping against the rocks of a distant seashore God had created, for Christian rock, and, with lovers of classical Christian in mind, for the theme song of *2001: A Space Odyssey*.

By the time Benny had found his way to the sound of Christian waves, the prelude was over and it was time for the reading of Scripture.

This time the choice was among the Parable of the Prodigal Son, the story of David and Bathsheba, selections from the *Tao Te Ching*, and a quiet moment of Christian yoga.

Benny expertly flipped back and forth between the *Tao Te Ching* and a quiet moment before settling on the quiet moment, which gave him the opportunity to enjoy his cigar.

Then it was time for the main event. The selection included a traditional message, a dramatic rendition of a Christian CEO's fatal attraction to a war hero's wife, a puppet show depicting two young women's search for world peace through the teachings of the Chinese sage Lao Tzu, and the steady repetition of the name of Jesus. This selection, the screen explained, corresponded to the various forms of activity on the stage. If you wished to listen to the senior minister deliver the traditional message, you should watch him at the pulpit occupying the right third of the stage. If the dramatic rendition was the entertainment of your choice, you should watch the action occurring at the center stage. If you happened to be interested in world peace, you should watch the puppet show on the left. The repetition of the name of Jesus was appropriate for all three presentations.

Benny chose a Christian CEO's attraction for someone else's wife. Within twenty minutes, the CEO had watched the woman sunbathe, had invited her over for a cappuccino, had seduced her, had gotten her pregnant, had conspired with her to assassinate her war-decorated husband, had become a proud father, and had wept and repented when the baby mysteriously died.

Benny did not stay around to find the cause of the child's death. He switched channels and heard the senior minister, a young man nearing thirty, present a stand-up comedy routine on the importance of volunteering time and money for the upcoming membership drive. Not yet feeling the call to become a member of the Church of the Wide Open Door, he switched to the puppet show, just in time to watch the two puppets embrace and agree that the key to world peace was LUTFT: love, understanding, tolerance, and flowing with the Tao.

The audience stood and applauded as the presentations of their choices simultaneously ended, as if by Divine Providence.

Benny lifted up his eyes to the overhead screen for his cue. Next on the agenda was a choice among three testimonies. The first was given by a professional athlete who had formed the national organization called Wrestlers for Christ, the second by a Hollywood actress who had abandoned a promising career as a cultural icon to become a motivational speaker, and the third by a fully-licensed sex therapist.

He chose the sex therapist, a dazzling blonde of uncertain age, who told a heartwarming story of how her faithful attendance at the Women's Bible Study Cell had led her to realize that self-criticism had been blocking her efforts to become emotionally intimate with her male friends.

After the postlude, Benny selected the country and western channel. Meanwhile, the screen flashed an invitation for newcomers to meet in Room 345C, where the senior minister would answer questions. There was, the screen promised, no obligation to join.

Benny put out his cigar and headed for the men's room.

§

Room 345C of the Church of the Wide Open Door was the size and shape of a small concert hall and was furnished with well-padded seats. Benny arrived late and seated himself at the rear. The senior minister, a young man named Sean, was listing the ministries a prospective member might choose to join. If your interest happened to be politics, he explained, there were cells of Christian Republicans and Christian Democrats, as well as a fellowship for the Christian Independents. If your interest happened to be the abortion issue, there were cells for both pro-lifers and pro-choicers, and oh yes, he remembered, a new cell was just getting underway, calling itself . . . the Christian Confuseds. The audience, following the script, laughed. True to its eighteen-month tradition of non-judgmental openness, the minister went on, the church sponsored chapters of both the National Organization of Christian Women and the Christian Promise Keepers. There was also a wide range of Christian support groups, for recovering alcoholics, substance abusers, sex addicts, wife beaters, husband naggers (laughter), gays, straights (more laughter), Jews (nervous laughter: was the minister being anti-Semitic?), Catholics (he was building up to something!), and oh yes . . . Baptists (an explosion of mirth that landed a quarter of the audience on the floor).

The laughter eventually died out; the recovering Baptists picked themselves off the floor, exhausted by their strenuous workout. The senior minister chuckled, clearly pleased with his performance. He wanted to know if there were any questions.

A somber woman introduced herself and said she had an Alzheimer father. Wiping a tear from an eye, she went on to describe in depth her family's grief at the mental vacancy of a loved one and ended up asking if the church sponsored a Christian adult day-care center.

The minister, moving effortlessly from comedy to the tragic mode, admitted that such a program was the one thing lacking in his church, but he promised to explore the matter.

After half an hour of questions, many of them about the restrooms, the minister introduced ten or twelve church leaders, including some who had taken part in the service. Then he announced that if anyone was undecided about which ministries would be appropriate for him or her, he or she could follow the leader of his or her choice to a special room where he or she would receive a free, confidential diagnosis.

Benny chose to follow one of the testifiers. This was the sex therapist who had earlier spoken of her pilgrimage toward mastering the art of intimacy and who, he was now certain, was the owner of the Jaguar, the woman for whom he was beginning to feel he had been searching for the better part of his life, or at least since his last conversation with Lucy.

§

The special room contained a dozen computer stations. The sex therapist introduced herself as Arielle and shared with her charges the information that she had a Ph.D in psychology but asked them not to call her Dr. Arielle, please, she preferred just plain Arielle. She then instructed her charges to choose a station.

This time Benny selected a computer at the very front of the room.

Arielle told her charges which keys to press in order to bring a questionnaire to the computer screen. She further told them how to answer the questionnaire, which was designed to match them with the ministry or ministries they felt they would be most comfortable with.

Benny pressed a series of keys that did not produce the questionnaire. He raised his hand. Arielle came over to help him. He looked her over. She was clearly a veteran of several face-lifts, but otherwise—

He flashed back thirty-some years. When he had raised his hand in grade school, his teacher would come over to help him with his math problems. Then he'd slip a mirror under her Amish skirt to catch a glimpse of a brave but forbidden new world that he hoped one day to conquer—.

"Here we go," said Arielle after she had retrieved the questionnaire from the depths of his computer.

Benny stared at the screen.

"Is something the matter?" asked Arielle.

Benny admitted that he didn't know how to operate a computer. "Trucks, yes. Computers, no."

"No probleme!" said Arielle, planting her still-firm breasts gently on his wide shoulders. "It's user-friendly."

"Glad to hear that. Which keys do I massage?"

She reached over his shoulder and gave him a quick lesson.

"Trucks?" she asked.

"I used to run a Peterbilt."

"How *int*eresting! All that power!"

"So you know about the Peterbilt. Maybe one of them has passed you on the Interstate. Maybe you've passed one of them. Maybe I was driving. Ships with the best of intentions often pass in the night. In the day, too, but nobody seems to find this fact worth mentioning."

She looked puzzled. "And what do you do now?" she asked.

"I run a talk show."

"Oh, *fa*scinating! Let me guess: politics!"

"Close. Religion."

"Religion! I'm im*pr*essed! I can just see the gifts you'll bring to this church!"

Before Benny could ask her which of his many gifts were obvious to the naked eye, some of his computer-literate companions were demanding Arielle's attention.

"I'll be back," she told Benny in a confidential tone, touching him lightly on the elbow with a ring-free hand.

While he was busy confessing the secrets of Benny Good to his computer, the other potential believers were having their personal profiles being printed out and analyzed and their gifts being properly distributed among the many ministries offered by the Church of the Wide Open Door. When he was finished, he looked up to find that he was the only one of the original twelve left in the room.

Arielle came over and stood behind him. "How are we coming?"

"We have met the enemy, and she is ours."

She leaned over the corner of his shoulder and flashed a puzzled frown.

"That's a Biblical quotation," he explained.

"I thought it sounded kind of familiar. What exactly does it mean?"

"In plain German, *Es ist vollbracht.* In English, It is finished. In French, none of the above. In Latin . . . but I'm boring you."

"Oh, no! I find this *fas*cinating, uh—sorry, I didn't catch your name."

"I'm Benny, but please don't call me Dr. Benny. I prefer just plain Benny."

"Good! Let's see what your printout says, Benny."

Arielle produced a printout of Benny's personal profile and looked it over.

"Leadership qualities, the ninety-fifth percentile! Wonderful! Linguistic skills, ninety-nine plus! You don't need a test to see that! Psychological outlook, healthy. Spirituality . . . well . . . I guess that's something we can work on."

Benny grunted.

"Capacity for emotional intimacy," Arielle went on. She paused, then nodded confidently. "That's something else we can work on."

"I'd certainly be willing," said Benny.

"Fine! Now let's see which ministry you'd be most comfortable with."

"Do you have something with the word *Christian* in it?"

"Oh yes. In fact, I was going to suggest a new cell group I'm in the process of forming. It studies Christian Tantrism."

"Sounds *won*derful," he said. "I've heard of Christian, but what's Tantrism? Worship of aunts?"

"Benny! You're putting me on!"

"I wish I was."

"Really? I thought maybe you'd know all about Tantrism, being this high-powered religious expert and everything. Tantrism happens to be a very big part of Eastern religion."

"My specialty is Midwest religion. What does it teach, this Tantrism? In three words or less."

"It's very simple, basically. Samsara is Nirvana."

"I see," Benny nodded thoughtfully.

"I'm using the Buddhist language."

"My specialty is English. Let's start over, from the top. What does Tantrism teach, in three words or less? Wait: let me guess. God is love."

"Well, that's one way to put it."

"What's another way? Just out of curiosity. Remember the three-word limit."

"Salvation through sex."

"I see," Benny nodded thoughtfully.

4

Benny Achieves Perfection

CURIOUS BY NATURE, Benny Good was always intrigued by new ideas. The idea of salvation was not of course new to him; he had run across it from his years with the Amish and his months with Reverend Barnabas. Neither was the idea of sex new to him. But the idea of combining sex with salvation—this was what caught his attention and kept him in the questionnaire room with Arielle past ten-thirty, discussing the possibility of joining her new cell group devoted to the teachings of Christian Tantrism.

"Before I give you the first lesson, Benny," Arielle said, "I've got to know something."

"I'm an open book. Read me."

"Have you been baptized?"

"Only twice."

"Really! Twice?"

"That I know of."

Arielle frowned, revealing several stray wrinkles that had been overlooked by the plastic surgeon's quality-control specialist.

"What's the matter?" said Benny. "Is double baptism against the rules?"

"Not that I know of. I've just never heard of anybody being baptized twice."

Benny stopped to think this over. "Well, maybe it was only once. Come to think of it, it *was* only once. The first time didn't take. Probably because they didn't do it right."

"They who?"

"The Amish. Ordinarily they're pretty particular about following the rules. No cars, no tractors, no Peterbilts, no electricity, no telephones, no TV, no talk shows, no window peeking. And absolutely no spectator sports, for example, rabbit-breeding. But when it comes to things like baptism, they've been known to make mistakes. I speak from experience. But you've got to hand it to them, they handled the situation well. They gave me some money and encouraged me to bug off."

Arielle was again puzzled. "Are you saying you were excommunicated? By the Amish?"

"I don't like to think of it as excommunication," explained Benny. "I like to think of it as being paid off. That's another thing about the Amish, they pay their bills. In my case, it was a hundred dollars. That may not seem like much, but it was a lot of money in those days. But I'm sure they'd agree I was worth every penny."

"So you've only been baptized once. For all practical purposes."

Benny again stopped to think it over. "Now that you mention it, I'm not sure I was ever baptized. The second one probably didn't take either."

"Who baptized you the second time?"

"Reverend Barnabas. An old man who ran a storefront church. The deal was, he'd take me in and feed me, and all I had to do was accept Jesus as my personal Lord and Savior, be baptized, pass out tracts, attend church regularly, sing hymns of praise in the right key, and seek the will of God for my life. And oh yes. I also had to help his wife around the church. Which I did, but not to his satisfaction."

Arielle continued to be baffled. "Bottom line is, you're not sure you've ever been baptized."

"Do I sense a problem?"

"The thing is," Arielle explained, "if you haven't been baptized, I'm not allowed to give you lessons. If you want to learn Christian Tantrism, you've first got to be baptized."

Benny paused. "Do I get a choice, waterwise?"

"What do you mean, waterwise?"

"I'm speaking of sprinkling versus immersion."

"Oh. We usually immerse, but if somebody insists, we can go the other way. Do you have a preference?"

"I'm flexible. Who does the honors?"

"One of the ministers."

"Are you a minister?"

"Well, actually—no."

"Oh." Benny's voice signaled disappointment. "When would this take place?"

"We could arrange for next Sunday, unless you've got other plans."

"Sunday's out. Kansas calls. I've got to be back at work the middle of next week. Keep them cards and paychecks comin' in, folks."

"How about Saturday?"

"I'll be in Reno."

"Friday? Thursday? Wednesday? Tuesday?"

"Reno. Reno. Reno. Reno. I'm planning to attend a divorce and a wedding. And who knows? Maybe even a baptism."

"What about tomorrow?"

"I was thinking of tonight," said Benny.

Arielle furrowed her intelligent brow and tapped her petite foot for several seconds. "And when were you thinking of taking the lessons?"

"Tonight."

"Tonight?!"

"I thought we could do the baptism and lesson at the same time," said Benny. "Kill two birdies with one cannon shot."

"In the name of the Father, the Son, and the Holy Spirit," said Arielle, turning on the spout.

Waterwise, Benny had chosen sprinkling. To do the honors, he had chosen Arielle, suggesting that this was a special situation, which called for immediate action. Timewise, he had chosen the stroke after midnight, when the Church of the Wide Open Door closed its doors. Sitewise, it was the women's shower room. Clotheswise, he had taken off his new suit and tie as well as his shirt for the occasion. He was superstitious, he explained to Arielle. During his first two baptisms he'd been fully clothed, and he wanted very much for this try to succeed.

Arielle had agreed with all these choices. In fact, she even agreed to go the extra mile and take off her own outer garments.

"Amen," said Benny, turning off the spout. "You look nice."

"Thanks," she said, playfully plucking at his wet tee-shirt. "So do you."

"Maybe we should take these things off. Put them in the sink to dry." They were both drenched to the skin.

"You think of everything."

"I try to plan ahead."

He helped her off with her intimate garments. She helped him off with his. They took these items of clothing and placed them over the sink to dry, as per his suggestion. Then they went back into the shower for the first lesson.

"In Christian Tantrism," she began, "there are Twelve Steps to Perfection."

"Could you cut them down to four? Remember, I gotta be in Reno tomorrow afternoon."

Arielle frowned and thought. "I'll try. . . . Okay, I've got it. Step number one. You've got to have a healthy body."

"I make it a point to eat three square meals a day."

"What about exercise?"

"Practically every night. My favorite is the trampoline, but a bed does just as well. Step number two."

"Step two, meditation on a mandala."

"Keep in mind," warned Benny, "that English is one of my better languages."

"A mandala is an icon. A picture. You start by meditating on it."

"I don't have a picture."

"Well, think of a picture."

Benny closed his eyes. "I'm thinking."

"What do you see?"

"I see a beautiful woman. She's on a beach, posing for a *Playboy* calendar. The month is June, I believe. She's totally nude, except for the grape between her teeth. She looks smashing. She reminds me very much of you. May I ask a personal question, Arielle? Yes. Thank you. Did you ever work for a guy named Hugh Hefner?"

"Never in June, and I'm allergic to grapes. I was Miss July, and I had seaweed in my hair."

"I *thought* you looked familiar. Step three?"

"Step three involves the contemplation of a ritual."

"Can this ritual be erotic?"

She removed his lips from her left breast. "Yes, but you can't perform it. You have to just contemplate it."

"Sorry." Benny closed his eyes and counted to one. "Okay, I'm contemplating. Now what?"

"Step four, the activity itself."

And so, standing in the shower shortly after midnight, they performed the activity. Three times they performed this well-known ritual, once in the name of the Father, once in the name of the Son, etcetera.

"And those are the four steps?" asked Benny when they were finished.

"That's all there is to it."

"Did I achieve perfection?"

"Well . . . there are some things we've got to work on."

§

The major problem, Arielle had gone on to explain, was that Benny did not yet grasp the philosophy behind the Tantric way to Christian perfection. This was why she decided to give him a second lesson, this time in the hot tub in the baptism room for those who chose immersion as their entrance into the mysteries of the Church of the Wide Open Door.

She was sitting on his lap facing him, still waiting for their intimate garments to dry. "You're probably wondering why you've never heard of Christian Tantrism."

"You are a mind-reader," said Benny. "Could you turn the heat up?"

Arielle reached around him and fiddled with the thermostat. "Have you ever wondered what Jesus was doing in that garden just before they arrested him?"

Benny thought a moment. "Planning his escape?"

"Wrong. He was with his women."

"You mean. . . ?"

"Exactly."

"I hadn't realized."

"It was in the Bible, originally. The Catholics took it out."

"If I remember, so did the Amish."

"An Indian guru followed Buddha into China, see, where he caught Buddha dancing with his harem. 'Stop!' he cried. 'This goes against the teachings of the ancients!' 'If you want to be saved,' Buddha said, 'go and do thou likewise.'"

"That's a great story," agreed Benny. "What's it got to do with Jesus?"

"Jesus and Buddha were both great religious leaders," she explained. "All the main teachings of the great religious leaders were basically the same. This means Jesus taught more or less the same things as Buddha. If Buddha taught it, Jesus must have taught it too."

"I can't argue with that. You have nice breasts."

"You have a nice chest. I like hairy men. This doesn't mean that Christianity and Buddhism are *exactly* the same."

"I'd always thought of them as different."

"For instance, the Buddhists don't let women be gurus."

"Christians are way ahead of them on that point," suggested Benny.

"Another difference is that Buddhists teach that samsara is Nirvana."

"I believe you mentioned that. What does it mean?"

"Samsara is the impure world of pain and suffering. Nirvana is salvation. When they say the two are the same, what they're basically saying is that if you want to find salvation, and who doesn't, you should embrace the world, including its flaws. Hold me around the hips and pull me towards you."

"Like this?"

"A little more. But Christianity teaches that God created the world, which means it is very good."

"In other words, He put his Good Worldkeeping stamp of approval on it."

Arielle giggled. "You know, Benny, you're very funny. Where do you come up with that stuff?"

"I used to listen to a lot of sermons. I got in the habit of paraphrasing, just to keep from going crazy."

"You have a lot to offer this church. Do you feel what I feel?"

"I've never felt this way before."

"Really?"

"It's approximately *won*derful. To paraphrase you."

"Be serious, Benny. Buddhism also teaches that the whole point of life is the pursuit of pleasure."

"Buddhism is a very wise religion."

"Not so fast. It also teaches that you have to pursue pleasure with a pure mind."

"So what's the point?"

"The point is, they're wrong. Christianity teaches that there's no such thing as a pure mind."

"That's always been my experience."

"Kiss me here," said Arielle.

He dutifully kissed her there.

"You don't know what that does to me. Feel me shiver?"

"Mmmm."

"Buddhism also teaches that in practicing the Tantric ritual, the woman should be active and the man should be passive."

"So far, so good."

"They stress that when the man is about to come, he should hold it back."

"I'm doing the best I can."

"But Christianity teaches the equality of the sexes."

"I know people who would disagree."

"They're wrong. The man and the woman should cooperate."

"That's always been my philosophy."

"It takes two. Take Adam and Eve, for example. Someplace in the Bible God tells them, 'Be fruitful and multiply.'"

"It's been a long time, but I believe that's in Genesis."

"You're probably right. Anyway, the point is, He's talking to them both. That means they're equal."

"I'm coming!"

"O BennybennybennybennyBENNY! . . ." Then, several long moments later: "Is your condom still on?"

Benny paused to catch his breath and to relieve tension. "I think so."

"Good," she said as they carefully disengaged. "My final point is that Buddhism teaches that you achieve salvation through satisfying your desires."

"And all these years I've been saved but didn't know it."

"On the other hand, Christianity teaches that you achieve salvation when you realize you can't be perfect."

"Fine. I'm covered there, too."

§

They went back to the women's shower room to retrieve their underwear, which was no longer wet. Time, which heals all wounds, also gives baptismal garb the chance to dry.

"I think this time it took," said Benny as he put on his shoes.

"Took?"

"The baptism."

"Oh I see. Third time's the charm."

"No, I mean it was finally done properly."

§

"You have leadership qualities," Arielle informed Benny. "That's what the computer says."

They were at her place, where they were in bed. They were discussing Benny's future role in the Church of the Wide Open Door while a Jaguar and an Infiniti stood guard in the parking lot.

"Computers can lie," replied Benny.

"Plus you have the gift."

"That's what my boss says. Bosses can lie too."

"I think you should stick around for a week. We can enroll you in the Outreach Program."

"Learning to spread the gospel of Christian Tantrism to the good people of Kansas?" guessed Benny.

"Exactly!" Her voice was gaining in enthusiasm. "Benny Good, missionary!"

Benny thought this over for a split second. "This would require money."

"We have a special fund earmarked for that kind of thing. I'll talk to Sean. He's the senior pastor."

"Fine."

"I'm making no promises," warned Arielle. "There's plenty of competition."

"Let me make a suggestion. Take the good man out to dinner. Explain the finer points of Christian Tantrism. Encourage him to develop a healthy body. Give him a *Playboy* calendar. Get him thinking about sex. Then go for it. But remember to remind him that samsara is Nirvana. And make sure he understands that you run a very Christian operation, and that you require he wears a condom."

"He already knows that."

"Great. I've got to make a phone call."

"At this time of night?"

Benny reached over to the phone and dialed.

"Lucy here," said a voice. "I can't come to the phone right now, but at the tone please leave your message and I'll try to get back to you in the morning, unless you want a wake-up call in the wee hours."

The tone sounded.

"Benny here," he said. "I can't come to Reno right now, I'm enrolled in the Outreach Program at the Church of the Wide Open Door, and in one week I'll be fully certified to become a missionary and teach Christian Tantrism to those who've been saved all these years but didn't realize it. This may or may not include you. For more information, please send $29.95 and a self-addressed stamped envelope to Benny Good, care of station KKKS, Kirkland, Kansas."

"Benny?" said Lucy's voice.

"Yes?" said Benny.

"Are you crazy?"

"Yes," said Benny, and hung up.

Arielle rolled over on him. She ran her fingers through his hair. She kissed his hairy chest. She straddled him. "God's been leading you," she whispered as she started to rock slowly back and forth. "You are a God-led man."

Benny gazed up at a pair of surgeon-sculpted masterpieces. "I guess I've never really noticed," he said, "but now that you men-tion it. . . ."

5

Priming the Pump

AND GOD CONTINUED TO LEAD BENNY GOOD. Upon awakening the next morning, Benny felt God's presence in his life; a voice advised him to stay in southern California another week to improve his grasp of the teachings and practices of Christian Tantrism with the aid of Arielle and several members of her fledgling cell group. God also went the extra mile, appearing to Pastor Sean in an exclusive Wednesday night vision. As a result, Benny's name found a place in the budget of the Church of the Wide Open Door under the line item, "Outreach: Salaries."

Then God led Benny back to Kansas to begin his radio ministry at KKKS.

On the way home to Kirkland, Benny felt certain that God was urging him to get a head start on this ministry. Why else would He be providing him with three potential converts, two waitresses and a state patrolwoman? One of the waitresses chose sprinkling. The other waitress and the patrolwoman chose immersion after they showed up simultaneously at Benny's door, and quick-thinking Benny invited them both to attend a baptismal party in the motel swimming pool.

Benny finally made it back to Kirkland, full of missionary zeal to capture his share of the Kansas religion market.

§

"Sit down!" said a furious Dennis Bright as Benny strolled into his office.

Benny started to sit down. He paused in mid-squat. "Will I need a lawyer?"

"Listen, Benny."

Benny parked himself on the edge of the chair. "Could I have a list of the offenses I'm charged with?" he asked, removing the wrapper from a panatela.

"You know how much this fuckin' trip cost me?"

"Watch your language. Remember, you are in the presence of the newly-anointed host of 'Religion Talk.'"

"Motel Sixes, total $447.98."

"Congratulate me on being frugal."

"The Marriott, Castle Inn, Executive Inn, total $675.18. I guess frugal can get pretty boring."

Benny sat back in his chair. "There was no room for him in the east-bound Motel Sixes."

"Food, total $2051.32."

"Man does not live by bread alone."

"Who the hell were you dining with, the goddamn president?"

Benny adopted a British accent. "I had a spot of tea several times with the ghost of Princess Di. Do tell me, Benny, was she as wonderful as they say? Mr. Bright, I'm happy to report that the media routinely underestimates the delight that woman, God rest her soul, brought to this world."

"Gas, $248.33."

"Contrary to popular opinion, Infinitis do not run on the air we breathe."

"Suit and tie and shirt, $679.66."

"A, I had to make a personal appearance. B, I was representing Dennis Bright and his band of merry men. C, the price of clothes has gone through the roof. D, all of the above. Circle the correct answer and move on to the next question."

"Speeding tickets, $129 and $105."

"Let us have a moment of silence to thank God for nice round numbers."

"Damn it, Benny, you know what all this comes to?"

Benny paused to light the cigar with a match. "What is mere money to the producer of a blockbuster?" Benny shook the flame off the match. "But just out of curiosity, what *does* all this come to?"

"Four thousand three hundred and thirty-six dollars and forty-seven cents is what it comes to. All I can say is, this blockbuster better be damn well worth it."

Benny filled the room with the aroma of inexpensive tobacco. "Guaranteed," he said, standing up to leave.

"By the way," said Bright, suddenly shifting from anger to curiosity. "What's this stuff about your mother?"

"My mother?"

"You wrote and told me your mother appeared to you in some kind of a vision. Remember?"

"Oh yes. The séance."

"Whatever. I'm curious. What did she have to say?"

"She reminded me to clean my plate and dress warmly."

"Seriously."

"Let's see . . . she said I had the gift."

"That's what I've been telling you. What else?"

"She told me to speak slowly and distinctly."

"Not bad advice. What else?"

"She predicted a stunning success for 'Religion Talk.'"

"Great! Anything else?"

"Oh yes. She also charged me $500." Benny sauntered toward the door. "I'll bring the bill in the morning."

§

Next morning Benny did not bring the bill for the fictitious séance. He did, however, launch "Religion Talk" on the maiden
voyage KKKS had been spotting for the last three weeks.

He began the show by speaking of Kirkland's deeply-felt,
long-standing need for an enlightening but lively radio show on
the topic of religion. He went on to acknowledge his lifelong interest in the subject, taking care not to mention his
excommunication from the Amish community and his adventures under the church pews with Lucy. He told about his recent
sojourn in California, where, he said, he had spent two weeks
visiting various synagogues, cathedrals, charismatic churches,
mosques, Buddhist monasteries, and spiritualist mentors, taking
care not to mention the imaginary episode in which he had gotten in touch with the mother he had never known. He spoke
glowingly of his experiences with a New Wave church and of the
many services it had to offer, taking care not to mention that he
was on its payroll.

"Now, let's get to the phones," he said confidently. "Hi, you're
on 'Religion Talk.'"

Benny's confidence sprang from the knowledge that his caller
would be Shannon Bright. The evening before, he had made
arrangements with Dennis Bright's willing wife to prime the
pump by making the first call.

"Hi Benny," said Shannon in a cheerful, pleasant soprano. "I'm
Sarah, and I'm visiting from Salem, Mass."

"Hi, Sarah from Salem. Why does that place sound familiar?"

"Salem is where they had all those witch trials."

"Witch trials? I thought it was where they made cigarettes."

Shannon giggled, on cue. "You're not even allowed to smoke
in Salem."

"And this is why you called?"

Shannon laughed, still on cue. "Actually, I'm calling to talk
about my religion."

"That's what we're here for. 'Religion Talk,' on KKKS, first in alternative programming in the Kirkland area. Which church do you attend, Sarah?"

"I'm currently Baptist."

"And what would you like to talk about?"

"I've been having trouble with my boy friend lately, because I want my other boy friend to move in with us, which my first boy friend doesn't think is a good idea, so I went and had a talk with my minister."

"Let me guess. He doesn't think it's a good idea either."

"Right. He thought I should repent and be saved and marry the guy."

"Which boy friend is that, Sarah? Number one or number two?"

"Number one. The guy I'm living with now."

"Didn't your minister offer you a choice?"

"No, and come to think of it, he put most of the emphasis on repenting and being saved."

"Let me ask you this, Sarah. How much are you paying this minister?"

"We're supposed to put ten percent of our take-home in the offering plate every Sunday."

"He gets a cut?"

"I believe so."

"How big is the church?"

"Very large. It takes up a whole city block."

The script called for laughter. Benny laughed. "I mean, what's the membership, numberwise?"

"It has oh, about a thousand members, but only a couple hundred show up Sunday mornings."

"That's not a high percentage."

"No, but the funerals are well-attended."

"That's a positive. But if I were you, Sarah, I'd shop around for a second opinion."

"The Baptist minister *was* my second opinion. I started out Presbyterian."

"And you had already talked to the Presbyterian minister about your problem?"

"Right."

"What did he say?"

"Pretty much the same thing. Except he thought I should go for boy friend number two."

"Why number two, if I may ask?"

"My guess is because the guy's an elder in his church."

"So, bottom line, the Presbyterians weren't much help either."

"Right."

"Well, you could always go someplace for a third opinion."

"Oh, I already got one. Last week I attended a Methodist church."

"Have you talked to that minister yet?"

"I did. She said to tell both guys to go to hell and get on with my life."

"She didn't mention anything about repentance and being saved?"

"No, she talked mostly about how we women of the female gender should stick together."

"Bad advice, Sarah. What I'd recommend is, join the Church of the Wide Open Door."

"I've never heard of it."

"You mean you don't have one in Massachusetts?"

"Not to my knowledge."

"In that case, you've got three options. One, you can move to California. Two, you can move permanently to Kansas, where I understand a new chapter is just opening up. Or three, you can stay right where you are and wait for them to set up shop. It won't take long."

"What's so special about the Church of the Wide Open Door?"

"It has lots of programs."

"Like what?"

Benny caressed the stem of the microphone. "We don't have all day, so I'll make it short. For somebody in your situation, I'd suggest Christian Tantrism."

"What's Christian Tantrism?" asked Shannon, and she put down her script and picked up the latest *Cosmopolitan*.

Benny proceeded to explain the basics of Christian Tantrism, starting with the Buddhist teaching that samsara is Nirvana, moving on to the English translation that God is love, and ending with the insight that salvation is achieved through sex. He cautioned that in order to put this insight to work, you should be at least eighteen and baptized. He went on to outline the four steps to Tantric perfection: (1) having a healthy body, (2) meditating on a mandala, which can be purchased at any adult bookstore, (3) contemplating an erotic ritual without feeling guilty, and (4) performing the ritual to your partner's satisfaction.

Shannon put down the *Cosmopolitan* and picked up her script and read, "But what's this Tantrism got to do with Christianity?"

"Have you ever read the Bible?"

"Everything up to the Ten Commandments."

"Why did you stop there? Some people consider the Ten Commandments very important."

"Actually, I got halfway through. To the one that said, 'Honor thy father and thy mother.' Which I figured didn't apply to me."

"Why not?"

"I'm an orphan."

The script again called for a laugh. Benny followed the script. "So you never got to the stories about Jesus?"

"No, but I saw the movie."

"Did you ever notice that they never report what Jesus did between the ages of twelve and thirty?"

"No I haven't, but now that you mention it. . . ."

"How would you explain that fact?"

Shannon paused, on cue. "Maybe he was going through a difficult period and they took it off his record."

"Good guess, but no. What he was really doing was, he was practicing Tantrism, which he got from the Buddhists."

"Yeah?"

"You remember John the Baptist?"

"Wasn't he the guy who got his head handed to the queen on a platter?"

"That's the one."

"I've always wondered about him."

"He was a Buddhist. He baptized Jesus after he taught him Tantrism."

"Really?"

"That's what scholars are now saying."

"You don't hear that very often."

"You know why? The clergy don't want the cat out of the bag. They specialize in sexual guilt. That's how they make a living, raking your guilt-ridden ten percent off the top."

The KKKS switchboard was beginning to light up. Benny said goodbye to Sarah from Salem and went to a commercial, an ad for the Christian Family Book Store, which specialized in Bibles, inspirational literature, children's books, computer software, and candles and had the distinction of carrying the largest assortment of American flags in the entire state of Kansas. Benny then spent the rest of the hour taking calls. Half of them were from offended ministers, priests, and a scattering of rabbis; the other half were from ordinary Kansans who were thirsty for more information on the Church of the Wide Open Door, especially the option of Christian Tantrism.

§

"Sit down!" said a furious Dennis Bright as Benny wandered into his office.

Benny sat down and reached into his T-shirt pocket for a pair of cigars. He offered one to his boss.

Bright waved his hand in refusal. "See that sign?" he said, pointing to nowhere. "It says 'No smoking.'"

Benny looked around at nowhere. "What sign?"

"Damn it, Benny."

"I sense a problem," said Benny, lighting the two cigars and inserting them into the left corner of his mouth and leaning back in his chair. "Would you like to talk about it?"

"Listen, Benny."

Benny leaned forward and cupped a hand behind an ear. "I hear it! I hear America singing." He puffed. "Do you hear America singing, Dennis?" Another puff. "Were you listening to my show?" Another. "Did you hear the clergy of Kirkland break into song halfway through the inaugural edition of 'Religion Talk'?" Another, and shorter, puff. "I did." Even shorter. "And what were they singing, Mr. Bright?" A long double drag, which Mr. Bright did not interrupt with an answer. "They were singing a song from *The Messiah*." Benny left off the puffing and became musical. "Despiséd and rejected," he sang.

"Cut the crap," said Bright. "We just got a cancellation. The Christian Family Book Store called and informed us they were no longer interested in sponsoring 'Religion Talk.'"

"You did the right thing, Denny. You talked about it. You unburdened yourself. Don't you feel better? That'll be a hundred and fifty bucks."

"We've got two options," Bright went on. "We can look for a new sponsor, or we can cancel."

"It's back to 'Benny's Begonias,'" sighed Benny.

"This is not funny. It's either a new sponsor, which means you've either gotta clean up your act or it's back to jockeying some eighteen-wheeler, which would be too bad, because you got the gift, plus the fact that I happen to like you even though you drive me absolutely nuts."

Benny thought about this for a long moment, between puffs. "Let's go for a new sponsor. Know of any Christian bordellos?"

§

That afternoon an enthusiastic person who wished to remain anonymous phoned Dennis Bright and offered to sponsor "Religion Talk."

Bright immediately called Benny into his office to break the good news and to work out the bugs of the temporarily suspended talk show. Bright suggested that Benny place less emphasis on the Church of the Wide Open Door and Christian Tantrism, and that he spend more time using his expertise to enlighten his audience on topics such as synagogues, cathedrals, charismatic churches, mosques, Buddhist monasteries, séances, the Amish, and the Holy Rollers.

Benny accepted these wise suggestions, and for the next month everything ran as smoothly as a Peterbilt on an interstate. Shannon Bright retained her position as the authorized first caller and pump-primer, establishing the subject of discussion for that day according to the script Benny had given her the previous evening. This worked very well, though the conversation frequently drifted back to the subject of Christian Tantrism, a subject Benny treated as dispassionately as a recent convert can be expected to treat his newly-adopted religion.

Soon Benny Good was a local celebrity. He became a regular at the best restaurants in Kirkland, where he never had to wait to be seated and where he was always placed at the best tables among the very best people. His autograph became a collectors' item. He became a popular speaker at the best clubs, whether men's, women's, or mixed. He was invited to give a series of Sunday morning lectures at the Kirkland Unitarian Church. He began to receive phone calls in the middle of the night from one or another of his growing band of disciples, requesting advice on such matters as whether or not pure Tantrism is best practiced in the missionary position. It was also rumored that he had become available for house calls.

So Benny was able to remain true to his religious calling, thanks to Arielle, who, at his suggestion, had talked Pastor Sean into placing that anonymous phone call.

§

"Come on in, Benny."

Benny obeyed. He followed Shannon into the den, taking the opportunity to admire the confident lilt in the gait of his leader.

"Sit down. What'll it be, a whiskey sour?"

Benny sat down on the white leather sofa. "You're beginning to know my intimate habits," he observed.

She flashed two rows of advertising-quality teeth and disappeared into the kitchen. Benny waited, paging through the latest *Cosmopolitan*. He looked around. "Where's Dennis?" he called.

She came out with the drinks, a whiskey sour and a Burgundy that matched her hair, and seated herself on the sofa within easy striking distance. "Denny's in New Orleans. Some convention or other." They clinked glasses. She showed her admirable teeth. "You know, Benny, Denny's very fond of you."

He took a long sip. "I'm making your husband lots of money, that's why." He took another sip. "Money makes the heart grow fond." Another sip. "Absence makes the heart grow fond*er*." Another. "As for what makes the heart grow fond*est*, it's probably a toss-up." And another. "The absence of money, however, makes the stomach growl."

Shannon laughed and held her glass aloft and peered over it at her welcome guest, one eye closed, the other narrowed. "It's not just the money. He goes around telling everybody you got the gift. He's a great judge of talent."

"Enough of Dennis," said Benny, finishing off his whiskey sour and placing the glass on an available table. "What should we do tomorrow?"

"You didn't bring the script?"

"I thought maybe we could wing it."

"I wouldn't have a clue what to say."

"You could begin with, 'Hi Benny, I'm Tanya from Tibet.'"

Shannon took a sip and squiggled up her nose. "Know something? You're funny."

"It's the cross I have to bear. Then you could go on and complain about your Buddhist monk who won't teach you Tantrism."

"I thought that's all Buddhist monks did, teach Tantrism."

"Where did you get that idea?"

"From you, silly," she said, nudging him with her glass. "Oh! Sorry," she said, showing a woman's concern for a man's shirt on which she has just spilled half a glass of Burgundy.

Benny inspected the damage. "That's all right," he assured her. "Whenever I put on this shirt, I'll think of you and Buddhist monks and Tantrism."

"Really? Always?"

"Sometimes I'll leave out the Buddhist monks."

Shannon giggled again. "Let me put it in the washer."

"That's what I admire about you. Your ingenuity. I bet if you thought about it long enough, you'd also put it in the dryer."

She helped him off with his shirt and disappeared with it into the laundry room. He heard the sound of running water. Soon she was back with a wet paper towel.

"Did I get some on your pants?"

"It depends. When will Dennis be back?"

She gave him the look of a woman weighing the risks. "I think he said something about tomorrow."

"In that case, you got some on my pants."

She helped him off with his pants and began to rub them in the logical place with the wet paper towel.

He confiscated the glass of wine from the end table and took a sip of what was left. "You're very funny," he said, nudging her with her glass. "Oh! Sorry," he said. "Did I get some on your dress? That's all right, Benny. Whenever I put on this dress, I'll

think of you and Tantrism. Really? Then let me put it in the washer. It'll go well with the shirt. They can spend the evening together, writing a script for their owners while their owners are in another part of the
house, winging it."

He helped her off with her dress and trotted off with it into the laundry room. He put it in the washer, which was getting ready to go into the spin cycle.

Very soon he returned with wetness in the logical place.

Shannon was not alone.

"Sit down!" said a furious Dennis Bright as Benny entered his den. "I wanna know just what the hell's going on!"

6

Touched by an Angel

As HE DROVE HOME FROM THE BRIGHTS', Benny Good sized up his situation.

He'd been on the ropes before. There was that first excommunication. Then the second, followed by the divorce. Then losing the Peterbilt on a calculated wager. And of course the begonias fiasco.

And now, being laid off from the best job he'd ever had.

But he'd bounced back. Every time. When the Amish sent him packing, he'd run across Reverend Barnabas. When Reverend Barnabas felt that his services were no longer needed, Lucy was right there to pay the bills. When the thing with Lucy didn't work out, he found employment as a trucker—eventually being able to go independent after he prophesied, correctly, that the Bulls would blow out the Lakers, a prophesy that won him the Peterbilt from a good buddy with a misplaced faith in the Magic Man. When he said goodbye to the Peterbilt after his gift for prophesy failed, temporarily—the Lakers hadn't beat the point spread and the Jazz had held Shaq to under thirty—he cashed in on his new-found knowledge of indoor plants and became a talk show host. When "Benny's Begonias" failed to meet expectations, he won that free trip to California and returned to a brief but glorious stint as the toast of Kirkland. Kirkland wasn't Big Apple country, but toast is toast, however you butter it.

There was no reason to think he wasn't up to *this* setback.

There were problems, of course. Not that the rent on his apartment was due tomorrow, or that the payment on his own new Infiniti was due the day after; he was still receiving checks from the Church of the Wide Open Door, checks that kept not bouncing. The big problem was keeping his cash cow from realizing that its missionary to Kansas had been deprived of his talk show and replaced, if Dennis Bright made good on his threat, with a priest, a minister, a rabbi, and some idiot professor known for his dandruff and the teeth marks on his tie. What if Arielle and Company found out? How would he finesse *that* one?

There was also another problem. He had not grown indifferent to the perks of being a local celebrity. He enjoyed eating in the best restaurants, not having to wait for a table, sitting with the best people, speaking to the best clubs, the best churches, giving advice on the best sexual positions, making calls in the middle of the night at the homes of the classiest ladies. Was all this history? Had God-led Benny Good exhausted his fifteen minutes of fame in one short but spectacular month?

§

Driving up to his apartment, his shirt still damp after its brief tumble in Shannon Bright's dryer, Benny suddenly remembered his new discovery, that God had been leading him all his life. This meant God was on his side. If this were true, wouldn't God come through for him again?

He went inside and checked his answering machine. Five messages. One was a dud, an abrupt hang-up; either a telemarketer or, possibly, a wrong number. One was a heavy breather; either a drunk or a nympho. One was a female admirer, wild to start a Benny Good fan club. One was a guy wanting to know if you had to be straight to be a Christian Tantrist. One identified herself as a talent agent. The fan, the inquisitive gay, and the agent gave their numbers and invited him to call back. He recorded these numbers on separate slips of paper and accepted their invitations.

Yes, he agreed with his female admirer, a Benny Good fan club would be a great idea. What exactly did it involve? Yes, he was a card-carrying Christian Tantrist, but there were other dimensions to him. No, he was not referring to indoor plants, he was referring, for instance, to his sensitivity, which not many people knew about. Yes, the point of life was personal growth. Through intimacy, yes of course. Divorce her husband, should she? He'd have to know more about the situation. No no, not now, not at this particular moment. Yes, they should probably get to know each other. On a personal basis? Possibly. Yes, he'd be delighted to come to the fan club's first meeting. By the way, what was her target market? Agewise? Oh. Well, why didn't he get back to her. Yes, he'd written the number down. Six-eight-two, and so forth. And thanks for calling. Thank you. Thank you. Thank you. You too. He had to go, sorry, the doorbell. Yes. Yes. Yes. He smelled a steak on the stove, burning itself to a crisp, he preferred his steak medium rare. She too? Great taste buds run in similar channels. Right. Right. Right. Fine. He thanked her for calling. He'd get back to her. He repeated the number. He again thanked her for calling. He said bye-bye and hung up.

Benny misplaced the phone-number-bearing slip of paper in the wastebasket and rang up the guy who was curious about the lifestyle requirements for Christian Tantrism.

As far as he knew, he told the guy, you didn't have to be straight to practice Christian Tantrism. He wasn't positive, but he'd ask. Oh yes, he had access to that information, in fact he knew the founder. On a personal basis. Yes, it was a she. Absolutely positive. Yes, he knew drag when he confronted it. No, he was not bi. But this didn't mean he wasn't a firm believer in the cause. Would he what? Sign a petition? Possibly, it depended on the wording. Had he made any what? Any contributions? Oh.

Yes, from time to time, he had, yes, but then of course he contributed to many worthy causes. Many many. Sorry, he had this principle, he did not divulge that kind of information. Of course, but the IRS was an exception. Comfortable, was he, discussing the topic of Christian Tantrism's inclusiveness on "Religion Talk"? Well, yes, except that tomorrow he would be going on leave. No, he didn't know exactly for how long. Would he be back? He wasn't positive, but he—. Oh no, no no no, nothing serious, not at all. Contract negotiations, that sort of a thing. Sure. Sure. Certainly. He was glad he'd called. Any time.

Benny tossed the number in the wastebasket and called the talent agent.

No he didn't, he told her. No, he'd never had one. Not that he was opposed to having one. He was sure many careers had gotten big boosts from having an agent. Well, to tell the truth he hadn't ever seriously considered the issue. No, the fee wasn't the problem. He was sure a good agent could earn her ten percent. Fifteen, was it? Oh. Well, he'd always handled his own business, pretty successfully, too, for the most part. Yes, of course there were tight spots, he realized that, he was no longer a child. Talk about it, at least? He guessed so. Nothing to lose, right? Tomorrow lunch would be fine, he happened to be off tomorrow, so twelve-thirty would be perfect. Make it Pepe's, that's where the best people hang out. Fine. Pepe's it was, twelve-thirty, he'd be hard to miss, he occupied more than his share of Newtonian space.

"Pepe's. 12:30. Esther Geld," he scribbled, adding "FOXY voice."

§

"Caught your act yesterday," said Esther Geld, lighting a cigarette. "Just happened to be in town. Funeral, you know. Mama went bye-bye."

"Sorry," said Benny, forgetting to light a cigar.

The voice, foxy though it was, did not begin to purvey the essence of Ms. Geld, around thirty, dressed in a black suit, in celebration of the life of a former mother, but with a white blouse, in celebration of who knew what. She could make the cover of any magazine, maybe even and hopefully the centerfold of one in particular. Comparatively speaking, Shannon was a mere warm-up, a Joan the Baptist preparing the way for one lovelier and more pulchritudinous, if that was still a word, than herself. Even Lucy in her prime was, comparatively speaking, a dog, to say nothing of Arielle and the Dollys and the Officer X's and the runaways that stretched from coast to coast over a period of twenty-some years.

Ms. Geld inhaled and threw her head back. "Life is short."

"*Human* life," he pointed out. "That's compared to the life of the giant turtle. Compared to the life of the average fruit fly, you might have an argument on your hands."

She aimed a perfect smoke ring at him. "You've got the gift."

"Unfortunately," he admitted as he fingered a Swisher Sweet, "I no longer have a tree to put it under. To quote my former boss."

"Meaning he canned you?"

Benny gazed at the end of the cigar. "Unfortunately," he said as he lit it, "great gifts often go unappreciated."

"Well. There are trees and there are trees."

Benny aimed a thick stream of smoke at the ceiling. "You got any particular tree in mind?"

She looked him over. "Maybe. Tell me about yourself, starting with the tadpoles in daddy's sperm."

Their waitress, one of Benny's recent converts to the teachings and practices of Christian Tantrism, came and got their orders and left with a frown on her doggy face, comparatively speaking.

He proceeded to give Ms. Geld an expurgated version of the adventures of Benny Good, starting with the buggy story and ending with the recent controversy over whether "Religion Talk" should still be jump-started every morning by a well-rehearsed question from Shannon Bright.

"So where do we go from here?" she asked when he was through.

"An excellent question," he said. "Congratulations. Few persons have the ability not only to recognize the shortness of life but to see the connection of this fundamental truth with the question of the future, which stands before us, ready to be embraced, either passionately or with a certain . . . panic."

Ms. Geld smiled faintly. "You are a natural communicator. Sometimes. So, where do we go from here?"

Their waitress arrived with two lunches and distributed them erroneously.

Benny dug into the small shrimp salad that Esther Geld had ordered.

Ms. Geld gently shoved aside Benny's more substantial order but sipped his vodka tonic. "If this is an example of where we go from here," she said, arching an eyebrow, "we are not going to make it."

"Oh," said Benny, realizing his mistake. "Did I mention my employment at Windsor Palace? I once served as food-taster for the Queen Mother. A woman of many fears. I ended up eating all her meals. I'm afraid it's become a habit. God has learned to forgive me, on a regular basis. Could you? Not that I put you and God in the same category." He leaned forward. "Just between the two of us," he said conspiratorially, "if I had to choose who should manage my career, I'd go with you."

She leaned forward. "I'll keep it a secret," she whispered.

"Easier said than done. Rumor has it He's got big ears."

Smiling briefly, she snuffed out her cigarette. She lit another and blew a thin, admirable smoke ring, which dallied in the mesosphere before quietly dispersing. "There are two kinds of people in the world," she said, shaking the flame off the end of her match. "Those who *have* talk shows, and those who *use* them."

"I couldn't agree more. What do you mean?"

"I mean you were wasting your time on 'Religion Talk.'"

"That's what I kept telling my boss. I kept saying, 'Let's go back to "Benny's Begonias." I was just getting to know the names of the plants.'"

"You belong on the other side of the mike," observed Ms. Geld.

"What's the pay scale? I ask this only because I'm concerned about your fifteen percent."

"Sure you are," she said agnostically. "Pay scale?" she added. "That depends on where we put you."

"I'm open to being put anywhere. I draw the line at coffins."

"We should stay in the religion business, definitely. That's where the future lies."

"I wouldn't want to leave Christian Tantrism. I have a special affection for it."

"Tell me more about this Christian Tantrism."

Benny spoke glowingly and at length about Christian Tantrism, ending his sermon with an altar call.

"Sorry," she said, "I don't screw my clients."

"Sorry," he replied in a voice just several millimeters this side of despair. "Any particular reason?"

She gave a toss of her hair. "I have my principles."

"Sorry," he repeated. He began to devour the meal he had ordered. Three mouthfuls later he wanted to know, "Where were we?"

"We had you in the religion business. The specifics had not been worked out."

Benny bit off half a loaf of French bread. "I could always start my own."

She arched a disapproving eyebrow. "You want to start your *own* religion?"

"I've been thinking about it for fifteen seconds."

The arch grew; the eye under its partner narrowed. "In the age of corporate takeovers?"

Benny quit chewing and raised a shrewd eyebrow. "Exactly what did you have in mind? The answer should probably end with the word *church*."

"Guess."

"Unitarian?"

"Think big."

"You don't mean Amish?"

"Don't think goldfish. Think whale."

"Church of the Wide Open Door?"

"Use your imagination."

"I was brought up not to. Especially in mixed company."

"I'll give you a hint. It has a pope."

Benny resumed eating. "That boils it down. What else?"

"Corporate headquarters are located in Rome."

"What else? Usually the contestant gets three clues."

"It has monks and nuns."

"That's what I was afraid of," sighed Benny.

"I'm serious. With your talent, sky's the limit."

"Which sky are we talking about?"

"Oh, bishop for starters. Then we go from there."

Benny hailed their passing waitress and requested the check.

"What would this involve?" he asked Ms. Geld. "Just out of idle curiosity."

"Reinventing Benny Good."

"And here I've always assumed that God had done one helluva job."

"Let's start with the name. How would 'Benny Good' look on a resumé?"

"It's got me where I am today."

"That's my point."

The check arrived. Benny moved a tentative hand in its direction. Esther Geld deftly beat him to it. He stood up and tossed a pocketful of small change on the table.

"Do yourself a favor," she said, snuffing out her latest cigarette. "Think it over. Then give me a ring." She handed him a card with a New York address and phone number.

"I'll pray about it," he said, placing the card in his wallet next to a disappointed condom.

"Fill me in on the results."

He nodded and headed for the men's room.

When he came back, she was gone. He glanced around for possible witnesses, gathered the small change on the table with a newly-washed hand, pocketed it, and left for home.

§

"Lucy here," said a voice. "I can't come to the phone right now, but at the tone please leave your message, etcet etcet."

The tone sounded.

"Lucy. Benny here. I need some advice. I'm about to be reinvented, and I thought you might have a few suggestions. Could you compose a five-minute speech on the subject and give me a call? This outstanding opportunity expires at midnight tomorrow. If I haven't received your views on the subject by that time, I'll be forced to remain the same old Benny—glutton, wastrel, vagabond, rogue, con man, etcetera."

"Benny?" said the voice.

"Today I am Benny, yesterday I was Benny, tomorrow I will still be Benny, but I don't know how long I can keep it up."

"Talk sense, would you?"

Benny talked sense. He spoke proudly and at some length of Esther Geld, talent agent, and her plans for his future, omitting comparisons to the other women who had played significant roles in his life.

"I'm jealous," she said with a pout on the edge of her voice.

"You have no right to be. Remember, you are a married woman."

"Were. Yesterday I kicked the kid out."

"This was Sal?"

"I don't recall the name. It's been such a long time."

"Anyway, you're jealous."

"Right. I'm jealous of any woman who has the slightest chance to reinvent Benny Good."

"I think she wants to make me pope."

"I wish her lots of luck."

"Will you marry me?"

"I thought they had this rule, no married popes."

"That was pre-Benny. I would, of course, reinvent the papacy."

"You're crazy."

"Thank you, Lucy. I hadn't realized it was so obvious. Maybe that's why she wants to make me pope. Will you marry me, or did I already say that?"

"Bye-bye, Benny, or did I already say that?"

"Consider what I could offer you. A nice clean cell in Rome. A life of contemplation, relieved by an occasional roll on the hard stone floor. Unlimited access to Italian monasteries, manned by multitudes of sex-starved Latin lovers. Unlimited world travel to visit the rich, the powerful, and the wannabes. I also understand there are plans afoot to put a pope and a dozen of his closest friends on the moon in the coming decade—conquer it for Christ, maybe even give Buddha a piece of the action. Think of it, Lucy, you could be among that select group."

"Lots of hard stone floor up there."

"That would also be my guess. Will you marry me?"

"I'm sorry, Benny, I can't." These words seemed to spoken in a serious, maybe even plaintive, tone.

"Give me one good reason."

"I could give you a hundred."

"Go with your best."

"I'm engaged."

"Congratulations, Lucy. That's a fine reason. I wouldn't underestimate that reason. I have great respect for it. But what about the other ninety-nine? On further reflection, forget it. I know them by heart. I would like to know, however, which of the remaining reasons no longer apply."

"Not now, Benny. I don't have time."

"Of course. I understand. In ten minutes you're due at work."

"As a matter of fact, in ten minutes I'm due at the altar."

§

Benny spent the rest of the day rambling around the apartment, sipping whiskey sours and wondering where God had gone wrong.

He woke up next afternoon with a slight headache.

He called the New York number printed on Esther Geld's card. Her secretary put him straight through.

"Have you thought it over?" asked Ms. Geld.

"I prayed about it."

"And what did God say?"

"He spake to me out of a whirlwind, saying, 'Go for it.'"

"Fine. Hop on over to New York and we'll come up with a strategy."

Benny acknowledged that this was a fine idea. He further acknowledged that he was, comparatively speaking, broke.

"Don't worry. I'll pop for this. I'm putting you on to my assistant. He'll work out the details."

Benny spoke to the assistant, a discerning young man with the world of airline schedules at his fingertips.

Early next morning, Benny was on a flight to New York, paging through the chapter on Catholicism in *Religion for Dolts.*

7

Some Minor Cosmetic Surgery

ESTHER GELD'S ASSISTANT had arranged for a limousine to retrieve Benny Good from JFK.

Throughout his many years on the road, Benny had always bypassed New York, preferring to stay down the coast in Atlantic City, which had many of the amenities he prized and was kinder to truckers, trafficwise. But here he now was, approaching the greatest city in the world in a stretch limo, wearing the suit and tie and shirt he had bought in Los Angeles and with his shirt pocket stuffed with cigars.

He leaned back and lit a Swisher Sweet.

"Mind if I smoke?" he asked the chauffeur, a handsome liveried male in his early- to mid-forties. "It's a special blend of fine noncarcinogenic tobacco leaves, carefully chosen for their gentle aromatic properties."

"Fine. What're you reading?" Benny was caressing a paperback book.

"*Religion for Dolts.*"

"That's what I thought."

"I recommend it for the uninitiated."

"Thanks."

"No disrespect intended, of course. In fact, I have a great deal of admiration for those in your profession. In leaner days, I myself was a trucker. Ah yes. As a poet once wrote, 'Alone and lighthearted, I take to the open road.' Much of my spare time on the highways of America was spent reading the great literature, which I also recommend."

"The poet was Whitman, and it's '*Afoot* and lighthearted,' and I meant thanks for liking my book."

"Whitman, of course. I was paraphrasing. *Your* book?"

"I wrote it."

"Congratulations," said Benny agnostically. "Have a cigar."

Benny leaned forward and handed the man a fine cigar, which the man pocketed.

"Turn to page 127," said the chauffeur. "Seventh full paragraph."

Benny turned to the recommended page and found the recommended paragraph.

"'Islam,'" quoted the writer by heart, "'considers Muhammad the last of God's prophets, which include Adam, Noah, Abraham, Moses, and Jesus.'"

"That's what it says, all right. How did you know?"

"I struggled with that sentence," said its author.

Benny shook his head in unagnostic awe. "You got it right."

"I got a lot of them right."

"A fine book," agreed Benny, "though it's a little weak in my area of expertise."

"Yeah? What's that?"

"Christian Tantrism."

"Christian what? Fill me in."

Benny gave the uninitiated a brief synopsis of his newfound faith.

"Interesting," said the chauffeur, stopping at a red light. "Do you have to be single to join?"

"An excellent question. I myself know of no married Christian Tantrists," said Benny, forgetting the half a dozen married but lonely women he had initiated into his chosen faith, "but then I've only been practicing the religion for several weeks. If you're interested, however, I can make inquiries. I personally know the founder, who is single—at least she didn't mention a husband when she baptized me. Perhaps I should explain that the true devotee isn't required to reveal his or her marital status. In fact, such information is considered private, and divulging it is frowned upon."

The chauffeur fought his way through a war zone indicated by a green light. "Could a guy practice it with his wife?"

"I suppose so, but I don't know why anybody would want to."

The chauffeur, stuck in traffic, played his steering wheel like a piano while he hummed bars from the Overture to *The Marriage of Figaro*.

"I didn't mean to offend you," Benny went on. "I was just giving my personal opinion, which the last time I checked was still covered by the First Amendment."

"Sure," said the chauffeur, moving on.

"If it's any consolation," confided Benny, "I've often thought of practicing it with my former wife."

Instead of answering, the author of *Religion for Dolts* broke into a whistled rendition of selected arias from *The Barber of Seville*, which he completed just as he deposited his loquacious passenger at the Madison Avenue address of the Esther Geld Agency, Inc.

§

Benny looked up and down the sidewalk. Never could he have imagined so many outstanding candidates for Christian Tantrism. Manhattan seemed to be an enormous mission field, teeming with attractive young women scurrying about looking, without realizing it, for a guru who would unlock their spiritual potential. Maybe Kirkland was not his place in the Grand Design? Maybe he was in New York for a reason?

He went up to the Esther Geld Agency to find that reason.

"She'll be with you in a minute," said the receptionist. "Have a seat."

Benny had a seat and thumbed through a dozen back issues of *Variety*.

Then he reread the *Religion for Dolts* chapter on Catholicism, underlining the key points.

He took his pulse.

He asked the receptionist for directions to the men's room, pointing out that he was still alive and would be back in a minute.

He was back in forty-five seconds, fresh of breath.

He sat down and memorized the key points of Catholicism.

As he was rechecking his pulse, a distinguished-looking gentleman emerged from the office of Esther Geld, followed by Ms. Geld herself.

"Three more years," she said. "I think you're right on schedule."

"On schedule," repeated the gentleman, beaming and shaking her hand.

He left.

"Mr. Good to see you," the receptionist informed Esther Geld.

Ms. Geld cast a professional eye on Mr. Good. "Come in," she said.

They entered her office and took turns sitting down and igniting the tobacco leaves of their choice.

"That was Governor Snow," she said matter-of-factly. "He'll be the Democratic nominee for president next go-round."

"Really? I'm impressed."

"Doesn't stand a chance. He'll be running against General Brewster."

Benny was confused. "Why would you back a loser?" he asked.

"We represent the general," she said, half-smiling. "We advise the governor. But let's get to the point, Mr. Good. It's Bunny, isn't it?"

"Benny," said Benny, accurately. "But I was named Kaninchen, which is Amish for Bunny."

"Oh yes. You're the gentleman from Kirkland."

"Correct. I'm the guy with the gift, looking for a tree to put it under."

"Refresh my memory."

"The former host of 'Religion Talk.'"

"Say more."

"Devotee of Christian Tantrism."

"It's coming. . . ."

"Salvation through sex?" he suggested hopefully.

She pointed an index finger at him "The one who ate my food!"

"It was nothing but a shrimp salad, ma'am. The lettuce lacked crispness. The shrimp were mere juveniles. The average American could pronounce the name of the dressing."

She nodded. "The bishop of Kirkland is on his last legs."

"Speaking of bishops," commented Benny. "How do you know?"

"Good news travels fast."

"What about the bishop of Manhattan? Is he also awaiting the Grim Reaper, God willing, or is he unfortunately in robust health, ready and eager to throw out the first pitch on opening day?"

"The main man here is a cardinal. That's something we work up to. We start with bishop. The Kirkland slot happens to be available, so we go for it."

§

Esther Geld led Benny Good down a hall and into a room and introduced him to a collection of consultants, all acknowledged as top-notch experts in their fields. They were Mike Bacchus, a round ex-priest with a red nose who was said to know the inner workings of the Vatican; Ron Something, a political advisor who kept consulting his wrist watch and was reputed to have his finger on the pulse of the American public; and Andrea Something, who was breaking in a pair of contact lenses and was known around town as a wordsmith. Ms. Geld had brought them all together for a brainstorming session. Their assignment, she informed Benny before excusing herself for lunch with an established client, was to reinvent her new client.

"Let's start with your life story," the red nose said to Benny in a tone both professional and casual. "Maybe there's something in it we can use."

Benny sketched an eloquent but accurate autobiography, from Amish foundling to host of "Religion Talk," placing special emphasis on his credentials as a licensed practitioner of Christian Tantrism.

"I like the part about being Amish," said Andrea. She was taking notes. Benny did not judge her to be a viable candidate for his particular variety of Christianity, though she was undoubtedly an expert in her own field. "How do you spell it?"

Benny did not get a chance to spell it. The other two experts, though approving of the fact that Benny had been a foundling and agreeing that Benny's Amish roots were indeed a human interest story, quickly vetoed this part of his past, Ron on the grounds that the Amish constituted a minuscule percentage of the American population and did not enjoy a political presence, Bacchus because the Vatican would not know who the Amish were.

"If not Amish, what?" asked Andrea.

"Let's think ecumenical," said Bacchus.

"There's the Buddhist connection," suggested Benny. "Tantrism was originally practiced by Buddha."

"How do you spell it?" asked Andrea.

"T-A-N-T-R-I-S-M," said Benny.

"I mean Buddha," said Andrea.

Before Benny had the opportunity to improve Andrea's mind, Ron and Bacchus shifted the conversation to American religion. Within ten minutes, they had given Benny a Jewish father (a rabbi) and a Christian mother (a Baptist Sunday School teacher) and were moving him along on his religious pilgrimage. It took them only ten more minutes to confer on him a theological degree from Harvard Divinity School and establish his career as a Unitarian minister in Kirkland, Kansas.

"Now," said Bacchus, "we've got to come up with a conversion story."

"What's wrong with the one I've got?" asked Benny. He went on to remind them of his recent discovery that salvation is attained through sex.

"Not a viable option," said Bacchus. "The Vatican is a bit behind the times."

Ron deferred to Bacchus's expertise on this issue. In fifteen minutes, Mike had composed the rough drafts, subject to Esther Geld's approval, of several alternative accounts of how Benny had shed the evils of his past ways and come to acknowledge the truth of Catholicism.

"Now for the name," said Ron, glancing at his watch. "I've got another appointment in five minutes."

"'Benny,'" mused Bacchus, staring at the ceiling and strumming two pairs of matched fingertips on each other, tip to tip. "Short for 'Benedict.' From the Latin, *bene*, good, and *diction*, speaking. 'Bene-dict': good speaking."

"*Love* it," said Benny.

"Remember, we gave him a Jewish father," pointed out Ron. "'Benny,' short for 'Benjamin.'"

"I vote for 'Benedict,'" said Benny. "But you can just call me 'Benny.'"

"Let's make it 'Benjamin' before the conversion, 'Benedict' after," said Ron, looking at his watch.

"Brilliant," said Bacchus. "Now the last name. 'Good,' right? That's okay, nothing wrong with it, but it's a little, what should I say, bland."

"Cut out an 'O' and you've got God," pointed out the man with the watch.

"Which 'O'?" asked Andrea.

"That would be too obvious," Bacchus said to Ron, ignoring the wordsmith's request for information. "Also, it's not Jewish."

"What's the Jewish word for 'God'?" asked Andrea.

"The Amish word is 'Gott,'" said Benny. "'Benedict Gott.'"

"Not bad, but it doesn't exactly come tripping off the tongue," said Ron, peering again at his watch.

"God is love," Benny reminded them. "Speaking of Tantrism."

"Love!" said Bacchus, struck by a new revelation. "The German word for 'love' is '*Liebe.*' Gott-lieb!"

"Very Jewish," said Ron, standing up.

"How do you spell it?" asked Andrea.

"Use your spell check," said Ron as he left, his watch in place and satisfied with its owner's timing.

"G-O-T-T-L-I-E-B," said Bacchus. "Gott-lieb. Lover of God. 'Benedict Gottlieb!' Good speaking lover of God!"

"*Love* it!" said Benny.

§

Esther Geld's assistant had arranged for Benny to stay at a hotel near Madison Square Garden. That evening Benny attended a game between the Knicks and the Blazers, accompanied by a Knicks fan, a potential convert he had run across in the hotel lobby. Sprewell had a difficult night; his wheels were rumored to be bothering him. The Blazers won, in overtime, much to Benny's delight. He used his winnings to treat his companion, an Esther Geld look-alike, to an after-game snack, during which he tried on his new identity as Benedict Gottlieb for size, bemoaning the tribulations of being the sole child of a Jewish rabbi and a

Baptist Sunday School teacher. Afterwards he used the opportunity to plant a cell of Christian Tantrism in Manhattan, baptizing his companion, first in the hotel swimming pool, then in the shower in his room, where she used his shoulder to bemoan the tribulations of being an unemployed lingerie model.

He awoke next morning alone and, he soon discovered, with an empty wallet.

He left a message on Lucy's answering machine and went to the offices of the Esther Geld Agency.

§

"'Benedict Gottlieb,'" said Esther Geld, looking through the stack of papers Andrea Wordsmith had recently deposited on her desk. "Didn't I tell you my people are tops?"

"You told me they were experts in their fields. I don't recall your using the word *tops*. But that's neither here nor there. What's important is that I have a new identity. The next item on the agenda is a new set of credit cards."

"I'll put my assistant on that." She picked up the phone and gave the order.

"Some cash would also be helpful. I lost a bet last night. The Knicks were defeated, in overtime. Sprewell had a difficult night."

She picked up the phone again and told her assistant to procure an ATM card.

She put down the phone. "We've got to make some lifestyle changes," she said. "Bishops don't gamble."

"Bishops don't *lose*," he corrected her. "A competent bishop will realize that the Knicks beat the point spread over sixty percent of the time. That's at home, of course. On the road, they have their problems. I'm not sure why. When I figure it out, I'll let you in on the secret. There will be a modest charge for this service."

"So don't gamble, okay?" she said, checking her appointment notebook. "Also," she continued without looking up, "lose some weight."

"I am a lover of the better things in life, of which I rank food number two. Does that include beverages, Bishop Gottlieb? It most certainly does. And what do you rank number one? Thank you for your curiosity, but on that question I'm compelled to take the Fifth."

"Try to be more discreet about your private life." She was still fascinated by her appointment book. "Last night you were seen with a hooker."

"Jesus himself commingled with sinners, some of whom may have been women, some maybe even harlots. And my evening companion was not a hooker, she was an unemployed lingerie model, a class of people for whom I have a great deal of sympathy and respect. I baptized her, in case you were wondering."

"Leave the girls alone, okay? At least in public. Which reminds me." She looked up. "Before you go, Mike wants to measure you for a priest outfit. Wear it."

"On job-related occasions, I would expect to. May I ask a personal question? Go ahead, Father Gottlieb. Do women find priestly garb a turn-on? Nuns, maybe. In that case, I'll also wear it for social occasions. But there's something I don't understand. Yes, Father Gottlieb? Do bishops live in monasteries?"

"You'd have to ask Bacchus. He'll be your Man Friday."

"Fine. I've observed that Michael Bacchus is a well-read man, an astute observer of the ways of the world, of the Vatican, and of the world in general. I'm confident he has a lot to offer."

"Mike is a drunk. Do what he says."

"I expect to get along with him famously."

She stared at him to make sure he was listening. "All payments will be made directly to him."

"Payments?"

"The Kirkland Diocese will have a budget."

"I've heard that word someplace. Where have I heard it? Oh yes. From my ex. She always urged me to live within our, what was the word? *Budget?* Which means it must be something like a cage."

"It's something like where we get our fifteen percent."

"That would explain Mike's interest in my career."

"Right."

"It might also explain *your* interest."

"You catch on fast."

Benny looked at his watch. "What's next for Father Gottlieb? Does he go home and wait for the good bishop to die?"

"The good bishop's funeral is tomorrow. Mike will take you."

"Funeral? Already? Did Mike have something to do with this?"

"Absolutely not. Mike has principles."

Relieved by this assurance of Mike's character, Benny got up to leave.

"Before you go," said Ms. Geld, "I've got something for you to sign."

She slid a piece of paper across the desk. It was a letter:

His Holiness the Pope
Papal Palace
Vatican City
Rome, Italy

Most Holy Father:

I was truly grieved to read of the recent death of Fr. James Duncio, Bishop of Kirkland, Kansas. Bishop Duncio has indeed been an inspiration to everyone whose life he touched. Though I did not know him in the flesh, only by reputation—word of his great piety and continual crusade for moral renewal has for several decades been passed along in hushed and awed tones in this diocese—I must nonetheless take this opportunity to add my own small voice to the chorus of those who lament his untimely passing. We are of course not left without the consolation afforded by the words of St. Paul in his Letter to the Romans: "I consider that the sufferings of this present life are not worth comparing with the glory that is to be revealed to us" (Rom. 8:18).

Undoubtedly the Holy See will be prayerfully seeking someone to fill Fr. Duncio's venerable shoes. It is with this in mind that I boldly approach the throne of grace, confessing that I feel led by God to offer myself most humbly as a candidate for the position of Bishop of the Diocese of Kirkland.

Enclosed you will find (1) an up-to-date *curriculum vitae* enumerating the particulars of my training and accomplishments, and (2) a narrative account of selected highlights of my career, including an account of my conversion to the one true form of Christianity.

Next week I will be making a pilgrimage to the European holy sites. Should you find my credentials suitable, I will be happy to make myself available for an interview any time from the late afternoon of the 4th to the early morning of the 6th, when, after prayers, I am scheduled to leave for Lourdes. I can be reached at the Rome Marriott; the number is undoubtedly listed in your local directory.

Thanking you in advance for your devout consideration of my petition, I am

Yours in Faith, Hope, and Charity,

Father Benedict Gottlieb

The letter had come through Andrea's spell check in fine order. Benny signed it. "What's this?" he asked, pointing to the phrase *curriculum vitae.*

"I believe that's Latin," explained Ms. Geld. "It refers to your resumé."

"My what?"

"Your statement of career and qualifications."

"Of course. Do you think it would be possible for me to take a peek at it? I feel I'm at a disadvantage, not knowing the details of my past life. How could I face His Holiness without that information? Would you recommend I plead amnesia? Maybe that's not a bad idea. It would explain why I forgot to kiss his ring—or will it be his feet? Does he shower before meeting bishop candidates, or do you have to be running for cardinal?"

"We're working on the final draft. We'll get it to you before the European tour."

"What about my conversion? Just curious, you know. Did I come to the truth through many years of serious study, prayerful contemplation, and drinking modest amounts of alcoholic beverages? Or did I get hit by lightning?"

Esther Geld stood up, signaling her opinion that the interview was at an end. "We'll get that story to you, too."

"If I have a choice, I'll go with lightning," said Benny as he lit a cigar and prepared to leave. "As a great poet once put it, 'Liquor is dandy, but lightning is quicker.'"

8

Pilgrim's Progress

FLYING BACK TO KIRKLAND, Mike Bacchus was looking out the window at the southern tip of Indiana. Benny Gottlieb was reading a catechism to prepare himself for the new job that he had every right to expect would soon be his. They had just finished their second whiskey sours when Benny said:

"I'd like to make a confession."

Mike said, "Shoot."

"I've never been to a Funeral Mass for a bishop."

"Nothing to it."

"I'd like to make another confession," said Benny.

"You've never been to a Funeral Mass, period. Or even to a Mass."

Benny shook his head in amazement. "You must be psychic."

"When you do a lot of confessions," explained Mike, "you get to know what's coming next."

"Really? You've done a lot of confessions? Which side of the curtain did you work? I don't mean to pry, but I have a sudden urge to know. As Plato said, 'All men by nature have sudden urges to know.' Being a man, I'm curious to know which side of the curtain you worked."

"It wasn't Plato, it was Aristotle, and I've done both sides."

"Do you have any preferences? I ask this only because I also have another sudden urge. I want know what the hell I'm getting into."

"Power is always on the side of the priest. If you like power, stick to that role."

"Tell me, Mike—I can call you Mike, can't I? Thank you, Mike. I appreciate your common touch, Michael—are you saying a bishop has to *make* confessions?"

"Only when he's sinned."

"I'll try to keep that in mind. And in case you were wondering, yes, I know all about sin. As you may remember, I was brought up Amish. You've probably been led to believe that the Amish are the most sin-free of all God's creatures. This is not true. Your typical Amish male commits 2.3 sins a day, on the average. Most of them are committed behind the barn, which explains why they write Bible verses on the sides of their barns, to keep the evil spirits away. The theory is, evil spirits cause sin. I don't know if that theory is reliable. There are arguments on both sides. Now, where was I? Oh yes, the statistics of sin. Your typical Amish female commits 2.7 sins a day, again on the average. How can this discrepancy be explained, you ask?"

"How?"

"All women by nature have sudden urges to *be* known. Compared to the urges of women, the urges of men—where are you going?"

"Excuse me," said Mike.

Mike lurched down the aisle toward the restroom. Benny reached up and pushed the button to attract the stewardess. She came. He ordered a pair of whiskey sours. Mike returned from the restroom and stumbled over Benny to get to his seat. The stewardess brought the whiskey sours and placed them at Benny's disposal.

"Here you go, Father," she said with a smile and an expectation.

Mike paid her. She left for other venues.

"'Father'," said Benny, shoving a whiskey at Mike. "You hear that, Mike? She called me 'Father'."

"That's because of the costume."

"I thought it was because of the drinks."

"Getting back to the Funeral Mass," said Mike, changing course.

"Yes. What do I do?"

"Just two things. One, grieve a lot. Two, do whatever I do."

"Grieve without ceasing. Monkey see, monkey do," repeated Benny, throwing down his whiskey sour and preparing to order another.

§

At the Funeral Mass for the former bishop, the officiating archbishop, citing Scriptural evidence, guaranteed the faithful that Father Duncio's exemplary life had won him a special spot in heaven. He also seemed to think that Father Duncio had a fair shot at sainthood, a thought that elicited fervent nods from those who had known him best.

As for our two heroes, the whole affair went off without a major hitch. The only blunder came near the end, when Nature called Michael and Benny followed them both to the men's room.

"What the hell are *you* doing here?" growled Mike.

"Monkey see, monkey do. How's my grieving?"

"Fine, just don't overdo it," growled Mike. They shared a nip from his flask. "Let's go out and press some flesh."

§

Next day the monkey and his trainer flew to Europe, disguised as American tourists. At De Gaulle, they were met by their tour bus driver, eager to escort them to every castle, cathedral, palace, museum, and monastery from Paris to Vienna.

They began their pilgrimage with a nap at a hotel. Then they floated up and down the Seine, listening to an amplified voice pointing out the famous landmarks while observing G-stringed sunbathers in the act of reading paperback novels. That evening the bus took them to the cathedral Sacré Coeur ("French for 'Sacred Heart,'" Mike explained), overlooking the city. Mike took a picture of Paris and Benny lighting up. They strolled around Montmartre, watching artists paint portraits of smiling, well-paying American pilgrims.

The following morning they went to Notre Dame ("French for 'Our Lady,'" explained Mike). Benny remarked how nice it was. He added that when he put his mind to it, it made him think of God.

They went to the Louvre, a famous museum. They took turns taking pictures of each other standing alongside a nude statue, admiring the artistry. ("The *Venus de Milo*," explained Mike.) Benny wandered off by himself and eventually found himself in a large room, where Mona Lisa was holding court. Their eyes met; she smiled at him. He winked back.

Benny and Mike strolled around the Latin Quarter, stopping at an outdoor café for several bottles of wine and a round of philosophical discussion.

"Life is good," said Benny.

"It'll get better," predicted Mike.

They attended the Folies Bergere and watched lovely semi-clad Frenchwomen on parade. Afterwards Mike took his client to visit some other semiclad Frenchwomen, equally lovely. Benny told two of them about Christian Tantrism. "*Monsieur professeur,*" one of them said with what appeared to be a French accent. "Do you want to talk, or do you want to screw?" It was a difficult decision, but Benny chose to take the vow of silence.

The tour proceeded to the city of Versailles, where it seems there was a palace. The two men left the group and strolled through the surrounding gardens. "I could see this as a golf course," observed Benny. They went inside the palace and fought their way through the foot traffic to the Hall of Mirrors. "Minia-ture golf," said Benny. "For the ladies."

They drove to Chartres to see a cathedral. A Brit with plenty of time on his hands gave them a guided tour, explaining the theological meanings behind the elongated statues of Bible char-acters and the figures depicted on the stained-glass windows.

"Why are we doing this?" whispered Benny an hour into the lecture.

"So you can say you've done Chartres."

"Who's gonna ask?"

"Maybe the pope."

Benny frowned. "Am I supposed to remember all this stuff?"

"Just the windows," advised Mike out of the corner of his still-wet mouth. "In case he asks, say the blue windows were ethereal."

Benny looked up at the blue windows. "They *are* nice."

"They're not 'nice,' they're 'ethereal'."

"Think he'd settle for 'stunning'?"

"Better play it safe and stick with 'ethereal.'"

"Gotcha."

The tour bus next took them to the Loire *châteaux* ("French for 'castles'"). Afterwards Mike gave Benny a quiz on the *châteaux* they had visited. Soon Benny could distinguish between Chenonceaux and Chambord. Chenonceaux was built over a river and had tapestries so delicate they could not be photo-graphed. Chambord was larger and harder on the *pied* ("French for 'foot'"). They were built in the same *siècle* ("'century'"), though one was somewhat older than the other. Benny was curi-ous about whether the pope spoke French. Mike said the French were of the opinion he didn't.

The tour bus drove to a minor *château*, owned by a member of the faded aristocracy, where the tourists spent the night. Most members of the group slept in the *château*, but Mike and Benny were assigned a tiny room above an adjoining horse stable. "'There was no room for them in the inn,'" quoted Mike, tossing his suitcase on a cot. "There was no room for them in the stable, either," growled Benny as he perched, sidesaddle, on the *toilette*.

Benny was awakened in the middle of the night by the sound of giggles. He went to investigate and discovered several French teenagers. He joined them to share their humor and their wine. Next morning he woke up in a strange bed, smelling of horses and able, miraculously, to speak a smattering of French. "Probably not the kind the pope would appreciate," warned Mike.

On the way to Dijon, Benny slept, Mike fooled with his Palm Pilot, and a tourist from Kansas made the driver stop so he could take pictures of a wheat field. That evening Benny had his first Latin lesson.

"*Credo*," said Mike.

"'I believe,'" said Benny.

"*Credo in unum Deum.*"

"'I believe in one God.' Give me a hard one."

"*Agnus Dei, qui tollis peccata mundi, miserere nobis.*"

"Latin is a dead language," said Benny. "Let's go have a drink."

And they did.

Next morning Benny woke up with the flu. The bus drove to Strasbourg, a fine German city in France. Everyone got off the bus and ate. Benny bought many bottles of wine, which were soon depleted. The wife of the tourist from Kansas spoke highly of herbal medicine and fed him some pills. Benny stretched out in the back of the bus. That night, in an inn deep in the Black Forest, his insides exploded. He sat on the commode, wondered who his mother was and why people weren't born with a knowledge of other languages. Becoming a bishop no longer seemed a worthwhile goal.

Several days later, they were peering up at a Disney-like structure perched on a promontory. "A B C," said the driver in a perfect Dutch accent. "Another bloody castle." The other tourists scurried off to explore it while Mike and the driver played poker. Benny slept.

They stopped in at a Munich beer hall, which brought Benny a measure of happiness. The Kansas wife stayed on the bus, preferring to knit booties for an impending granddaughter. When the group got back, her husband took pictures of American tourists proudly displaying their Black Forest cuckoo clocks.

They went to Salzburg, where the tour group followed an itinerary designed for fans of the Trapp family.

"Who were the Trapps?" asked Benny. He was beginning to feel better. He was back in the tourist mode.

"They were the ones in *The Sound of Music*," said Mike. "Ever see it?"

"I started to. I got to the part where they were being chased by the Nazis. How did it turn out?"

"They escaped."

"Too bad," sighed Benny.

The Kansas wife turned around and glared at him.

They explored the Melk monastery, an especially fine example of the synthesis of the Gothic and some other kind of architecture. The library contained many old but important books that no one was allowed to open. Outside, they were able to purchase wine and cheese. Afterwards they got on a boat and floated down the Danube. The boat had a bar, which the two new friends found useful. They sat on the deck and watched the world of vineyards glide by. Benny was coming around to being his old self. Becoming a bishop regained its status as his number one priority.

In Vienna the bus circled St. Stephens. "A B C," said the bus driver. "Another bloody cathedral." The American tourists voted, thirty to two, not to stop. Instead they went to a palace in which the great Mozart had played a piano at an early age. Mozart had an ambitious father. Vienna had the highest ferris wheel in the world. Everyone in the group except the Kansas wife went on it. At the top of the world, Benny complained of dizziness but was told by a physician in the group that this was quite natural. They went somewhere and drank wine and watched sprightly waltzers pay homage to the Strauss family. Benny tried to climb up on the stage to add his own homage, but wiser hands plucked him from his perch and helped him back to the bus.

The following day, they toured an area between Vienna and Hungary. One village had a high population of storks, most of which resided in nests atop chimneys. Another village had a gypsy café, which played gypsy music and served gypsy food and much gypsy drink. Then they went to a church where the great Haydn was buried. After viewing his tomb and being told that after Haydn's death, they had cut off his head in a vain effort to discover what made him a musical genius, the pilgrims followed the stations of the cross, which took them to the roof of the church and a view of the surrounding countryside. Benny proclaimed this experience a high point of the pilgrimage.

"'If thou be who thou sayest,'" he said to Mike in a Biblical voice, "'cast thyself down. For he shall give his angels charge concerning thee.'"

Mike peered skeptically at the street below. "No way, José."

That evening was the tour's last. The group celebrated by going to Grinzing, an area of Vienna specializing in beer gardens. Benny entertained a cast of hundreds by singing "Home on the Range," accompanied by the Kansas man. Shortly thereafter Benny attempted to dance with the man's wife, who kicked him in the shins and called him a repulsive ass— *Un imbécile répugnant*, Mike translated. Benny cried, "Bring on the pope!"

§

Several days later, Benedict Gottlieb had an audience with the pope. He would have preferred waiting a few extra days for his copy of the story of his conversion to arrive, as promised, which would give him the advantage of knowing how his life had changed, whether through a slow process of prayerful contemplation or through being struck by a bolt of God-sent lightning.

But Mike Bacchus counseled him that the pope waited for no man and that they should wing it and hope for the best.

Rattled somewhat by the sudden change in his circumstances, from being a holy pilgrim to kneeling in the presence of God's viceroy on earth, Benny suffered a sudden bout of amnesia. Not remembering whether he was to kiss the pope's feet or his ring, Benny covered all his bases and did both. He followed these acts of humility by kissing the hem of the papal garment, which, as he had just discovered, covered a pair of aging Birkenstocks.

Several elderly but well-dressed ecclesiastics appeared to be dozing in a corner. The pope was sitting on what appeared to be a throne. Benny sat down on what appeared to be a chair. Mike, who through his old contacts had been able to work his way into the role of interpreter, positioned himself next to the pope's good ear.

The pope stared straight ahead. He nodded.

"The ball's in your court," said Mike. "Keep in mind he doesn't speak a word of English."

"*Credo in unum Deum*," Benny informed the pope.

"*Credo in unum Deum*," agreed the pope, nodding slowly and thoughtfully.

There was a long silence.

"Though I have to confess," Benny went on, "I've often wondered where God came from."

Mike spoke what appeared to be Latin into the pope's ear.

The pope put a finger alongside his cheek and looked pensive. He finally turned to Mike and said something in much the same language.

"He says it's a great mystery," said Mike.

The pope cast his eyes heavenward and appeared to sigh.

"Ask him if he's ever come up with a revelation on this subject," suggested Benny. "I'd kind of like to know."

Mike spoke again into the pope's ear.

The pope looked startled. He vigorously shook his head No.

"There's another thing I've often wondered about," Benny went on. "Do evil spirits cause sin? I was brought up to believe they do, but I have my doubts. What thinks Your Holiness about this question? Or does it really make a whole lot of difference?"

Mike spoke more Latin into the pope's ear.

The pope put a finger alongside his cheek and frowned. He turned to Mike and spoke a few incomprehensible words.

"He says he doesn't understand the question," said Mike.

"Tell him to skip it," said Benny.

Mike spoke yet again into the pope's ear, apparently telling him to skip it.

The pope frowned and shook his head in puzzlement. Then he turned to Mike and said something, probably in Latin.

"He says he enjoyed reading the story of your conversion," said Mike. "I think he wants you to make a comment."

"Which version did Esther send him?" asked Benny.

"He didn't say."

"Try to draw him out."

Mike spoke into the pope's ear.

The pope gave Mike as startled a look as an aging pope can muster.

Mike shrugged. "He's not showing his hand," he said.

"Tell him that after many years of prayerful contemplation, I was struck by a small bolt of lightning."

Mike made a long speech to the pope. By the time he was finished, the eyes of the pope were closed. He was nodding, either out of fellow-feeling or because he was asleep.

Mike and Benny waited around for several minutes. The pope's head slowly dropped onto his chest. He suddenly awoke with a start and smiled in what could have been interpreted as a sheepish manner. He leaned over to Mike and whispered something.

"He says it's time to go."

"Did I get the job?"

"I can't ask him that."

"So what do I do now?"

"Say something appropriate," counseled Mike.

Benny paused, seeking *le mot juste* ("the right word"). "Ask him what he thinks about Christian Tantrism."

"I don't think that would be wise," advised the more experienced man.

"You're probably right. Tell him I like his hat."

The pope muttered something to Mike in their secret language. Mike said something back. Then the pope nodded and made a faint gesture with his frail right hand, indicating that the interview was over.

When they were out of earshot, Benny asked Mike what the pope had said.

"He said, 'He's got the gift.'"

"So he noticed. Good. And what did you say?"

"'Pray for us sinners, now and at the hour of our death.'"

§

"Lucy here," said a voice. "I can't come to the phone right now, but when that tone sounds, you know what to do."

The tone sounded. Benny knew what to do.

"Lucy. Benedict here. Benedict Gottlieb. Are you happily married? I'm not. I am, however, happily employed. They made me archbishop of Kirkland. I was going for bishop, but they saw me as archbishop material. One of the rules is that I can't get married. I do, however, oversee a large diocesan budget and expect in the near future to see a large turnover in our current work force. Would you happen to be seeking a new position? We are an Equal Opportunity employer."

"Benny?"

"Lucy?"

"You threw me off for a minute there."

"I threw you off for many years. But I've repented of my evil doings. After many years of prayerful contemplation, I was suddenly struck by lightning. I'm free from sin for the first time since my last baptism." Benny broke into song. "'Oh, the unsearchable riches!'" he sang.

"Benny, you're an idiot."

"I believe the phrase is *imbécile répugnant.* Do you speak French?"

"*Oui* and *non.*"

"Are you happily married? You may answer that question in either language. Your reply will be held in strict confidence."

"What did you say your name was?"

"Benedict, from the Latin, meaning 'good speaking.' Gottlieb, from the Amish, meaning 'lover of God.' Benedict Gottlieb. 'Good speaking lover of God,' in the Amish dialect of Latin. A committee in New York gave me that nickname, and it's stuck with me for several weeks. The pope seemed to like it. He wears Birkenstocks. Are you happily married?"

"The pope wears Birkenstocks?"

"Yes, but his toenails needed a good clipping. Are you happily married?"

"Were they ingrown?"

"I didn't notice. It was dark down there, and there was a faintly disgusting odor. Did I ask if you were happily married?"

"I don't want to talk about it."

"Come visit me. I now take confessions."

"You always took confessions."

"There's a difference. I now have a license. Nothing you say can or will be used against you in a court of law."

"What happened to that Esther person?"

"She's my agent. She lives in New York. I've never taken her confession. I doubt that she has anything to confess. She got me that interview with the pope I may have mentioned. I asked him where God came from. He didn't seem to know. He said they're working on that problem. When they come up with a solution, they'll be able to stake a strong claim to being Number One. I'll be proud to be a part of their team. Come join me. We're listed in the Yellow Pages, under 'Churches, Synagogues, and Mosques.'"

There was silence on the other end of the line. Benny's soul filled with an emotion akin to hope.

"I have a vacation in two weeks."

"I go to New York in three weeks, where I'm scheduled to appear on national TV and tell the inspiring story of my conversion. Come with me. Join the festivities. Win a trip to my private Kirkland apartment, where I've set up a confession booth and a well-stocked bar."

"Maybe I should first get a divorce."

"That would probably prevent complications."

"On *my* end, anyway."

"I'll try to do my part at this end."

"Goodbye, Benny."

"Goodbye, Lucy."

"Two weeks."

"Two weeks."

9

Benny's Conversion Story:
The Revised Standard Version

THE STUDIO AUDIENCE WAS ALIVE WITH ANTICIPATION. All eyes were on the row of four talk show guests. Three of them were dressed in Leavenworth pinstripes. The fourth wore a cassock; his head was covered by a black hood, with slits for his eyes and mouth. The camera crew members were roaming the aisles, seeking the most advantageous positions for shooting the upcoming proceedings.

And there, at the center of things, was Crock. Crock the host, Crock the celebrity, Crock in his sixties (already!) but young in spirit, Crock the master, Crock the sensitive, open-minded thinker. Crock wielding a microphone. Crock peering at a cameraman, waiting for the signal.

The signal came.

Crock put on his professional face. His eyes flirted with the camera.

The audience held its breath waiting for Crock to speak. "Preachers . . . in the Pen!" he finally announced.

A camera zeroed in on the first two guests, a handsome couple in their thirties.

"Bonnie and Clyde Bilk," introduced Crock. "They engaged in fraud, and the law caught up with them."

The camera moved past the fraudulent couple and settled on a sad-looking man in his forties.

"Jimmy Joe Sassin," said Crock. "He poisoned his disciples and is now serving a life sentence."

The camera tarried on the disciple-free man before settling on the last and largest guest.

"And our mystery guest today, a man of the cloth, as you can see." Crock paused for effect. "What do our guests have in common? They're all preachers, and they've all spent time in the penitentiary. 'Preachers in the Pen': that's the focus of today's edition of 'Crock!' We'll come back and hear their heart-warming stories, right after these messages."

The studio lights dimmed slightly. Bonnie and Clyde Bilk whispered while Sassin adopted a stoic pose. The studio audience went back to breathing. Crock fiddled with his tie. The mystery guest retrieved a cigar from someplace inside his cassock, inserted it through the bottom hole in his black hood, lit it, puffed, and blew a smoke ring that ascended, then dissipated on its way to heaven.

§

Several minutes later, the lights returned to normal. Bonnie and Clyde and Jimmy Joe came to attention, Crock forgot about his tie, and the mystery man put out his cigar.

Crock began by asking the Bilks why they had just signed a long-term lease with a prominent minimum-security federal housing project.

The Bilks told their story.

Back in the 'Eighties, they had both attended the College of Christian Entrepreneurship (CCE) in Mudhut, West Virginia, where Clyde majored in fund-raising and Bonnie majored in cosmetology. They met in a prayer class. Clyde noticed Bonnie right away, because of her good looks and her request that God send her a queen-sized waterbed. Clyde said to the Lord, "Lord, send me a sign. If this young lady gets her waterbed, I'll know You want me to be a big part of her life." A week later, a furniture truck rounded the corner near Bonnie's dormitory and a queen-sized waterbed came tumbling off.

This was both an answer to her prayer and the sign Clyde had sought. It was then that he knew Bonnie was going to be a winner in the game of life, and he wanted to be a big part of her success story. Bonnie, however, had her doubts. She had her eye on another young man, Billy Bob Greede from Nashville, a major in Christian country. She was attracted to Billy Bob by his boldness in coming before the Lord's throne, specifically, his request that God send him a Rolls-Royce. Fortunately—"All things work together for good," said Bonny, quoting Scripture—fortunately the Lord only came through with a Volvo, reserving a better gift, a cream Jaguar, for Clyde. As a result, Clyde picked up ninety credits and was able to graduate.

The Bilks explained that at CCE, a student needed at least one hundred credits in order to graduate. For example, you got ten credits for a new dress, twenty-five credits for a waterbed (thirty if it was queen-sized), fifty for a Volvo, eighty for a Mercedes, ninety for a Jaguar, and the full one hundred for a Rolls. Bonnie had earned her degree by getting the waterbed (thirty points), a fur coat (twenty), a strand of perfectly-matched pearls (forty), and a French poodle (ten). Clyde had graduated with the highest distinction by acquiring the Jag (ninety points), a closetful of clothes (forty), and a quarter section of rolling hills in Western Kentucky (a hundred and fifty points!).

"Nothing," explained Clyde under gentle questioning, "is too good for the work of the Lord."

After graduation, the couple followed the Lord's bidding and went into business, selling life insurance to all His people in Televisionland. Their problems with the law arose when the clients started to pass away and the relatives, due to a slight misunderstanding, found themselves unable to collect. Ordinarily, agreed the Bilks, when a person owns a life insurance policy and then dies, the relatives are the ones who collect. But, they took pains to explain, with true believers it is different. When *they* buy life insurance, they, and only they, collect when they meet the Lord face to face. The whole point of buying Christian life insurance is to guarantee you everlasting life. "Why do you think they call it life insurance?" asked Clyde, palms extended upward to betoken his recognition of an obvious truth.

Crock played devil's advocate. He could imagine people saying, "Hey, they got exactly what they deserved. They defrauded thousands of their faithful followers of millions of dollars, which they used to buy luxury automobiles, five or six palaces, a dozen yachts, and trips around the world. If I'd have been the judge, I'd have given them two hundred years apiece." What would the Bilks say to those people?

The Bilks would say that the whole thing was blown out of proportion by the media. They didn't have five or six palaces; they had only four or five.

A lump appeared in Crock's throat. "Audience," he said, "let's show them we care."

The studio audience pulled out its handkerchiefs and wiped its eyes.

"Don't go away," said Crock, almost in a whisper. "We'll be back."

The lights dimmed slightly. Bonnie and Clyde held each other's hands. Sassin's posture remained as stoic as ever. The studio audience shook its head in disbelief at the injustice in the world. Members of the camera crew chewed gum. Crock fiddled with his cuff links. The mystery guest retrieved a notebook and pencil from under his cassock and proceeded to take notes.

Minutes later the lights returned to normal. Bonnie and Clyde let go of each other's hands, Sassin stirred, the audience snapped to attention, the camera crew returned to work, Crock forgot about his cuff links, and the mystery man inserted his notebook and pencil into a hidden pocket.

Crock shifted his attention to Reverend Jimmy Joe Sassin, the charismatic leader whose current address was Leavenworth, Kansas. He asked the good reverend to tell his story.

His story, said Sassin, had been scripted by the Lord. He had only been following the Lord's plan for his life.

When he was in college back in Florida, Sassin began, he was quarterback on the football team, captain of the basketball team, student body president, and chairman of the Beta Eta Pi social committee. He was a Big Man on Campus. He had everything. But he was beginning to feel unhappy. He had not yet found the Lord. He couldn't sleep days. His ends kept dropping his passes. He couldn't hit his free throws. He was facing a recall election. His fraternity was under investigation for date rape.

Then he found the Lord, and he changed. Totally. Overnight. He could remember the details. His basketball team was playing Alabama Christian. They were down by one with ten seconds to play in the game, he was fouled in the act of shooting, he stepped up to the line, the first shot hit the back of the rim and rolled around and then dropped in, the crowd went wild (they were playing at home), the ref flipped the ball back to him, he was getting ready to shoot again, then he looked up at the basket and happened to see this sign behind the glass backboard (he could read through glass), it was one of those signs often displayed at sporting events—John 3:16, Thessalonians 6:23, a passage from First Galatians—somebody witnessing with a placard referencing Matthew 10:1.

He went home and consulted his Bible. He read Matthew 10:1, the verse in which the Lord gave His disciples power and authority to heal the sick and cast out unclean spirits. He knew instantly that this verse applied to him, that the Lord was calling him to do great things for Him. Why else would He be flashing that sign at him, giving him the go-ahead to wipe out unclean spirits?

So he quit school and moved to California, where at the Lord's bidding he started a church. No no, it was not a cult, it was a church, a regular church, with its own five-hundred-voice choir and mass weddings. And prophet: Reverend Jimmy Joe Sassin himself, who delivered the Lord's instructions to His people. Those instructions included moving God's people to an off-shore island to get away from their legions of persecutors, urging them to protect themselves from the feds who were investigating them for tax evasion, and serving them orange juice that turned out to be lethal.

Crock returned to his role as devil's advocate. Critics of Sassin had said, "The bottom line is, Sassin ordered the poisoning of hundreds of his innocent disciples. And let's not forget that Sassin's boys killed a dozen feds, who were only doing their job. Hanging's too good for the guy." How would Sassin answer those critics?

Sassin would answer that he was simply doing the Lord's will. He would answer that both the feds and the disciples had unclean spirits, which he had been ordered to cast out. He would answer that the media was out to get him. He *would* admit, however, that mistakes were made.

Crock proclaimed that it took a real man to admit that. He further expressed his admiration for the good reverend for taking responsibility for his actions.

The audience showed its own admiration by applauding.

Crock went on to say that he personally admired the way Sassin had stood up to the press. He then asked the audience if they agreed with his assessment that Sassin, whether or not he was a bona fide prophet, had been crucified by the media.

Sassin wiped a tear from an eye. Several members of the audience followed suit, some even weeping openly.

Crock suggested to the audience that his guest had suffered enough.

The audience showed its total agreement.

Crock suggested that they show his guest some support.

The studio audience broke into rhythmic clapping. Some of them looked at each other and nodded knowingly.

Crock paused. "We'll be back in a minute with our last preacher in the pen."

The lights dimmed slightly. Bonnie and Clyde whispered. Crock went over to Sassin and shook his hand. Many members of the studio audience came down from their perches and touched Sassin. The camera crew stretched out and relaxed. The mystery guest went back to taking notes.

§

The lights returned to normal and all eyes focused on the fourth preacher.

"Our final guest," announced Crock, and here he indicated the hooded cleric, "is the mystery man of the hour, who is none other than—"

The mystery man removed and discarded his hood as the camera zeroed in on him.

"—the Most Reverend Benedict Gottlieb, Archbishop of Kirkland, Kansas!"

The audience greeted Archbishop Gottlieb with hearty and sustained applause.

"Father Gottlieb—that *is* the correct form of address, isn't it?"

The archbishop shook his head No. "It's 'Your Excellency.'"

"Your Excellency," said Crock, and he began to read from a card in his hand, "it says here that you're the son of a rabbi—"

The audience sat up straight.

"— that you went to Harvard—"

Half the audience opened its mouth. The other half frowned.

"—that you spent a number of years in prison for persecuting Christians—"

The audience booed. Crock held up a hand to quiet them.

"—and that you've just recently been inaugurated as the archbishop of Kirkland, back in Kansas. Is that correct?"

"That's right," said Archbishop Gottlieb with a hint of a smile.

"Tell me, Your Excellency, isn't it rather unusual for the son of a Jewish rabbi to become a Catholic archbishop?"

"I'm also the son of a Christian," explained Archbishop Gottlieb. "My mother was a Baptist Sunday School teacher. Also, let me remind you that the very first pope was a Jew."

"That would be. . . ?" said Crock.

"Peter," said the archbishop.

"That's right, I'd forgotten about that. I tend to think of Peter as a Christian. I think we all do. But what about persecuting Christians? Just how common is it for someone with that particular background to become a Catholic archbishop?"

"The first great missionary was famous for persecuting Christians," Archbishop Gottlieb pointed out, "and he did time."

"You're referring to. . . ?"

"I'm referring to the Apostle Paul. Rather, *St.* Paul—you'll have to excuse me, I'm new at this Catholic game. I'm still learning all those titles, which hat to wear for what occasions, where the wafers are kept."

"Harvard," said Crock, moving on. "You went to Harvard."

"Yes," admitted Archbishop Gottlieb. "The Divinity School."

"First you went to Harvard Divinity School, then you got into the business of persecuting Christians. Excuse me," said the slightly confused Crock, "but I don't see the connection."

"Know thy enemy. The First Commandment."

"Aha!" said Crock. "The Trojan horse strategy."

"Exactly."

"Let's focus on this persecution angle for a minute. Tell us about it."

110

"I was a Unitarian minister at the time. There wasn't that much to do, not very many Unitarians in Kansas, so with lots of time on my hands I took up this hobby, persecuting Christians."

"Lots of Christians in Kansas," said Crock brightly.

"Mostly Protestants," explained Archbishop Gottlieb. "I specialized in Protestants, though I enjoyed doing a Catholic now and then. For a change of pace."

The collective mouth of the audience fell open.

"You say *doing*. What exactly did you do to them?"

"Mostly I held them for ransom."

"Aha!" said quick-thinking Crock. "Supplementing the modest paycheck."

"Actually," admitted Archbishop Gottlieb, "I didn't do it for the money. Holding people for ransom is not a paying proposition, especially when their relatives are Kansas Christians. They are a frugal lot."

"You wouldn't recommend it for young people, then, the ransom business?" asked Crock. "I mean, as a career path?"

"Definitely not," agreed the good archbishop. At this he looked directly into the lens of an available camera. "Stay in college. Finish your education. It's something they can never take away from you."

The audience applauded.

"I second that," said wise Crock. "We all do. Now, getting back to the subject of persecuting Christians, a subject I personally find fascinating—you didn't actually *hurt* those people, did you? I mean, you were pretty humane about the whole thing, weren't you? For instance, you didn't put them in rat-infested cages and sear their flesh with burning cigarettes, did you?"

"Yes and no," said Archbishop Gottlieb. "Of course I put them in cages—where else would I put them? On my modest ministerial salary, I couldn't afford penthouses. There were, oh, a few rats, but no, I didn't brand my hostages with hot smoldering cigarettes. I wouldn't do that. I don't smoke."

The audience looked puzzled.

"What I did is this," continued Archbishop Gottlieb, "I ran colored toothpicks up their fingernails."

The audience groaned.

"*Colored* toothpicks?" asked Crock. "Am I missing something here? Why colored?"

"I enjoyed the irony: torture, with *hors d'oeuvre* toothpicks."

"I see—," said Crock. Then quickly, "Did *they* enjoy the irony?"

"Only a select few," replied Archbishop Gottlieb. "For instance, I remember one attractive young woman with whom I engaged in spirited conversation on a wide range of topics—the ethics of torture, the wide range of techniques used by the professional torturer, the symbolic significance of certain toothpick colors, the master-slave relationship, the bond that often develops between the torturer and his victim, the pros and cons of various forms of birth control. But, and I have to emphasize this, only a select few."

"Are you saying that by and large, Christians don't have a sense of humor?"

"Let me ask you this. Are *you* a Christian?"

"Well . . . yes, yes of course, in my own particular way," replied Crock. "But let's not get into the problem of definition."

The audience applauded.

"Do *you* have a sense of humor?"

Crock replied that he liked to think so.

"We'll be back," said Archbishop Gottlieb, smiling into a camera, "right after these important messages."

The lights dimmed as the audience broke into laughter. Bonnie and Clyde Bilk engaged in private conversation, Rev. Sassin reverted to his stoic pose, several members of the camera crew lit cigarettes, and Crock combed his hair. Meanwhile, Archbishop Gottlieb took a Swiss Army knife out from under his cassock and cleaned his fingernails.

§

The lights returned to normal and all came to attention.

"This is 'Crock!'" said Crock. "We were just talking to Archbishop Benedict Gottlieb about his past life as a persecutor of Christians. Tell us, Your Excellency, how did you change from a persecutor of Christians to you yourself *being* a Christian—and, I might add, a very fine one? Why did you give up what has to be one of the most controversial and fascinating hobbies around?"

"I got hit by lightning on the road to Topeka."

The audience gasped.

"Sounds like there's a story here," guessed Crock.

"There is," agreed Archbishop Gottlieb. "I was heading up I-35 to Topeka, I was planning to apprehend certain young women of the Methodist persuasion and bring them back to Kirkland, imprison them temporarily in the cages in my basement, and seek ransom for their eventual release, when I stopped to shoot a few holes of golf. I had read somewhere that Jack Kennedy used to do that—when he was campaigning for president he'd park by the edge of a golf course, climb over the fence, and shoot a few holes of golf, say from Hole Seven to Hole Nine, replacing all divots of course. He found this a marvelous way to prepare himself for the appointed task ahead, it cleared his mind of extraneous detail, which was exactly why I did it, why I stopped by for just a few free holes of golf, being low on cash."

"You were a big fan of Kennedy's?"

"At first. Then he got us into Vietnam, which was the point at which Jack and I parted company—I could see what was coming down the pike, he apparently could not. Call it luck, call it instinct, call it genius, call it whatever you want, I somehow sensed, early on—"

"So you were hit by lightning," interrupted clock-aware Crock. "This was on the golf course?"

"Yes," replied Archbishop Gottlieb. "A high percentage of those who are struck by lightning are downed while scurrying around the links. Lee Trevino, for example—"

"And this was a revelation?" interrupted Crock. "I'm referring to the lightning bolt."

"No," replied Archbishop Gottlieb. "It was more of a warning. It was supposed to catch my attention, so that when God spake to me out of the tornado I'd be ready to sit up and take notes."

"Which is what you did," suggested the host of "Crock."

"Exactly," agreed the guest. "I took notes of our discussion. I have them here someplace." The good father fumbled around under his cassock. "The pope wanted to see them, too—during the interview—a very nice man, by the way—such *wisdom*—makes you proud to be Catholic—speaks pretty good English, would you believe it?" Archbishop Gottlieb extracted an American flag from under the cassock. "Quite knowledgeable about American politics—" Here he pulled out a stuffed toy lion. "Follows the Lions—"

"A Christian?" asked Crock with mock disbelief. "Cheering for the *Lions*?"

The audience chuckled at this incongruity.

"If you can't beat 'em, join 'em," explained Archbishop Gottlieb. He pulled out a pair of white panty hose and quickly stuffed them back. "Follows the White Sox, too—guess I must've left the notes in my other cassock—these things are called cassocks, did you know that?—I didn't—I kinda like them—they lend a certain air of authority—a little old-fashioned, of course—maybe we ought to have someone like, oh, maybe Bill Blass redesign them—if he's still alive—have to bring that up with the powers that be—hmm, that's funny—Jeez, I could have sworn I brought the damn things along—"

"Never mind, we'll take your word for it. Just tell us what God told you."

"He said, 'Benedict. Quit persecuting my people. Give yourself up. I've got big plans for you.'"

"Is that all? Didn't He say anything about prison?"

"Oh yes," recalled Archbishop Gottlieb suddenly. "He said if I'd cooperate with the feds, He'd try to get me a reduced sentence, but He was making no promises."

"What else?"

"He also told me that when I went to prison, I should take along my Bible, the teachings of the Fathers, and an extra pair of pajamas."

The audience howled with laughter.

At this Crock returned to his role of devil's advocate, with his customary apology and explanation. "And what about God's advice? Do you think of this as a revelation? Not just a casual conversation with an old and trusted friend, or practical advice on the art of living along the lines of, say, Miss Manners?"

"I'd classify it as a revelation," replied Archbishop Gottlieb thoughtfully. "Yes. Definitely. Not just chit-chat."

"On that note," said Crock, "we have to take a break."

The lights dimmed slightly. Bonnie and Clyde returned to their private conversation, Rev. Sassin adopted his stoic poise, the studio audience was abuzz, the members of the camera crew stifled yawns, and Crock rediscovered his cuff links. Archbishop Gottlieb went over to the studio audience and shook hands and visited, paying special attention to an attractive matron, whispering something in her ear while she nodded.

§

The lights returned to normal and all came to attention.

Following this cue, Crock began to leap up and down the studio stairs like a mountain goat, shoving his mike in people's faces.

"Here," he said, indicating a young man.

The young man stood up. A camera zeroed in on him. "This is for Mr. Sassin," he said. "I just wanted to know if you made that free throw."

"No," admitted Rev. Sassin. "I missed the free throw, it was an air ball, Alabama Christian won in overtime. I fouled out, incidentally. I couldn't keep my mind on the game, trying to remember the Bible verse, Matthew 10:1."

"Maybe the fact of your missing the free throw was the sign, not the Bible verse," suggested the young man.

The studio audience hissed its disapproval at this suggestion.

"I was just playing devil's advocate," said the young man, sitting down.

"Here, this young lady," said Crock, indicating a formerly-young lady. "Hopefully with something on a more positive note." He put his arm around her and patted her on the back, lower lumbar region.

The no-longer-young lady stood, and a camera picked her up.

"This is directed to Bonnie," she said. "I'd just like to say I've found the Lord too, and it's just like you say, before it happens you can't sleep nights, but after it happens everything changes, you experience true joy, for instance before it happened I was heavy into make-up but after it happened I sat down and had a talk with the Lord and He said 'Vanity, it's either me or it's Maybelline,' and I chose Him, and I never regretted it for one minute, and that's all I have to say. Praise the Lord!"

The former young lady sat down to applause from the studio audience.

"Here, this young lady," said Crock, indicating a young woman who did not appear ever to have had the problem of having to choose between God and the modeling profession.

The young woman stood. The cameraman decided on a long shot.

"I have another question for Bonnie."

"Yes?" said Crock.

"How long does it take, on the average, to pick up a hundred credits to graduate from the College of Christian Entrepreneurship, that's on the average, and number two," she said, blushing, "what's the percentage of guys versus girls?"

The young woman sat down.

"It all depends on how fast the Lord honors your requests," explained Bonny. "There's often a long backlog. I've seen cases of people graduating in less than one semester, but I'd say that on the average, it all works out so that you graduate about the same time you find the right man, or vices versus."

"The young man again," said Crock. "Wants to redeem himself."

The young villain stood up. The cameras vied for the best shot of him.

"This one's for Archbishop Gottlieb. How could you tell it was the voice of God and not just a loudspeaker?"

The studio audience hissed its disapproval at this question. The young man quickly sat down.

His Excellency raised his hand to calm the audience.

"He had all the classical attributes," he replied, speaking of God. "For example, He had a deep, rolling voice, He used good English but spoke with a slight German accent. He was obviously giving me classified information."

The audience applauded.

"Another young man," said Crock.

Another young man stood up. "This is for the archbishop again. How did you make it to archbishop so quick? Don't you first have to be a bishop?"

His Excellency nodded as if he had been expecting this question. "Ordinarily that's the case," he admitted. "But they counted the Harvard degree and previous experience."

"You mean as a Unitarian minister?" asked Crock.

"Exactly," said Archbishop Gottlieb, nodding.

"Including your persecution of Christians?!" asked Crock.

"They were mostly Protestants," replied the archbishop.

Crock nodded Of course. "Another young lady," he went on, indicating the matron in whom Archbishop Gottlieb had shown some interest during the break.

The matron stood up. She seemed perplexed.

"Yes?" encouraged Crock.

"I forgot what I was supposed to say."

"My charisma does this to them," said Crock, winking at the audience.

"Oh yes, now I remember," said the matron. "This one's for the archbishop."

"Archbishop Gottlieb," said Crock.

"Right," agreed the matron. "Archbishop Gottlieb. What I want to know is, do you think you'll ever make it all the way up to, uh, cardinal?"

Archbishop Gottlieb looked directly at the camera and flashed a benevolent smile. "I'm, ah, very happy to be exactly where I am now, serving the fine Catholic people of Kirkland, in my capacity as archbishop. That's all I have to say on the subject."

"Well," said the matron, "I just want you to know that if you ever decide to run for cardinal, you'll have plenty of good old American support, and I'm not just speaking for myself, lots of people think the way I do."

The matron sat down to wild applause from the audience, who were whistling and screaming and stamping their feet and striking their hands together and crying "Cardinal Gottlieb!" and "Gottlieb for cardinal!" with an occasional "Gottlieb for pope!" long after the cameras had been put to rest in favor of an important message.

10

A Miracle of Rare Device

"LUCY HERE," SAID LUCY'S VOICE. "I can't come to the phone right now, but if it's good news, let's hear it."

The tone sounded.

"Lucy. Archbishop Benedict Gottlieb here. I used to be Benny Good. We were once married. Something happened and we parted ways. I'm left with nothing but precious memories. The good news is, I've come up in the world. I wish for nothing more than to have you join me and share my good fortune and my bed."

"Benny?"

"Please call me Benedict. It may be my imagination, but I seem to recall that you didn't show up last week. I was planning to take you to New York, where yesterday I appeared on 'Crock' and told the American people about my sordid past. Where were you? Did the divorce fall through? Do you still have precious memories of our all-too-brief marriage? Select one question. Your answer will be judged on the basis of accuracy, conciseness, and aptness of thought."

"I'm sorry, Benny."

"Accurate, concise. Apt. Which question are you answering?"

"I'm telling you why I didn't show."

"And why didn't you show?"

"I guess I just didn't believe all that stuff about you being an archbishop and going on TV."

"With Benny, all things are plausible."

"That is the one precious memory I have of our much-too-long marriage."

"You skipped a question. Didn't the divorce come through?"

"The divorce came through. I was going to come, Benny, I really was." This was spoken in a plaintive tone. "But."

"You met a guy."

"I met a guy."

"And you can't remember his name."

"We're seeing each other."

"How much?"

"A lot."

"Let's get this straight. You didn't show because you didn't believe Benny, but you were going to come anyway, but you met this guy, who shall remain anonymous, and you're seeing a lot of each other, probably everything."

"Uh . . . right."

"Benny forgives you. You and this mysterious stranger can leap into bed at your convenience with the comforting knowledge that Archbishop Benedict Gottlieb, following God's example, forgives you. Did you happen to catch my show?"

"I saw the reruns. It was on all the stations."

"I'm now a celebrity. I sign autographs. Soon I'll be an icon. Then I'm scheduled to become a national treasure. After that, who knows?"

"Maybe a cardinal."

"I've gotten lots of e-mail on the subject. It's running eighty percent in my favor."

"Won't you need more than just e-mail? I don't pretend to know anything about the Catholic religion, but don't you need to work a miracle or do some good works or something like that?"

"Good point, Lucy. That's where you come in. I'm starting a new convent, and I was thinking, who would be the perfect candidate for mother superior, when my mind lit on you."

"Really."

"My mind often lights on you."

"It's a good thing you have a small mind."

"Thank you, Lucy. Just think about it. Lucinda Good, mother superior."

"I don't have the background."

"If you can do a madam, you can do a mother superior."

"I mean I've never even been a nun."

"We'll rewrite the job description."

"Sure."

"Think about it."

"I'm thinking."

"Keep in mind that, to quote a very wise archbishop, 'With Benny, all things are plausible.'"

"I'll let you know."

"I'm serious."

"I believe you," she said with apparent skepticism.

"I'm in New York. I'll be back in Kirkland tomorrow. Think about it for a couple of days, between marriages."

"I always weigh all offers."

"Put your finger on the scale for me."

"I've got delicate fingers."

"That's part of the new job description."

"I'll let you know."

"That's all I'd expect. Bye, Lucy."

"Bye, Benny."

§

Before the "Crock" adventure, Benny had of course met with the brain trust at the Esther Geld Agency, Inc., for a strategy meeting. Afterwards he met with them again.

The first item on the agenda was an evaluation of Benny's performance on "Crock." Esther was concerned that Benny had maybe shaded over a little too far into the area of farce, at the same time conceding that that was a large part of his appeal. She was also worried about Benny's off-the-cuff statement that he had been a fan of Kennedy's until Vietnam, when he had somehow sensed "what was coming down the pike." She hoped that not many viewers would be able to figure out that Benny wasn't even a teenager at the time he was supposed to have had this marvelous insight. Ron Something, not his real name, questioned Benny's advice to the youth of America to stay in school, noting that Benny was taking the risk of losing the support of the sizeable and rising percentage of the current population who were high school dropouts. Mike Bacchus could offer nothing but praise for Benny's narration of the conversion story, which, he reminded his colleagues, was *his* idea. Andrea Something (Wordsmith?) was critical of Benny for straying from the script, on which, she reminded her colleagues, she had spent an entire weekend. All of them agreed, however, that Benny had the gift, and that he had done an excellent job overall, and that he was now a viable candidate for cardinal.

The question now, said Esther, tapping her pencil on the desk, was how to proceed in that direction. "How," she asked, "do we go about placing this talent in its next logical slot?"

Ron pointed out that a spot check of his focus group showed that Benny had scored big, but that they were inclined to take a wait-and-see attitude, pending his performance as an archbishop. They wanted to see if he could pull off a miracle or two in the good old American can-do spirit, show a little creativity in the good works department, and jack up the waning interest in Catholicism.

"Sounds good," said Esther.

"Right," said Mike.

"Is there a hyphen in 'can do'?" wondered Andrea.

"I have an idea," said Benny.

"You're not here to have ideas," snapped Esther. "That's why we have these high-priced consultants."

"All top-notch experts in their fields," noted Benny.

"Right," agreed the three experts.

"Okay, Mike," said Esther. "Float one by us."

"I do my best work with a whiskey sour," said Mike.

"You had two before you came in. What about it, Ron?"

"It?" said Ron.

"Your idea," Esther said.

"I think he should start out with a miracle or two, plus a few good works. Otherwise, he's history, the story lacks legs."

"Which miracle? Which good works? Let's talk specifics," thundered Esther. She was growing angry. She was a born task-mistress. Had she and God so chosen, she would have done well as a parochial school teacher.

"That's something maybe we should work on," answered Ron. "Specifics."

"Andrea!" said Esther in a near-scream. "Specifics! S-P-E-C, and so on."

"I like Benny's idea," said Andrea with her customary meekness.

"A perceptive woman," observed Benny.

"Okay," sighed Esther. "Put it on the table."

"We Catholics," observed Benny, "have a problem with the numbers. Specifically, the dwindling population in the convents, which are now practically empty. My idea is, fill them with a new generation of nuns. Teach them the elements of Christian Tantrism. Then put them to work. There's a big market for the service they can provide. We have lots of businessmen in Kirkland, also an Air Force base."

"Refresh our memories on Christian Tantrism," said Esther.

Benny repeated his stump speech on the virtues of Christian Tantrism, dwelling on the phrase *salvation through sex*.

"Where do you plan to get the nuns?" asked Esther.

"There are lots of underappreciated hookers out there. I say we convert them. Retrain them along Tantric lines. Run them through the vows of poverty, chastity, and obedience."

Mike frowned. "I see the poverty and obedience factors," he said. "What I do not see is the chastity factor."

Benny raised his finger in the spirit of wisdom. "In Christian Tantrism," he pointed out, "you think chaste thoughts during the act of congress."

"I understand that. What I do not see is how this goes over with certain elements in the Catholic Church."

"Here's what we do," explained Benny. "We persuade them to see it as a ministry to the downtrodden. We remind them that it gets the girls off the streets. We point out that it's a money-maker."

"It'll also look great on your resumé," chimed in Ron, consulting his watch.

Then they disbanded, but not before agreeing that Benny's idea showed creativity in the good works department, that it could be interpreted as a miracle in the good old American can-do spirit, and that it had great potential for jacking up the waning interest in Catholicism.

§

The next morning, Benny and Mike caught a flight back to Kirkland. While Mike slept, Benny conducted a talent search among the stewardesses. He inquired into the personal job satisfaction of a chosen few. He engaged those chosen few in conversation about religion. He moved on to describe the tenets of Christian Tantrism. He ended up with three telephone numbers and six free whiskey sours.

At the Kirkland airport, Benny was mobbed by a crowd consisting of media types, sheep from the faithful flock that had recently been entrusted to his loving care, and potential converts (former agnostics, atheists in the process of reevaluating their lives, disaffected Baptists, but no Amish) who had recently been hit by lightning while watching "Crock."

"What's it like, being hit by lightning?" bellowed a loud media-type voice.

"When did this happen?" bellowed another.

"Where was this golf course?" bellowed a third.

"Which hole? The seventh?"

"About this persecution business. What's the statistical breakdown, denomination-wise?"

"What brand of toothpicks did you use?"

"Do you still have those cages in your basement?"

"Would you consider making them into a shrine?"

"Your meeting with the pope. Does he follow the Chiefs?"

"Which penitentiary were you in?"

"How were the meals?"

"What are your thoughts on prison reform?"

"Are you planning to run for cardinal?"

"Have you been approached by anybody in the hierarchy?"

"What else did God tell you?"

"Anything you can repeat?"

The newly-ordained Archbishop Gottlieb raised his hand and smiled beatifically. The media momentarily stopped baying, stopped nipping at his heels. "I'm writing a book," said the good father cheerfully. "It'll answer all your questions."

"Say, aren't you the guy who used to do 'Religion Talk'?"

"Yeah, whatever happened to it?"

"Is it true they canned you?"

"Wasn't there some kind of scandal?"

"Didn't it involve the boss's wife?"

Archbishop Gottlieb blinked through the lights at the offending jackals. At the edge of the crowd he caught a glimpse of a familiar face. It had the California look. It reminded him of the Church of the Wide Open Door. It made him think of Christian Tantrism. It caused a stirring in his lower regions.

"I'd be happy to answer these questions," Archbishop Gottlieb told the reporters, "but I have priorities, and my top priority is my flock. If you'll excuse me, I've got to go listen to a few confessions. Unfortunately, people are still sinning. One of my goals is to cut down on the sin rate among Kirkland Catholics. I plan to appoint a commission to study the matter—find out the actual effectiveness of confession, take a good hard look at the old definitions of sin. This will, of course, take money. No, I'm not talking about raising the tithe rate. As far as I'm concerned, that's off the table. No new tithes! In fact, I'm thinking of an across-the-board tithe cut. What I'm talking about is upping the contributions. We'll be looking at how other institutions do it: Democrats, Republicans, Protestants, Buddhists, the Red Cross, the Girl Scouts. If we have to, we'll even sell cookies from door to door. Maybe even fudge, if studies show that the interest in cookies has dropped off. But it will be worth it, even if the sin rate drops only, say, ten percent. My goal, incidentally, is forty percent. My Nobel-prize-winning advisors tell me forty percent is do-able."

The archbishop strode toward his waiting limousine, pressing flesh as he worked his way through the crowd.

Mike cleared the way.

The archbishop waved at the masses. The masses waved back.

Mike opened the door of the limo.

The archbishop climbed in, still waving.

Mike closed the door and climbed in after his charge, remembering to do these in the reverse order.

The archbishop looked around. There was a woman alongside him.

§

"Mike, this is Arielle. Arielle, Mike Bacchus."

"Sorry," said Mike as the limo drove off, "I didn't catch the last name."

"She's from California," explained Benny. "People from California don't have last names. They're like the pope in that respect. In other respects, I suspect there are differences. For example, I don't know of many Californians with Roman numerals attached to their names. Probably because it wouldn't be feasible. Take Arielle. Could she be called Arielle XXIII? I doubt it. You see the problem. It would cause—"

"I caught you on 'Crock,' Arielle interrupted Benny. "I thought you were working for us." There was disapproval in her voice.

"Us?" repeated Mike. Then, at a higher pitch, "*Us?*"

"I believe she's referring to the Church of the Wide Open Door," explained Benny. This woman," indicating Arielle, "taught me everything I know about Christian Tantrism. You've heard me speak of Christian Tantrism. There was approval in my voice. This man," indicating Mike, "is teaching me about Catholicism. You've heard of Catholicism. It's a controversial religion. I myself have mixed feelings."

"What's the deal?" said Arielle. "You're still on *our* payroll, and you're working for the *Catholics?*"

"I'm still working for you," said Benny in a consoling voice. "The Catholics are a front."

"Holy Jesus!" exclaimed Mike.

"I'm writing a book," explained Benny. "It'll answer all your questions." He was speaking both to Arielle, who was seated at his left, and to Mike Bacchus, who was slowly descending from the roof of the limo onto the seat at his right.

"You're still working for us?!" said Arielle.

"The Catholics are a front?!" said Mike.

"Explain," said Arielle and Mike in chorus, eyeing Archbishop Gottlieb with distrust.

"It's like this," said Benny. Then he went on to explain what it was like. It took him twenty minutes, but he got the job done.

His four major points were: (1) that he was committed to the principles of the Church of the Wide Open Door, especially the theory and practice of Christian Tantrism; (2) that he was also committed to the principles of Catholicism, to the extent that they could be made compatible with those of the Church of the Wide Open Door, especially the theory and practice of Christian Tantrism; (3) that he still considered himself in the legitimate employment of the Church of the Wide Open Door, under the category of Outreach; and (4) that he was still a Catholic arch-bishop in good standing, with the implicit understanding that the Catholic Church was a fertile mission field for spreading the gospel of Christian Tantrism, which had been the main selling point of early Christianity but which the Catholics had come in later times to overlook, forget, or neglect, for whatever reason.

He went on to inform Arielle of his plan for rejuvenating the convents, hinting that she would make a superb mother superior, which was, he indicated, a high-salaried position.

When he had finished his explanation, Mike and Arielle looked at each other.

"I think we three can work together," said Benny, placing his substantial arms around his two companions in a show of pastoral concern.

Arielle and Mike again looked at each other.

Arielle laughed and said, "We're a team!"

Mike nodded and said, "We've got the right stuff!"

Benny leaned forward and said, "Turn left at the next stop light."

§

Mike, Benedict, and Arielle were indeed a team. Acting quickly, Mike booked a flight to Paris, where he coaxed the finest dancers of the Folies Bergere and the finest girls in the finest brothels to follow him back to Kirkland. Archbishop Gottlieb adopted the disguise of a trucker and went on the road, where he converted many of his favorite Dollys to the doctrines and practices of Christian Tantrism. When the two men arrived back in Kirkland, each with his quota of twenty-five attractive, healthy specimens of female pulchritude, Arielle had an empty convent ready for its new occupants. She had already placed the convent's three leftover conventional nuns in a retirement living center, where, they were assured, they could spend their golden years in prayer, contemplation, playing dominos, learning the art of macrame, and keeping their blood pressure within the acceptable range.

Arielle's next task was to teach her novices the rituals of Christian Tantrism. Archbishop Gottlieb took time off from his initiation—learning where the wafers were kept and which hat to wear for which occasion—to help her. It was Mike Bacchus's responsibility to line up a high class of discerning clients for this new service, a duty that was quickly discharged.

The Kirkland diocese was soon a thriving enterprise. The *Kirkland Beagle* ran an appreciative series on the revitalization of Catholicism under the new archbishop, neglecting to explain the principles of Tantrism and remaining discreet about the true nature of the convent. The national media followed Father Gottlieb's career with more than a little interest. The Esther Geld Agency, Inc., pleased with the success of its rising star, began to plan the next step in his spectacular career. They had him placed on the cover of *Up and Coming*. Soon afterwards, *Life-Style* named him "Best Dressed Archbishop," a new category created especially for him. Mike Bacchus accompanied him on another pilgrimage, this time to the holy spaces of Spain, after which he had a second audience with the failing pope (now totally deaf) and told the Holy Father about his miracle and his good works.

On returning to America, Father Gottlieb found that he had been promoted to cardinal and transferred to Las Vegas.

§

"Benedict Cardinal Gottlieb here," said the voice. "I can't come to the phone right now, but at the tone, please leave your message, and God bless."

The tone sounded.

"Benny? Lucy here. Lucy Good. We used to be married. I've been thinking about your offer. Lucinda Good: mother superior. I'm beginning to like the sound of it."

Cardinal Gottlieb picked up the phone. "Lucy!" he cried. "Are you between husbands again?"

"I've given up on marriage. I'm thinking of becoming a nun."

"Congratulations, Lucinda. I wish you the best of luck."

Lucy paused. "You said something about, uh, rewriting the job description."

"Did I say that?"

"You did."

"My, my. I must have been misquoted. I find that often happens. Isn't the media terrible?"

Lucy paused. "We now live in the same state," she suggested in a timid voice that did not do her justice.

"How can that be? You live in the state of sin. I live in the state of grace."

"Aren't you in Nevada?"

"Is Las Vegas in Nevada? I hadn't realized."

"Like I say, I've been thinking about your offer. I'd love to be a mother superior. You were starting a new convent. Remember?"

"Oh yes. The convent. It's doing very well. I hired a mother superior, or did I mention that? She's doing a splendid job. I hired the best. Then I rewrote her job description. Please don't quote me. Cardinals do not like being misquoted. Neither do their bodyguards enjoy having their boss misquoted. Did I mention that I now have bodyguards? I didn't? Well, I do. I hired the best. They used to work for the Mafia, but I promised them forgiveness of past misdeeds and limited access to my private convent. I also rewrote their job descriptions, in accordance with their preexisting talents. They used to be butchers, or did I mention that? Please don't quote me. They have maintained their animal instincts. Again, this is just between the two of us."

Lucy paused. The sound of the gnashing of teeth was conveyed over the phone line. "You bastard!" she said with conviction.

"I may be a foundling," said the former Benny Good, "but I am not necessarily a bastard."

"Get help, Benny!" screamed Lucy. "Get professional help!" And she hung up.

11

Benny Seeks Professional Help

VIRGINIA SWEET, Ph.D., carrying a pencil and a legal-sized pad, entered her office, followed closely by Cardinal Benedict Gottlieb, carrying a pocket-sized Latin phrase book.

"Just make yourself comfortable, Your Eminence," said Dr. Sweet, pointing to the patient's couch.

His Eminence looked at the couch skeptically. "Is this for me?"

"It's brand new," said Dr. Sweet proudly. She sat down in the therapist's chair and demurely crossed her legs, which were nifty by any cardinal's standards.

The cardinal put his hand on the back of the couch, testing for firmness. He stood back and frowned. "Don't you have something with a bit more lumbar support?"

"It's only for fifty minutes."

"Have you ever suffered from lower back pain?"

"Nnnno, I can't really say that I have."

Cardinal Gottlieb remained standing and skeptical. "Are you sure? I thought I noticed a certain . . . lilt in the hip area as I followed you up the stairs."

She blushed. "I'm quite free of discomfort in that area," she assured him.

"Maybe you were being . . . how should I put it . . . seductive? Subconsciously?"

Dr. Sweet tugged at the hem of her skirt. Her blush remained intact.

The patient looked longingly at the chair. The therapist noticed this. She stood up.

"Would you like to trade places?" she asked brightly.

"If you don't mind. It's only for fifty minutes."

He assumed the chair. She sat self-consciously on the edge of the couch.

"Let's see," she began. "This is your first time, correct?"

"I believe so."

"Now." She smiled at him as any freshly-certified therapist might smile at any new client, as if he were five years old. "Where would you like to begin?"

"Ask me a question. I'll give you an answer. You'll find I put a high premium on fidelity to the facts."

"I'm sure you do, but that's not the way we're taught to operate. I'm supposed to let the client take the conversation in whichever way he or she wishes. This method is designed to get us eventually to the root of the—"

"I prefer the Gottlieb method," he interrupted. "I work best when I'm totally at ease, sitting in an orthopedically correct chair, answering questions that go directly to the point."

"Well—you're the client."

"Exactly. I can see we're going to get along famously."

"First question," she said, quickly regaining her confidence. Her pencil was poised above the yellow pad. "What seems to be the problem?"

"This is probably a good time for a break," he said.

"Break?"

"I do best in a talk show format, which includes frequent commercial breaks."

"But—"

"Trust me. I have lots of experience."

"Okay," she said with a puzzled half-smile, "a break it is."

He reached over to the switch and turned off the light, leaving the room in semi-darkness.

§

When Lucy had suggested to Benny that he get professional help, he was highly insulted. It wasn't that he had anything against getting help. What offended him was the idea of getting *professional* help. Never in his entire life had he paid anyone for help. Not his Dollys, not Arielle, and of course not Lucy herself. He was proud of the fact that the subject of money had never arisen between him and the ladies in his life. This even included the woman who had accompanied him to Madison Square Garden to watch Sprewell have a difficult night. She had made off with the contents of his wallet the next morning, a fact that didn't make him feel good, but he could still honestly say he'd never had to pay a woman to keep him company, which was how he understood Lucy's advice to get professional help.

Well, maybe there was one exception—the night he'd spent in Paris. But that hardly counted. In the first place, Bacchus was the one who paid for it, and in the second place, he had the distinct impression that even if Mike hadn't flashed plastic, those French girls would have gone right ahead and given him all the help he wanted, *gratis*, from the Latin, meaning free.

After several weeks of thinking about Lucy's strong recommendation, however, he changed his mind. He was now a cardinal, he reminded himself. He had an expense account. Why not go ahead and get professional help, even if it meant going against his principles?

The thing that changed his mind was a piece he noticed in the *Vegas Voyeur* concerning the longstanding nationwide epidemic of mental illness. The story featured Dr. Virginia Sweet, a freshly-coined Ph.D. who was new in town but who already possessed, according to the writer, "a professional demeanor" as well as "a firm grasp of the serious mental problems facing our country." The piece was accompanied by a half-page picture of the young woman, who reminded Cardinal Gottlieb of Lucy at her floor-rolling stage.

So he had had his secretary call for an appointment, and now there he was, in the young woman's office, looking forward to fifty minutes of professional help.

§

"Ever wondered what they do when they're off-camera?" asked Cardinal Gottlieb in a low, soft voice.

"I, uh, can't say that I have," replied Dr. Sweet.

"What would be your guess?"

"Oh, I don't know. . . ."

"Engage in sparkling repartee?"

"Probably."

"No no. That's a common misconception. Make insensitive remarks about race, color, creed, gender, or sexual preference?"

"It wouldn't surprise me."

"Sorry, wrong again."

"Well, what do they do?"

"They light up, or adjust their ties or hemlines, or look at the ceiling, or blow their noses. If they're asthmatic, they take whiffs on their inhalers."

"I guess that makes sense," she nodded uncertainly.

The cardinal gazed at his professional help.

"Another thing they do is, they size each other up."

"Size each other—up?" she asked guardedly.

"In case they have time later for a moonlight walk."

"Maybe we should get back to our regularly-scheduled program, Cardinal Gottlieb," she suggested tactfully.

"Fine. But one more thing."

"Yes?"

"My intimate friends call me Benny."

"Benny?"

"What do your intimate friends call you?"

"Well...."

"Virginia?"

"Uh, yyyyessss."

"What a lovely name."

Dr. Sweet said nothing.

"Lovely, lovely name. The Commonwealth of Virginia was named for the first Queen Elizabeth. Do you happen to know why they called it Virginia and not Elizabeth?"

Dr. Sweet remained silent.

"Virginia." Benny flipped through his phrase book. "From the Latin, *virgo*, meaning 'young woman.' Often translated 'virgin.' As in Mary." Benny put the book aside. "Women are very important in our religion."

To this observation Dr. Sweet had nothing to say.

"Were you brought up Catholic?" asked Benny.

Dr. Sweet thought about this for a moment. "My mother used to go to Mass."

"Regularly?"

"Religiously."

"Your father?"

"Dad spent a lot of time sitting on toadstools."

"Toadstools!?"

"Oh! Did I say toadstools? I meant bar stools."

"Aha. A Freudian slip. And you?"

"I guess you could say I'm, uh, an agnostic."

"An agnostic. A gentle, peace-loving agnostic. I see absolutely nothing wrong with that. In fact, I have a lot of respect for you people. I've noticed you're often a cross between Catholics and ne'er-do-wells. Ordinarily the mother's Catholic, prays for the salvation of her only child, weeps with joy when he finds his way back to the Church. The father's usually the ne'er-do-well, cheats on his pious wife, drinks to excess, plays the ponies, and has absolutely no conscience."

"'Ne'er-do-well'? What's that?"

"You don't hear that word much any more. A ne'er-do-well is a bum."

"Bum? You don't hear that word much any more."

"It tends to be regarded as insensitive. You also never hear the word 'drunkard' anymore. Or 'lecher'."

"Maybe we should get back to our regularly-scheduled program," she suggested with all the tact she could summon.

Benny leaned over and turned on the light. "Okay, let's have another question."

"Where should I begin?"

"I asked about your parents. Now you can ask about mine. You might start with my mother. Her physical appearance."

"Could you describe your mother's physical appearance, uh, Benny?"

"Five foot eight, a hundred and twenty-five pounds, statuesque—there's a word that fit her precisely, *statuesque*—and a coquettish smile, which I can still see. A perfect ten, if I do say so myself."

"Perfect . . . ten," she said, writing it down. "What color was her hair?"

"She was blonde."

"Blonde," she said, writing it down.

"Come to think of it, in the dark she became a brunette. We spent a lot of time in the dark together, Mommy and I. Strolling along the river under the moon, holding hands, reciting Mother Goose, asking profound questions."

"Hmm," she said, writing it down. "Profound questions?"

"Actually, some of them were mundane. Maybe, oh, fifteen percent. The rest were pretty profound."

"For example?"

"Mundane or profound?"

"Let's start with mundane." Her pencil was poised.

"'Benny, do you have to use the bathroom?'"

"'Benny . . . bathroom.' I see. What about a profound one?"

"'Do you know why I named you Benedict? Because it's the name of a long line of popes. And I want you to grow up to be pope.'"

"'Grow up to be . . . pope.' Very interesting. But there's something here I don't understand."

"Ask away. That's what I'm here for."

"I thought I read someplace that your mother was a Baptist Sunday School teacher."

"That's right."

"Why would she want you to grow up to be pope?"

The cardinal beamed. "She thought it would reflect positively on her."

The therapist frowned. "I still don't understand. What's the connection between Baptist and pope?"

"The connection is religion. Baptist is a religion, and a pope is a religious leader. It's as simple as that."

"I know, but—"

"We've got to take a break, we'll be right back."

Benny turned off the light and pulled his chair closer to the couch.

§

Benny's answers to Dr. Sweet's questions were not completely faithful to the facts. But they were, it must be said in his favor, faithful to his imagination. When he spoke of the moonlight strolls he and his mother had taken, he was thinking of what might have been, if only she hadn't gone and planted him in old Eli Good's buggy. There was also more than a kernel of truth in his description of what they might have done on those hypothetical strolls. He knew many of the Mother Goose rhymes by heart, from having read them to the twins. This was before he discovered that God was not leading him toward the demands of fatherhood.

On the other hand, his claim that he and his mother had spent a good deal of time exploring profound questions was a complete fabrication. In his youth, Benny was a typical American boy, having little interest in profound questions. With two exceptions. The first exception was, "Where do babies come from?" The second and later one, "What about God? Where did He come from?"

§

"Mind if I smoke?" asked Benny. Without waiting for an answer, he took a cigar from under his cardinal's robe, unwrapped it, and lit up. Dr. Sweet opened the table drawer and pulled out an opened pack of Virginia Slims.

"Ah yes," said Benny. "Virginia Slims. They remind me of my girl friend."

She shook a cigarette from the pack and looked at him quizzically. "I didn't know cardinals were allowed to have girl friends."

"You must be Protestant."

"Agnostic, remember?" She lit her cigarette.

"Oh yes. A gentle, peace-loving agnostic. I have a lot of respect for you people."

"Did you ever think of getting married?" she suddenly wanted to know.

He blew a smoke ring. "It's frowned upon."

"How about secretly? In Reno?"

He shook his head. "Reno gives me bad vibes. My ex lives there."

"What about here in Vegas?"

He smiled wickedly. "Actually, I prefer living in sin."

"Sin?"

"Just a technical term we theologians sometimes use."

"I see." Then Dr. Sweet had a sudden inspiration. "Benny. Could you describe your girl friend's physical appearance?"

Benny leaned back and gazed at the ceiling. "Five foot eight, a hundred and twenty-five pounds, statuesque—there's a word that fits her perfectly, *statuesque*—and a coquettish smile, which I can still see. A perfect ten, if I do say so myself."

"Blonde?"

"It varies. Come to think of it, in the dark she's usually brunette. We spend a lot of time in the dark together, Arielle and I. Strolling along the river under the moon, holding hands, discussing the poetry of Allen Ginsberg, asking profound questions—that kind of a thing."

"What about your ex?"

"Lucy? Five foot eight, a hundred and twenty-five pounds, statuesque—there's a word that fits her perfectly, *statuesque*—and a coquettish smile, which I can still see. A perfect ten, if I do say so myself."

"What about the hair color?"

"In her better days, she was your quintessential redhead."

"What did you discuss on your moonlight walks? Mother Goose or Allen Ginsberg?"

"Neither. Woody Allen."

"Hmm," said Dr. Sweet. "Do you notice anything unusual about your descriptions of the women in your life?"

"Of course. But it probably wouldn't interest you."

She ignored this remark and went on. "Your mother, your girl friend, your ex-wife—they're remarkably similar."

"Really?" said Benny, affecting puzzlement. "You think so?"

"Except for the hair color and subject of discussion, I could hardly tell them apart."

"*I* certainly could."

"How?"

"Take the nipples, for example. The colors range from pink—that's Lucy—to light brown—that was Mommy—to dark brown—Arielle."

"Amazing."

"What? The differences?"

140

"No. The fact that you'd remember the color of your mother's nipples."

Benny winked. "I came into the world with my eyes open."

Dr. Sweet blushed slightly, then recovered. "On that note, let's get back to our regular program."

§

Here Benny was being faithful to the facts, largely. He had once taken a moonlight stroll with Lucy. He could remember the event clearly—she had used the occasion to compare the lunar cycle with her own and to inform him that she was going to have a baby. His description of her physical appearance was also quite accurate, as was his description of Arielle, whose hair often became brunette in the dark, much as Virginia Sweet's now did when he extinguished the light.

Benny was also being more or less truthful when he spoke of Allen Ginsberg and Woody Allen. Lucy always compared him (not unfavorably, he thought) to Ginsberg, and Arielle once suggested that he would be just right for a role in one of Woody Allen's films.

As for his references to profound questions, Benny was no doubt thinking of Lucy's frequent mention of child support laws and Arielle's lessons on the ins and outs of Christian Tantrism.

§

"You haven't mentioned your father," said Dr. Sweet, her pencil again poised.

"Say, I'm getting a little thirsty. How about a cup of coffee?"

"Sure." She stood up. "Cream? Sugar?"

"Give me the works."

Dr. Sweet left the room.

Benny got up from the chair and went over to the couch, on which he reclined. He was still smoking his cigar.

"We're talking to Dr. Sweet here," he said, "and she's just getting ready to ask me about my father—. 'Benny,'" he said, mimicking the therapist's voice, "'could you describe your father's physical appearance?'—'He looked pretty rabbinic.' —'Could you be more specific?'—'Well, let's see. Put the right hat on him, he could have passed for an Orthodox patriarch.'—'Yes?'—'Another hat, you'd have yourself an Amish farmer.'—'He wore a beard, is that what you're saying?'—'Beard, hair growing out of his ears and nose: the works.'—'Brought you up in the traditional way, did he?'—'Spare the rod and spoil the child.'—'Any outstanding memories along those lines?'—'Now that you mention it, he didn't exactly appreciate it when a bunch of us kids sneaked over the fence one night and stole a few pears from Farmer Brown's orchard. Didn't eat them, of course. Threw them to the very swine.'—'Thou shalt not steal. Those were his sentiments, right?'—'Actually, he put the whole episode under the category of eating what's on your plate.'—'I bet it didn't help that you threw them to the swine, he being a rabbi.'—'That didn't seem to bother him, the swine part. On the other hand, if the pears would have been pearls. . . .'"

Dr. Sweet silently appeared in the doorway. She stopped, stepped back, and listened, apparently unseen by her soliloquizing patient.

"'There's something here I don't understand,'" said Benny, emulating his therapist.—"'Yes, Virginia?'—'Dr. Sweet, if you please.'—'Yes, Dr. Sweet?'—'Why wouldn't a rabbi be concerned about you feeding the pigs?'—'Sorry, I don't see the problem.'—'The problem is the relation between rabbi and pigs.'—'We've got to go away, we'll be right back.'—'No you don't. It's time we got to the bottom of this.' —'How much time left on the meter?'—'Quit avoiding the issue. Your father wasn't really a rabbi, was he, Cardinal Gottlieb?'— 'No.'—'He *was* an Amish farmer, wasn't he?'—'Yes.'—'In fact, you were originally an orphan, weren't you?'"

Benny broke into a sob that may or may not have been genuine.

"'You never knew your real mother, did you?'—'No,'" he sobbed, holding his head in his hands. "'No . . . No.'"

Benny suddenly composed himself, wiped his eyes, and got up from the couch. Then he walked back and resumed his position in the chair as if nothing had happened.

§

In this soliloquy, Benny was no doubt being faithful to the facts. The only questions are why he chose to reveal himself in such a poignant way, and whether he was aware that he had an audience for this self-revelation.

This is a difficult issue. Benny's motives are not always clear, and he seems to have a boundless capacity for amazing us, and by "us" I include myself as an author. All I can say with certainty on this point is that Benny has a talent for mimicry, and that he has some knowledge of the practice of therapy—not that he had ever been subject to it, or even that he had read Freud and his ardent band of followers, but that in his travels across the length and breadth of our great land, he had encountered many of its victims.

§

Dr. Sweet entered the room with a cup of coffee.

"Here you go," she said. "I hope this will quench your thirst."

"Ah. Just in time for a break." Benny turned off the light and pulled the chair even closer to the couch on which his professional helper had just placed herself.

"You follow the Cardinals?" he asked her, sitting down.

"Who?"

"A baseball team."

"Baseball's not my sport."

"Just out of curiosity, what *is* your sport?"

"Wrestling."

"Wrestling!" said Benny, standing up.

"I don't mean I *do* it," she said quickly and preventively, "I just watch it, in fact I have a friend who's—"

"Have a friend who does it, do you? You'll have to give me her number."

Dr. Sweet rose without answering and firmly turned on the light. She returned to the couch. Benny sat down.

"Our guest is Cardinal Gottlieb, and the topic is early childhood memories. Say, Benny, I've been meaning to ask you this question about—"

Benny got up and turned off the lights. He nudged his chair closer to her couch and then sat down on the chair. "Have you been reading the latest about the pope?"

"I understand he's in a bad way."

"Preparing to meet his Maker. You know what this means?"

"It probably means they're going to have to choose a new pope."

"That's the way I've got it figured." He paused. He looked at her closely. "What would you say," he said, "to the idea of Cardinal Gottlieb as pope?"

"You, uh, certainly have the credentials."

"Thank you."

"Just out of curiosity, how would you bring it off?"

He took a long drag on his cigar and inspected the ceiling.

"I plan to form an exploratory committee, then announce that I've given it a lot of thought but that I need to spend more time with my family, etc. When they ask if I'll accept a draft, I'll hedge. This will be a clear signal to the deep pockets that I'm ready to roll, and the money'll start pouring in. Then I'll appoint a campaign manager, visit some naked old guru in the Indian jungles to beef up my credentials in the area of foreign policy, get my picture taken with an assortment of television evangelists, visiting dignitaries, CEOs of major multinationals, converted terrorists, and simple Central American peasants. Finally, I'll wine and dine a few of my fellow redbirds, sandbag my main competition, old Geronti, put out several position papers on topics of contemporary interest, and wait for the will of God to take over."

"Very impressive plan."

"Thanks. Well, Doc, what do you think? Am I up to the job?"

"I, uh, see no reason why you wouldn't make a representative pontiff."

"Really?"

"In my professional opinion, you could pope with the best of them."

"You don't know how good that makes me feel!"

Dr. Sweet did not reply.

"What about you?" he asked. "Want to know whether you're up to your job?"

Again Dr. Sweet did not reply.

"My only observation," continued Cardinal Gottlieb, getting up from his chair, "is that you've been a little timid. You've got to work on being more aggressive. Not just assertive, aggressive. For instance, when I came into this room and started to complain of lower back pain."

"I seem to remember that. I probably have it in my notes."

He stood over her. "Then you suggested we switch chairs."

"I'm patient-oriented."

"Shouldn't have done it."

"Why? I was only trying to be helpful."

Benny sat down next to his professional help. "You've got to remember that the name of the game is control. The minute I worked you onto this couch, I took over. I began to dominate. You were dead in the water."

"I see what you mean. I'll try not to let it happen again."

Benny ran a hand up and down her slender, vulnerable arm. "You could have pressed me harder on many issues. On the issue of the quote-unquote 'chance' similarities among my mother, my ex, and my girl friend, for one thing. Not to speak of my interest in the papacy. Lots of very rich material in both those areas. Just think how bad you could have made me feel!"

"I'm sorry—"

Benny touched her face. "Uh uh. There we go again. See what I mean?"

"I'm not prepared—"

Benny put a finger on her lips. "Shhh," he said softly. "Neither am I."

"I wouldn't want to get—"

Benny again put his finger on her lips. "There's always abortion," he whispered.

"What?"

Benedict Cardinal Gottlieb began to take off his robe. "There's always abortion," he repeated.

"Could you speak up?"

"THERE'S ALWAYS ABORTION."

"Well—"

"Virginia Sweet," said Benny, fiddling with a button on her blouse. "What a lovely name. Perfect for a pope's mistress."

Dr. Sweet suddenly extricated herself from his grasp, quickly switched on the light, and made a beeline for the phone. "We're back," she said. "Let's get to the phones."

"Phones?"

"Isn't this a talk show?" She picked up the phone and dialed.

Benny sat on the edge of the couch. He was half undressed.

"Is that you, Bruno?" said Dr. Sweet into the phone. "Come on up. There's somebody here who wants to meet you."

"Who was that?" asked Benny.

"My boy friend. He's that wrestler I started to tell you about. Six foot four, two hundred and forty pounds, statuesque—a perfect ten, if I do say so myself."

Benny headed for the door, with his hat but without his robe and cigar.

"Where are you going?" asked Dr. Sweet.

"I've got an appointment," he cried back.

Virginia Sweet, Ph.D., went over to the bookcase and reached behind some books on the lowest shelf. She rummaged around for a time and pulled out an audio tape. She tapped it three times with her finger. Then, smiling, she turned off the light and followed her client down the stairwell in which the echo of his terrified voice still reverberated.

12

The Will of God at Work

RUMORS ABOUT THE POPE were beginning to circulate. That His Holiness was refusing to eat his vegetables. That His Holiness was forgetting to sign the encyclicals that appeared on his daily breakfast tray. That His Holiness was leaving Latin words out of his prayers and replacing them with bad French.

Then the *New York Times* reported that His Holiness had not blessed a crowd of believers in two weeks.

Esther Geld called a meeting of the brain trust to formulate a strategy for placing her star client in his next logical slot.

Cardinal Gottlieb arrived in New York, disguised as Benny Good. He was met at JFK by the author of *Religion for Dolts*, disguised as a limo chauffeur. Stuck in traffic over the East River, the two spent a leisurely hour discussing the beneficial effect of Christian Tantrism on marriage. The chauffeur reported that Tantrism had proved to be an inexpensive and practical method of birth control. Benny presented him with a cigar and lit one himself. The chauffeur had five children, he admitted, and he was hoping to send them to college so that they would be in a position to achieve the American Dream. Benny suggested that he write another book, perhaps a short history of the papacy from Peter to the present. The chauffeur agreed that this might help, but confided that he had made less money on his first book than on tips from his more generous patrons.

The chauffeur let him off at the Esther Geld Agency, Inc. Generous Benny gave him a tip:

"Are you a gambling man?" he asked.

"I only bet on sure things," said the chauffeur.

"You can bet the farm on this one. The next pope will be named Benedict XVI."

§

The brain trust spent a leisurely afternoon planning the upcoming campaign.

There was quick and general agreement with Benny's idea that he take a world tour, accompanied by a sizeable percentage of the world's media. Ron Something suggested that on his return, Benny should appear on "Perry Plug Live" to announce his candidacy for the papacy, pending, of course, the demise of the current pope. Mike Bacchus approved of this idea, offering a friendly amendment that instead of making a bold declaration, Benny should play coy and merely drop a handkerchief in the vicinity of the College of Cardinals. Mike then suggested that Benny compose a series of position papers on the torrid issues of the day—abortion, birth control, women in the priesthood, physician-attended suicide, and any scandals that may arise. Ron approved of this idea, offering a friendly amendment that instead of composing the position papers, which nobody but the opposition would read, Benny should write a book, detailing the story of his conversion and setting out his vague hopes for the future of the Church, perhaps including a few touching stories of how lost women had achieved inner peace in a convent founded by Archbishop, now Cardinal, Gottlieb. Andrea Wordsmith added an equally friendly amendment to this amendment, suggesting that she had a free week in which she could help Benny put his words in proper order. Benny declined this invitation, pointing out that he knew an underemployed author who needed the money to place a large but safe wager that would enable him to send his five children to college so that they would be in a position to achieve the American Dream. Esther Geld herself closed this stage of the planning session with the strong recommendation that the touching stories of the lost women not mention their adoption of the practices of Christian Tantrism; she insisted that those practices were a private matter.

"Now, are we overlooking anything?" asked Ms. Geld, flicking an ash from her slender cigarette.

"I have an idea," said Benny, flicking an ash from his slender stogie.

"Let's hear it," sighed Esther, looking at her watch.

"I say we get somebody to name a cigar after me," said Benny. "As you may have noticed, all the best people have adopted the cigar as the tobacco of choice. My experience with cardinals is that they are among the best people, ranking only slightly behind converted hookers. I speak comparatively, of course. The very best people are sitting at this table. But back to the point. If the vote for pope were close, a cigar named 'The Gottlieb' could conceivably tip the scales in our favor. That cigar should be the cheroot. The cheroot is cut square at both ends. Your average cardinal, besides being square in his dealings with the rest of the population, is astute and would immediately grasp the connection. I rest my case."

"Benny," said Esther, "you are an idiot."

"I agree," said Mike, who had already reached his quota of whiskey sours. "The cigar industry is hurting. But I still think Benny's got a point. I say we hire somebody to name a drink after him. 'The Benny.'"

"Two idiots," said Esther.

"I agree," said Ron. "I say we settle on a candy bar. 'The Benedict XVI.' Recent polls have shown that thirty percent more people eat candy bars than drink whiskey. Fifty-four percent more people eat candy bars than smoke cigars."

"Three idiots," said Esther.

Andrea said, "Could you run those numbers by me again?"

"The number is now four," said Esther. She pounded the table with her cigarette-free hand. "Let's get serious. Let's think damage control."

"Damage control?!" sang a quartet of accused idiots.

"Preemptive," explained Esther.

"What have I done wrong?" asked Benny, throwing up his hands in a show of innocence.

"Maybe we should make a list," suggested Esther.

"We don't have all day," Mike pointed out.

"Let's think worst-case scenario," said Esther. She turned to Benny. "Which skeleton would you most prefer to remain hidden in your immense closet?"

Benny called for a moment of silence.

The brain trust ceased speaking.

Benny meditated on an answer.

The brain trust respected his privacy.

Benny cleared his throat.

The brain trust collectively leaned forward.

Benny finally spoke. "Lucy," he said.

"Who's Lucy?" wondered Esther.

Benny told his friends about Lucy, beginning with the roll on the floor of Reverend Barnabas's store-front church and ending with the phone call in which he had withdrawn his offer of a lucrative mother superiorship. The story took thirty minutes, including Andrea's requests for correct spelling. Benny, sensing the importance of this episode in his life, told the truth as he saw it. He ended with the stipulation that Arielle not be kept abreast of this news.

"Mike," Esther said sharply when the story was laid out on the table. "Deal with Lucy."

"Mike," begged Benny. "Pay her well. She's the mother of my twins."

"Twins?" sang the brain trust in three-part harmony.

"Who are they? Where do they live?" inquired Esther.

"I don't remember their names. One is a boy, one is a girl—or it may be the other way around. I also don't know their present whereabouts. They never write. We never bonded. I left shortly after I taught them about Mother Goose and many of the other facts of life. It was an amicable divorce. I'm slightly in arrears in my child support payments. Would that be a problem?"

"You pig!" screamed Esther. "Mike! Deal with the twins!"

"Mike," Benny said gently. "Pay them well. They're the children of my wife, speaking retrospectively."

§

The pope was reported to be unable to eat pizza. Benedict Cardinal Gottlieb began his campaign.

Immediately on his return to Las Vegas, the good cardinal flew to Seattle, accompanied by both Mike, attired as a priest, and Arielle, attired in the modest dress of a mother superior. In Seattle he purchased a Boeing 747 and loaded it with members of the press known to be sympathetic to the causes Mike wished His Eminence to be thought of as espousing. Before commencing his world tour, the cardinal invited a celebrated software mogul aboard to discuss the question of bringing the Vatican into the Information Age.

After the photo op, they flew to Brazil, where His Eminence kissed the infants of Amazon settlers and, citing the teachings of St. Thomas Aquinas, delivered a grave pronouncement on the problem of the environmental changes brought about by the destruction of the rain forest. His main point was that the settlers might think about relocating to Nevada, pending changes in America's immigration policy.

They flew to St. Moritz, where His Eminence shared the slopes with a rising young starlet who had been compared to the late Princess Di. During the ensuing press conference, he announced that they had discussed the possibility of her becoming a mother superior in the convent of her choice.

They flew to Israel, where, after a pilgrimage to the Wailing Wall, His Eminence met with the Prime Minister to discuss the problem of the Arab world's threat to world peace.

They flew to a secret destination in the Middle East, where His Eminence met with a select group of Arab leaders to discuss the problem of Israel's threat to world peace.

They flew to Moscow, where His Eminence held a pep rally for true Christianity and thousands of Communists-turned-Russian-entrepreneurs answered his altar call.

Then, after Mike instructed the pilot to fly to Vladivostok, His Eminence led a motorcycle caravan across the Siberian wastes to check on the plight of the Russian peasant, stopping to allow him to dip his big toe in Lake Baikal.

They flew from Vladivostok to Hong Kong, where His Eminence held an open-air forum on the problems of integrating free-market capitalism into the Chinese system.

§

Before heading back to New York, they stopped in Sri Lanka, where His Eminence engaged in a high-level ecumenical consultation with the saffron-robed abbot of a small Buddhist monastery. This frank exchange of ideas took place in a cave dating back to the third or fourth century B.C.

Mike and Arielle accompanied His Eminence, polylingual Mike to act as an interpreter, monolingual Arielle to act as a resource person.

The abbot made a graceful gesture to indicate that his guests should adopt the lotus position. His guests dutifully squatted on the dirt floor. The abbot nodded gravely to indicate that the consultation could begin. Mike and Arielle nodded equally gravely in acknowledgment.

"I understand you're a Buddhist," began Cardinal Gottlieb.

The abbot smiled.

Mike translated the cardinal's sentence into a strange language, either Sanskrit or Latin.

"I am," replied the Buddhist abbot to the question of his religious affiliation.

"Do you speak English?" inquired a surprised cardinal.

"I'm originally from North Dakota," said the abbot in a good upper-Midwest accent.

"I used to drive my Peterbilt through Bismarck," said the still-surprised cardinal. "I believe it's the capital."

The abbot nodded and stared into space.

"He's meditating," Arielle whispered.

The abbot sighed.

"He's approaching Nirvana," Arielle whispered.

The abbot cast a steady gaze on the trio before him.

"He's achieved Nirvana!" whispered Arielle.

"It's been a long time," the abbot said slowly and with a wise nod.

"Twenty years," agreed the cardinal. "I was hauling sunflower seeds out to the West Coast. I have no idea why. I don't associate sunflower seeds with California. I associate them with grade school. We used to split them open with our teeth and spit the hulls on the floor. It drove our teacher crazy. I attended a one-room school. I was brought up Amish. If you don't mind my asking, what's your religious background?"

"Lutheran," said the abbot.

"That would have been my guess," said the cardinal with a wise nod of his own. "Not many Buddhists in North Dakota. What made you switch?"

"Went to Berkeley," said the abbot, coming out of his shell. "Took a course in World Religions. Professor showed this documentary. 'Footprints of the Buddha,' I believe it was called." The abbot paused to reflect. "These Buddhist guys were achieving this incredible high just walking around, no dope involved. I was brought up in a very strict environment, totally

154

religious, 'Your body is the temple of the Holy Ghost,' stuff like that, so this emphasis on dropping out and getting high without the use of dope was a big selling point. Lutherans get high on Bach, Johann Sebastian, but with me it never took. His music is so damned mathematical you have to be a genius to understand it, and my SAT scores in that area were, what should I say, 'improvable,' to quote my advisor. Also, my parents were going through a midlife crisis, and I couldn't deal with it, so I split and came here. I've never been sorry. The only thing I really miss is the Beatles."

"They were before my time," put in the cardinal. "During their heyday I was still into Amish hymns, singing praises to my Lord. But that got to be a drag, so I took off. Ended up hooked on the Grateful Dead. I was a big Jerry Garcia fan, until. Care for a cigar?" At this point the cardinal offered his host a panatela.

"Thanks," said the abbot, accepting. "It's been a long time." He paused to reflect. "Say, the U.S. ever lift that embargo on Cuba?"

"I don't really keep up with politics." His Eminence lit three cigars, one for each male truth-seeker. "Being a cardinal takes up most of my time." He extinguished his match and flipped it on the dirt floor. "It's a helluva job, but somebody's got to do it." He offered a smart cigarillo to Arielle, who accepted. "I just happened to be available." He lit her cigarillo with the tip of his cheroot in expert fashion.

The four sat for a while, smoking, achieving a high which, though perhaps not incredible by either Buddhist or Lutheran standards, was sufficient for the occasion.

"Say," said the cardinal, breaking the silence. "What can you tell us about Tantrism?"

"Tantrism?" said the abbot.

"It's a big part of Buddhism," explained Arielle.

The abbot paused to ponder this information. He shook his head slowly. "I'm drawing a blank," he finally said.

"Salvation through sex," explained the cardinal, hoping to jog a Berkeley memory.

"You're probably thinking of Hinduism," said the abbot. "They do all sorts of really weird stuff. We Buddhists, on the other hand, are a pretty straightforward outfit. Lots of sitting, lots of meditating, a joke here and there to break the monotony, and of course an occasional cigar."

"Oh," said the cardinal, showing signs of disappointment. He looked at Arielle. "I must have been misinformed."

The abbot paused to reflect and blow a smoke ring. "If you want to know the truth, most of us came here to get away from women." He looked at Arielle. "No offense intended."

"My God!" said Mike under his breath.

Benedict Cardinal Gottlieb untied himself from his version of the lotus position and stood up and stretched. "Okay," he yawned, "let's go get our pictures took."

They went for a photo op, in which the monk, at Cardinal Gottlieb's suggestion, merely nodded and smiled, keeping his autobiographical reflections to himself.

§

The cardinal and his entourage took off on an unscheduled trip to India, where, according to Arielle's vibes, a holy man was awaiting them. The vibes reported that he would be in a forest outside Benares, eager to fill them in on the details of Hindu Tantrism. Her vibes were highly accurate, said Arielle. Usually, she added.

En route to Benares, they heard the news. The pope was dead.

They changed course in mid-flight and flew to Rome, where the media recorded His Eminence in the act of mourning and Mike made arrangements for the candidate to make a timely appearance on "Perry Plug Live." Then they flew to New York, where His Eminence was scheduled to share his fondest memories of the late pope with a live television audience and sell his new book and be prepared to assess his own chances for a transfer to the Vatican.

§

"The late pope," said Perry Plug. "Could you share your fondest memories of him?"

"Perry, I considered him not only an excellent pontiff but a close friend. This is not widely known, but I met with him on several occasions. We exchanged correspondence on the hot-button issues of the day. We were like two peas in a pod. You no doubt have heard that expression. It refers to soul mates, which is what we were, the late pontiff and I. We thought alike on the great issues. He was a moral conservative, number one, and a political activist, number two. He wanted to return the Church to its primitive state, morally speaking, just as I do. He shared with me his plans for saving the world through a missionary campaign, plans I not only approved but also, I like modestly to think, had a part in planting in his fertile mind. His legacy was the building of bridges to both the past and the future. It will be our task, as cardinals, to replace him with someone who will honor his legacy as well as continue it, with slight modifications. I speak about this subject at some length in my book."

"Time for a message," said Perry Plug.

The cameramen took an evening siesta.

"Hold up the damn book!" Gottlieb advised Perry Plug. "Ask me about it. Feel me out on the question of my becoming pope. And for chrissake call me 'Your Eminence.' Care for a cigar?"

Perry Plug cared for a cigar. They smoked in silence for a time. Then the cameramen awoke from their brief siestas and the smokers extinguished the evidence.

"Here's the book," said Perry Plug, holding up a hastily-printed copy of *Cardinal Gottlieb and the American Dream* for a nation to see. "Could you tell us about it, Your Eminence?"

"It's the story of my conversion to Catholicism," said His Eminence. "It sets out my general hopes for the future of the Church. It also includes a few touching stories of how lost women have achieved inner peace in a convent I founded back in the days when I was just an archbishop."

Perry Plug fumbled for words. Quickly surmising that his host had already forgotten the instructions, His Eminence leaned forward and gravely whispered in Plug's ear. Plug nodded and asked his guest:

"What are your general hopes for the future of the Church?"

His Eminence smiled. "Number one, we've got to go back to the moral teachings that made our nation great. Number two, we've got to do a better job of getting our message across."

"Tell us about the lost women."

"Most of them have achieved salvation."

"Most of them?"

"I'd say, oh, a good three-quarters of them. Of course that's just an educated guess. Only God knows for sure."

Plug glanced down at a piece of paper. Then he looked at his guest and said:

"There's speculation that you and Cardinal Geronti are the top candidates for pope. One, is that accurate, and two, what do you think your chances are?"

"That's just speculation, and I wouldn't want to say anything more on the subject. In the last analysis, it's all up to God. If He so willed it, I'd have a hard time saying No. What was the second question?"

Plug stole another glance at the list of questions, then spoke:

"What do you figure your chances are?"

"If I were a betting man, which I'm not, I'd find ten to one odds very attractive. Geronti of course is more experienced. He enjoys the esteem of the entire College of Cardinals, including me—I'm just proud to be mentioned in the same breath as old Jerry, as we affectionately call him. And of course he's Italian. If I'm not mistaken, no American has ever been pope, so he's got the precedence factor on his side. On the other hand, there's that lightning strike, plus the salvation of those lost women, which, I'm told, my fellow cardinals just might count as another miracle. But the bottom line is, it's in God's capable hands. *Che sera, sera.*"

"Whatever will be, will be," hummed Plug.

"Right," said His Eminence, holding up the book for America to see. "*Cardinal Gottlieb and the American Dream.* Available at your local bookstore."

"We'll be back after these important messages," said Plug.

13

The Eighth Deadly Sin

ESTHER GELD AND THE BRAIN TRUST were pleased with the campaign to date. The press reports on the world tour had been highly favorable, though there had been some negative references both to the poorly-explained stopover in Sri Lanka and to the aborted flight to India. Benny's presentation on "Perry Plug Live" had been widely hailed in the media, though the *New York Times* religion critic had complained that Benedict Cardinal Gottlieb's answers to Mr. Plug's questions were, in her words, "somewhat succinct, especially considering the prominence of the office to which the good cardinal apparently aspires."

"All in all," summed up Esther Geld, "a bravura performance."

Andrea Wordsmith scrambled for her dictionary and began flipping through the B's.

"Now," said Esther, sipping on her second Manhattan, "where do we go from here?"

"Vegas," said Benny, sipping on his third whiskey sour.

Esther turned to Benny. "I was thinking of the cardinals," she explained, a noticeable scowl on the leading edge of her voice. "How do we line up the votes?"

"I was also thinking of the cardinals," explained Benny, ignoring the scowl. "How we line up their votes is, we invite them to Las Vegas. We wine them. We dine them. We show them the sights. We entertain them. We send them back to Rome happy and ready for the election."

"Las Vegas?" said Esther with a noticeable frown.

"Cardinals?" said Ron Something, waking up from a nap.

"Everybody loves Vegas," explained Benny. "That would include cardinals."

"Doesn't Las Vegas have a certain—reputation?" asked Andrea.

"That was then, this is now," said Benny. "Vegas is not what you'd expect. In fact, it's really a family town. It caters to families looking for paradise. Most Catholics would qualify."

"Do cardinals gamble?" asked Andrea.

"Catholics are big on bingo," explained Benny, raising one finger to indicate a point being made. "Cardinals are Catholics." He raised a second finger. "Therefore, cardinals are big on bingo." A third finger. "Bingo is gambling." A fourth, leaving logical space for one more point, which was: "Therefore, cardinals are big on gambling."

"That's what you call Aristotelian logic," observed Mike Bacchus dryly.

"What's Aristotelian logic?" asked Andrea.

"Proof by means of bullshit," explained Mike.

"Thank you, Mike," said Benny as Andrea wrote down this definition. He continued. "Another thing. There's a need for a strong Catholic presence on the Strip."

"We already have a presence on the Strip," Mike reminded his latest meal ticket. "Rome doesn't know it, but we own a resort with a casino and an escort service. It's called The Deadly Sins."

Benny turned to his guide in the affairs of the Church. "Really, Mike?"

"Have you forgotten? We plowed most of the profits from the Kirkland convent back into that resort."

"I'd forgotten. Was everything above-board?"

"Let's just say it's taken care of."

Benny turned to the woman who had set him on the road to this latest adventure in his life. "Did you hear that, Esther? It's taken care of. Mike takes care of things like that. He's a detail man. I'm a big-picture man. I don't take care of things like that. I'm not a detail man. Resorts with casinos and escort services are beyond my area of expertise. Not that I disapprove. Hit me with another drink," he said, pushing his glass in her direction.

"No," said Esther.

Benny shrugged. "Back to the subject of cardinals," he continued. "Cardinals are people. They're just like everybody else. Occasionally they need refresher courses. I'll invite them to Vegas, put them up in The Deadly Sins, and give them a refresher course."

"The deadly sins?" asked Andrea.

"Pride covetousness lust anger gluttony envy and sloth," recited Mike, mimicking the voice of a parochial schoolboy.

"Can you run those by me again?" asked Andrea.

"Andrea has a point," mused Benny. "Seven sins—that's too many to memorize. When I'm pope, I'll suggest we cut them to five. Two will have to go. My thinking is lust and gluttony. They're too difficult to enforce."

"You won't have to suggest anything," said Mike in an authoritative voice. "All you'll have to do is say the word."

"Really?" said Benny. "How does this work?"

"It's simple. You issue an encyclical."

"Tell me more," said Benny, eagerly leaning forward in his chair.

"Geronti," interrupted Esther, tapping her pencil on the desk. "How do we deal with Geronti?"

"Who's Geronti?" asked Andrea.

"He's the competition," Esther explained.

"The competition?"

"He wants to be pope, too," she said to Andrea. "Lord, save us from fools," she said to the ceiling.

"Oh," said Andrea, nodding in innocent wisdom. "Can't they have two popes?"

"Not at the same time," Esther informed her. And then, to the other experts in their fields: "So how are we going to deal with him?"

"Leave the old bastard to me," said Benny, lighting his prop.

§

They came. The cardinals came. They flew in to Las Vegas, first class, and were immediately whisked away in a fleet of white limousines that stretched from the airport to the palatial resort called The Deadly Sins, where their host greeted them serenely, one by one, with a holy kiss.

They wandered among the slot machines, dressed in their flagrant red costumes. Arielle and her charges demonstrated the workings of the one-armed bandits, being careful to mention that this exercise, classified under covetousness, was optional. Arielle and her charges furnished the guests with quarters. Some abstained; some played, with uniformly good results. Soon the area, measuring the size of several soccer fields, rang with the clatter of silver settling on tin. It was not long before the number of players exceeded the number of abstainees. Cries of pious joy mingled with the sound of clinking metal. Cardinal Gottlieb made a hostly appearance, moving among his guests with grace, dignity, and a subtle hint of *joie de vivre*.

They were taken by their individual escorts to the roof of the palace, to which a bungee jump was attached. Arielle gave a demonstration and challenged them to follow in her steps, explaining that this exercise, a test of pride, was not required. Some abstained; some climbed to the top and cast themselves down. Fortunately, none were injured. Soon the air was filled with diving cardinals and the sound of terror mixed with glee. In some cases the glee was dominant, in others the terror. The split was fifty-fifty. Cardinal Gottlieb cast the deciding vote in favor of glee.

They proceeded to the Fighting Marines, a war-game gallery, where Arielle and her charges outfitted them with electronic vests and toy laser guns. They peeked out from behind their posts and took deadly aim at one another. Sometimes they missed, sometimes they scored direct hits. Cardinal Gottlieb congratulated them, remarking jovially that he hoped his good colleagues had worked out all their hostility.

They ate. Seated at the banquet tables piled high with fresh lobsters and other harvest from God's oceans and vineyards, they gorged themselves. Arielle and her charges roamed among them, seeing that their every gastronomic need was met. None fasted, though many spoke apprehensively of the coming season of Lent. Cardinal Gottlieb made an after-dinner speech in which he welcomed them and congratulated them on their appetites.

Attended by Arielle and her band of escorts, they proceeded to the two-thousand-seat showroom. A famous comedian made lewd jokes. They tried not to laugh. Afterwards Cardinal Gottlieb inquired if they envied the comedian's freedom of speech. Several confessed that they did.

They floated in a swimming pool shaped like Lake Michigan and nearly as large, donned in flagrant red swim suits, their round bellies protruding, in a display of sloth. Arielle and her nuns, dressed in shy bikinis, hurtled down a wet slide and splashed into their midst. Some averted their eyes; some made naughty remarks; some went so far as to make indelicate suggestions. Soon the pool was almost empty, as Their Eminences were escorted to their individual suites, in each case by a nun trained in the art of Christian Tantrism. Cardinals Gottlieb, by now in his late forties, and Geronti, in his late nineties, chose to stay in the pool, where, under the God-made stars, they discussed the problems of faith and morals in the new millennium.

§

At the end of the long day, Cardinal Gottlieb and Arielle retired to his suite to take a refresher course in the third deadly sin. They found an uninvited guest perched on his goddess-sized bed.

"Lucy!" exclaimed the cardinal.

"Benny!" exclaimed the stray guest. "Who's the new squeeze?"

"Lucy, this is Arielle. Arielle, this is Lucy," introduced Cardinal Gottlieb, though with less grace and dignity than he had demonstrated earlier in the day.

Arielle said nothing.

"I like your mirror," said Lucy, looking up at the ceiling. "Maybe you could demonstrate."

Benny wondered whether she was using the word *you* in the plural, or whether she was volunteering. But he did not give voice to this question. Instead he inquired what she was doing there.

Lucy spread out on the bed and raised her legs toward the ceiling and moved them about as if operating a bicycle. "I've decided to take the job."

"The job. . . ," said Benny.

"Mother superior. That convent. Remember?" said Lucy.

Benny looked at Arielle. Arielle looked at Benny. They both looked at Lucy, who was beginning to bounce up and down.

"What's going on?" asked Arielle, her gaze shuttling between Lucy and Benny.

"What's going on?" asked Lucy, her gaze shuttling between Arielle and Lucy.

"Anyone for a whiskey sour?" asked Benny, his gaze shuttling between the floor and the ceiling.

The two women were not thirsty. They were, instead, curious.

"Who is this broad?" asked Lucy.

"Who is this tramp?" asked Arielle.

"Didn't Mike speak to you?" asked Benny, addressing the tramp.

Mike had spoken to Lucy on the subjects of silence and money and their intricate relation. Lucy had showed a predictable deal of interest in the subject of money but wished to take up the question of silence with Benny directly, which explained her presence on his bed.

Benny found himself faced with two choices. He could retain Arielle as the mother superior of the convent, also known as the escort service, thus provoking the ire of both Lucy and the media. Or he could replace Arielle with Lucy, a move that could bring unforeseen but equally unpleasant consequences. He chose to finesse his way between the horns of this dilemma by (1) keeping Arielle and (2) offering Lucy a well-paying but behind-the-scenes position in his coming administration.

Arielle was pleased with this solution. Lucy was somewhat less pleased, wondering aloud how Benny could be certain of the results of the papal election. Benny replied that she herself could help assure the attainment of the desired goal. "Have you ever sandbagged a cardinal?" he inquired. She confessed that she had not. Upon further explanation, she began to show enthusiasm for the project.

Thus an agreement was reached, a crisis averted.

The three of them ended up under Benny's mirror, watching themselves engage in what Arielle's vibes told her would be a complex but especially gratifying form of Tantrism.

§

Next morning at ten o'clock, Lucy showed up in Cardinal Geronti's suite, dressed as a nun and bearing a breakfast tray on which were perched a plate of Belgian waffles, the fruit of the day, and a glass of orange juice fortified with vodka.

The cardinal was kneeling alongside his bed, asleep after a marathon conversation with God.

She awakened the devout man and helped him to his feet and manipulated him back into bed.

The cardinal rubbed his eyes in preparation for a smile.

"I'm Fluff," said Lucy, flashing a set of sparkling teeth, "and I'll be your escort today."

The cardinal smiled back. "I no speak a good English," he said.

"You're being modest," she said, smoothing the bedspread in preparation for placing the tray on his lap.

He smiled again. "In Rome," he said, "There's a no women in a room. It's a not allowed."

"When in America," she said, "do as the Americans."

He nodded in perplexed agreement and proceeded to eat his breakfast.

Lucy next prepared the cardinal for his day. She helped him shave. She helped him bathe, averting her eyes. She helped him don his garments, patting him tenderly on the chest to make sure that he was comfortable and that a small computer was firmly attached to his person, hidden behind his crucifix.

They ventured forth into the world.

They strolled along the streets of Las Vegas, arm in arm. A photographer strolled alongside them, doing what photographers are paid to do.

Cardinal Geronti turned to Lucy. "Fluffa," he said, "you have a the paparazzi too in America?"

"*Oui,*" she said.

"*Parlez vous français?*" he asked in non-Parisian French.

"I give it a shot," she said.

"I too give it a shot," said he.

They returned to The Deadly Sins for lunch. It was only one o'clock, but Lucy was already hungry.

She ordered a small salad with Italian dressing.

"I'm on a diet," she explained to her guest.

"What is it, a diet?"

"It's the same as a fast. Practically."

"I too then do a the diet. I have a the glass of water."

Lucy winked at the waiter, who went. Soon he was back with a small salad and a double vodka. After the nourishment had been properly blessed, the soul mates consumed their lunch, conversing in a mix of non-Parisian French and American slang.

They wandered into the full-service casino, followed by the lone paparazzo. Lucy guided her guest to the blackjack section.

"What is it?" asked the cardinal.

"It's a game," she said.

"It's a game," he repeated. "And what is a name?"

"Blackjack."

"Oh yes," he nodded. "Jack Kennedy. He is a the great Catholic martyr."

"Wanna play?"

"I do not know. Is it a gamble?"

"Not if you know what you're doing. Here, I'll help you." She winked at the dealer, who dealt.

In twenty minutes the good cardinal was happy and clapping his fine liver-spotted hands with something like true ecstasy. The paparazzo was busy preserving this charming scene for posterity.

Soon afterwards, the paparazzo recorded a series of events: a floor man approaching the cardinal; the floor man pointing to the cardinal's crucifix; the cardinal removing this crucifix and finding a small computer; the cardinal showing, or feigning, surprise; the floor man calling for the pit boss; the pit boss inviting the cardinal to leave the premises; the cardinal stumbling toward the exit.

The cardinal recovered from this humiliation in a time-tested way, ordering a double water with the help and encouragement of his mentor.

"I have a the worry," he said.

"Don't," she said. "We won a mint." She retrieved a small fortune from her cleavage and gave him a small share.

"It is a paparazzo," he explained in a nervous tone, pointing to the busy photographer.

"Just a damned tourist. He wouldn't know a cardinal from a magpie."

"What is it, a magpie?"

"A bird. Let's go for a swim."

They floated in the pool under the desert sun, she sipping on a ginger ale, he sipping on either a water or a double vodka. She threw her head back and smiled at him. He smiled back uncertainly. The paparazzo also smiled.

They went for dinner in a restaurant that warned against service to minors. A bare-chested waitress took their orders: pizza and a tonic for the lady, ravioli and a glass of wine ("very small please") for the gentleman. A nimble dancer, equally bare-chested, performed lewd acts with a pole rising from a table, then ended up on the Cardinal's lap, offering to give him suck. The crowd urged the confused man on. His Eminence bit. The crowd howled. The paparazzo snapped away.

Lucy called for a wheelchair. She helped her wavering guest aboard and wheeled him to the wedding chapel.

"What is it, a 'Wedding Chapel'?" asked the cardinal. He was still able to read.

"It's where you get married," she said.

"I am a Cardinal Geronti," he said, stiffening slightly. "I do not get a married."

"It's an old American custom."

"Is it for a entertaining or is it for a the eternity?" he inquired skeptically.

"It's make-believe. Nobody takes it seriously."

"Are you for certain?"

"I do it all the time."

She wheeled him inside. The paparazzo recorded her act of charity.

Several minutes later, she wheeled him out the door and lavished him with kisses. The paparazzo recorded this display of affection.

"Let's go for a ride," said Lucy.

She wheeled him to a waiting limousine, which was covered with graffiti and to which were attached various items of intimate apparel. The chauffeur opened a door and helped Fluff deposit her guest in the much-decorated vehicle to the accompaniment of quick, bright flashes.

Soon they were driving at excessive speeds up Interstate 15 in the direction of Salt Lake City, pursued by three patrol cars, which were followed at a prudent distance by a lone paparazzo.

§

Next morning at ten o'clock, Arielle's charges arrived at their cardinals' bedsides bearing breakfast trays containing a plate of Belgian waffles, the fruit of the day, a glass of orange juice fortified with vodka, and the morning edition of the *American Enquirer.*

"My God!" said the cardinals under their breaths.

They left. The cardinals left. That afternoon they were whisked away in a fleet of limousines that stretched from the palatial resort called The Deadly Sins to the Las Vegas airport, where their jovial host bid them adieu with a firm American handshake and a slap on the back. Then their jovial host climbed aboard his 747 and took off for the next stop on his career itinerary, accompanied by his entourage, including Mike, Arielle, and the newly-christened Fluff.

Several days later, the nation awoke to learn that it had every right to be proud. The College of Cardinals had just announced the election of the first American pope.

14

Vatican House

"I THINK," MUSED POPE BENEDICT XVI as he padded about his new living quarters in his Birkenstocks, clad in boxer shorts and a T-shirt advertising the cigar industry, "that there have got to be some changes."

The changes envisioned by the new pontiff included the installation of a bar, a poker table, a slot machine, a bed large enough for a pope-sized man and half a dozen novice nuns, a monumental mirror above that bed, and, to remind him of his humble beginnings, a dozen potted begonias.

"I think," mused Benedict XVI as he strolled leisurely through the Vatican grounds dressed in the raiment emblematic of his spiritual majesty, "that we could make this area a little more user-friendly."

What Christ's vicar on earth had in mind was the installation of a heated swimming pool, shaped like the Mediterranean Sea but not quite as expansive, in which he and the faithful members of his entourage could spend their precious leisure hours meditating on the grandeurs and joys of God's creation.

"I think," mused His Holiness after he had met the staff that had served his predecessors long and faithfully, "that we can do better than this."

Mike nodded and went to work checking out the credentials and records of those faithful servants. He found, to his surprise and delight, that each and every one of them had at one time or another been guilty of some kind and degree of sin, and that they were also not the kind of people who would appreciate the special genius of their new master.

The kind of people Mike had in mind were people like himself, who had served His Holiness long and faithfully and, for this, deserved to be rechristened Michael Cardinal Bacchus. They were people like Arielle, who was put in charge of the far-flung system of convents over which the Catholic Church had for centuries exercised strict control; Lucy, who was put in charge of the newly-created Vatican Intelligence Agency; Esther Geld, Ron Something, and Andrea Wordsmith, who became, together with Cardinal Bacchus himself, the major part of the Vatican brain trust; and an underemployed chauffeur from New York, who was valued for his ability to put the complex, innovative thoughts of His Holiness into accessible and G-rated prose.

Later additions to this core staff included Lucy's twins. After flying all the way over from Santa Monica and San Francisco in the pontiff's specially-equipped Boeing 747 to be happily reunited with their long-estranged father, they were presented with unspecified sums of money and placed in charge of the Travel Office and encouraged to keep their special relationship with His Holiness to themselves.

§

After all these things had been accomplished, Esther Geld called a meeting of the successful brain trust to discuss the matter of finances and whatever else might arise. This meeting was held in the Sistine Chapel, where the principals to this discussion could be surrounded and inspired by frescoes painted by Botticelli, Ghirlandaio, and especially Perugino, whose finest achievement, *The Deliverance of the Keys*, composed by that great master in the Year of Our Lord Fourteen Hundred and Eighty-Two—a painting that depicted the transfer of all earthly and spiritual authority from Christ Himself to St. Peter and, by extension, to all of that humble saint's duly elected successors and their agents—had struck Ms. Geld's cool, discerning eye as most appropriate for the occasion.

Ms. Geld began by reminding His Holiness that the Esther Geld Agency, Inc., was by contract entitled to fifteen percent of the take, which, according to the interpretation of her bevy of lawyers, included the vast holdings of the Catholic Church.

"That's probably a lot," replied Pope Benedict XVI. "Mike, how much would you say it would come to?"

"Quadrillions of liras," said Michael Bacchus.

"Italian is a fine language," observed Benedict XVI, placing a pair of Cifuentes y Cia Partagas 1845 Limited Reserves in the far corners of his mouth and searching in the folds of his holy robe for a match, "but it's seldom used in the *Wall Street Journal.* I'd appreciate it, Mike, if you'd speak English, especially when you're talking about my money."

"Trillions of dollars," said Michael, finishing a whiskey sour, "and I'd appreciate it, Benny, if you'd call me Cardinal Bacchus."

"Thank you, Cardinal Bacchus, and I'd prefer being called Your Holiness, Pope Benedict XVI. Except, of course, in private. Then you can just call me Sixteen."

"Cut the comedy," said Esther Geld. "What's fifteen percent of trillions of dollars?"

"I don't have the exact figures at my fingertips," confessed Mike.

"Probably enough to buy Texas," guessed Benny. "Or would you prefer Brazil?" he asked Ms. Geld. "Before you decide, let me warn you about Brazilian winters. They are hell. You don't mind? Mike, make a note to sell off fifteen percent of our holdings and use the proceeds to buy Brazil. Make sure Rio is included. Then transfer Brazil to the Esther Geld Agency, Inc. The meeting is adjourned."

"Not so fast," said Ron Something. "We've got to strategize. Don't forget we have an election in four years."

"Strategize?" said Benny. "Four years? For God's sake, this isn't the presidency, Ron. Sorry, I didn't catch the last name. This is a lifetime position."

"Are you sure?" said Ron.

"That's always been my impression," said Benny.

"I think Benny's right," said Mike diplomatically.

"We've achieved our goal," Benny went on. "So don't speak strategies to me. Strategies imply sin. When you get to heaven, sin goes out the window. We're in heaven, which means strategies follow sin out the window. That's basic Aristotelian logic. Tell, him, Mike. Fill the man in on Aristotelian logic."

"On this point I agree with Ron," said Mike. "This is politics. Politics requires strategy. If we want to maintain our current lifestyle, we've got to play it down and dirty. That's basic Machiavellian logic."

"Aristotelian? Machia what?" said Andrea, who was busy taking notes and waving her hand in front of her face to dispel the smoke being emitted by a pair of Cifuentes y Cia Partagas 1845 Limited Reserves.

"Don't bother to take notes," advised Esther.

"Maybe I should tape this?" suggested Andrea.

"God no!" said the others.

"Strategize away," said Benny, throwing up his hands.

"I have an idea," said Mike.

"Mike has an idea," announced Benny. "Listen closely, friends, Romans, and my fine colleagues. Lend him your ears. Just be sure to charge him the going rate. Didn't somebody mention fifteen percent?"

Mike's idea pertained to reading an encyclical over world television, preferably on something other than "Perry Plug Live," preferably on the subject of moral renewal. As for the exact topic of this encyclical, he would defer to Ron, who kept his finger on the public pulse and had a better idea as to what facet of moral renewal the public's heart would throb with the greatest eagerness. Ron's finger told him that the public secretly yearned for a return to the good old-fashioned classical traditional Christian virtues. The strategists immediately turned their attention to this topic. The first question, raised by Andrea, concerned the identity of those virtues. The first answer, offered by Ron, was that the twelve virtues were trustworthiness, loyalty, helpfulness, friendliness, courtesy, kindness, obedience, cheerfulness, thrift, bravery, cleanliness, and reverence. The first criticism of this answer, offered by His Holiness, was that, though this was an excellent list and twelve was a sacred number, these items wouldn't fit on a bumper sticker. The second criticism, offered by Mike, was that the list was similar if not identical to that of the Boy Scouts and might be construed as copyright infringement. This led Esther to offer a second answer, which was that the encyclical simply call for a return to the cardinal virtues. This answer led in turn to the question of the number and identity of those virtues, a question that was deferred to the next meeting because Mike was the only one who had been subjected to the promptings of parochial school nuns and he was suffering a temporary lapse of memory and the whiskey sours were not opening up the floodgates of his memory.

"I have an idea," said Benny.

"Let's hear it," sighed Esther in deference to her highly-placed client.

Benny's idea pertained to the possibility of moving the papacy to Monte Carlo. Andrea wondered if Monte Carlo didn't have a certain—reputation. Mike pointed out that there was a precedent for the movement of the papacy, that in the fourteenth century—or maybe it was the thirteenth?—it had been moved to Avignon, a French city with an active wine market, but that this move had turned out badly in the sense that the Catholic Church ended up with a pair of competing popes. Esther pointed out that fifteen percent of half of the trillions of dollars was exactly half of fifteen percent of the trillions of dollars. Benny pointed out that the smaller amount could still purchase half of Brazil and went on to suggest that the Amazonian jungles would be an excellent half to forego. Esther advised Benny to get serious. Benny then suggested that Ron place his finger on the pulse of the public to determine if world opinion would support the movement of the papacy to Monte Carlo. In Mike's expert view, such a study was unnecessary. Benny amended his original idea by suggesting that the papacy be moved to Monte Carlo while the new swimming pool was being installed. Several members of the brain trust glanced at their watches and called for a vote. The ayes had it. The meeting was adjourned.

§

And thus it was that the papal office was moved to Monte Carlo for a time. There the brain trust enjoyed themselves while collaborating on an encyclical, which was put into lucid, impeccable prose by the author of *Religion for Dolts* and which the new pontiff announced to an eagerly-waiting world on "An Hour with Maven Plum," an American television program that had the reputation of being sympathetic to its guests and that featured a venerable woman whose face had been kept current by the finest plastic surgeon in Southern California.

Because the encyclical, "The Virtues," ran two and a half pages, double-spaced, Benedict XVI and Maven Plum agreed that it was too long to read on the air. They further agreed that the best way to proceed was to discuss it only in the most general terms.

"The encyclical," began Maven Plum after a brief introduction and several commercials. "What would you say is its gist, Your Holiness?"

"It's about the virtues," reported Benedict XVI with a fatherly smile.

"How *fascinating!*" said Maven Plum, her eyes searching the depths of the new pontiff's soul.

"We—and I think I can speak for the entire Catholic Church, including everyone from the highest cardinal, Michael Cardinal Bacchus, down to the simplest peasant family scratching out a meager living on a hillside in Nicaragua—we are embarking on a campaign to return the world to the good old-fashioned classical traditional Christian virtues that we all learned at our grandmother's knee but that have unfortunately gone out of fashion. We're calling this campaign 'Back to the Basics.'"

"How *mar*velous!" said Maven Plum. "And what are these virtues?" It had been a long time since she had sat on her grandmother's knee. Also, her grandmother had been a trapeze artist whose knees had been rendered inoperable by the imperfect performance of a difficult maneuver.

"I brought along a list," said His Holiness, reaching under his surplice and retrieving a 3 x 5 card.

Ms. Plum leaned forward in rapt anticipation.

"Number one, abstinence," read His Holiness. "Number two, benevolence. And number three, chastity." His Holiness looked directly at the correct camera and lectured the world. "Abstinence, benevolence, and chastity. We like to refer to them as 'The ABC's of Morality.'"

"How *won*derful!" said Maven Plum. "But is that all? I was brought up to think there were seven virtues. What happened to the other four?"

"A very good question," said the pope, nodding sagely. "Of course this is an extremely complex issue. We've spent a great deal of time, my spiritual advisors and I, reducing the number to something the average person, raised in the age of the television sound bite, can remember and put into practice. We started with a list of oh, about twenty-five virtues—Greek, Biblical, monastic, Boy Scout—and ended up with these three." His Holiness returned his gaze to the camera. "Abstinence, benevolence, and chastity. The ABCs of Morality. A, for abstinence: just say No to foreign substances, whether they be alcohol, tobacco, marijuana, or the heavy stuff. B, for benevolence: give fifteen percent of your pre-tax gross to your favorite charity, which, in the case of you Catholics, would be the Church. C, for chastity. Perhaps I should say I've appointed a task force to study this mother of all virtues. We expect to issue an important encyclical very soon, 'Chastity in an Age of Rampant Permissiveness.'"

"How *interesting!*" said Maven Plum. "Could you tell us what will be in it?"

The pope smiled mysteriously.

"Oh come! Just a hint?"

The pope folded his well-ringed fingers over his ample abdomen and continued to smile.

"Will it be controversial?"

"All I can say," he said, "is that it will be ground-breaking."

It was time for a series of commercials.

After the commercials, the two celebrities exchanged reminiscences about personal encounters with other celebrities. And so, in keeping with the program's reputation, nothing further of substance was said by either guest or host.

§

Several days later, a handsome young man with a razor-skinned pate and a silver-studded earring in the lobe of each ear and identifying himself only as the senior pastor of the Church of the Wide Open Door, in Southern California, appeared at the temporary quarters of the papacy and requested an audience with Benedict XVI. The audience was quickly granted.

The man did not choose to kiss either the pope's ring or the hem of the pope's garment. He chose instead to shake the pope's hand and introduce himself as Sean. He also chose to address the pope by his given name and to inform him that he, Sean, had "caught his act," a quaint American phrase that in this case referred to the pope's recent guest appearance on "An Hour with Maven Plum."

Benny invited his unexpected guest to be seated.

The two men, who had never been formally introduced, sat down for a relaxed dialogue, during which Benny went so far as to remove his formal headgear.

Sean immediately got to the point. "I believe you're still on our payroll."

"Right," said Pope Benny I. "Though I wouldn't want this to be widely known. Care for a cigar?"

"I understand," nodded Sean, accepting the offer.

Benny lit the cigars.

"So, what are we getting for our money?" asked Sean, studying the glowing ember at the end of his Jose Gener Hoyo de Monterrey Excalibur.

Benny confided that his plan was to reform the Catholic Church, more or less along the lines of the Church of the Wide Open Door. "This might take some time," he went on to explain. "Rome was not built in a day."

Sean signaled his agreement with a vague tip of his cigar.

The two smoked in silence for a few minutes.

"Christian Tantrism," Benny went on, "is a major part of the big picture."

"That's what I'd expect," said Sean. "The Arielle connection."

"The woman is doing one hell of a job," reflected Benny, studiously tapping the ash from his cigar into one of the available ruby-studded ash trays. "One hell of a job indeed." He returned the cigar to its natural position, monitoring the left corner of his mouth. "I just wish there were more like her." He blew a near-perfect smoke ring. "And I don't mean that in a sexist sense."

"Didn't think you did," said Sean.

"Christian Tantrism," Benny went on, making a grand gesture with his cigar. "I'm beginning to see it as the solution to the big Catholic issues. Abortion. Birth control. Women in the priesthood. Maybe even physician-attended suicide. And of course any scandals that might rear their ugly heads."

"Yeah?"

"Let's start with abortion," said Benny, leaning forward. "If we get everybody to practice Christian Tantrism, what happens to abortion? There's no need for it."

"I see your point. No pregnancies, no abortions."

"Watch the ash," warned Benny. "These are Persian rugs."

"Sorry," apologized Sean, looking around for his own ash tray.

"Birth control," continued Benny. "Same thing. When you do it right, on Tantric principles, no danger. Am I right?"

"I'd never thought of it that way."

"Don't be too hard on yourself. Not many have." Benny paused to reflect. "Of course there are always bound to be a few slip-ups. Maybe one, two in a lifetime. But that's compatible with zero-population growth."

"I see lots of bipartisan support."

Benny inspected his cigar, turning it around in his great fingers. "Women in the priesthood," he went on. "Arielle is Exhibit A. Who could argue with that?"

"Maybe a few misguided cardinals."

"There are ways to deal with them," chuckled Benny. "Remember old Geronti?"

"It was in all the papers. Whatever happened to him?"

"We put him in charge of a task force," reported Benny with a sly smile. "They're busy translating Aquinas into all the Amazonian languages that begin with S."

The two new friends enjoyed a long moment of merriment. Then:

"Physician-attended suicide," said Sean.

"Yeah?"

"I fail to see the connection to Christian Tantrism."

"That's a tough one," acknowledged Benny. "We're working on it."

"I'd be curious to see the results."

"We hope to wrap up the entire project by Epiphany. Then watch the encyclicals come rolling off the press!"

Benny quashed the stub of his cigar in the ash tray and abruptly stood up. "You play roulette? It's very big around here."

Sean stood up too, but in a more tentative fashion. "Isn't that playing it a little dangerously? I mean, your position and image and everything."

"Around town," said Pope Benedict XVI, "I go by Benny Good."

§

The two ecclesiastics went to the casino, where His Holiness Benedict XVI, alias Benny Good, was treated with the consideration and deference consistent with his reputation as an American billionaire.

Sean got lucky and broke even, roughly speaking.

Benny dropped something in the neighborhood of $1.2 million.

On the way back to the papal palace in an unmarked limo driven by the ghost author of "The Virtues," Sean voiced his concern over his employee's run of ill fortune.

"Don't worry," Benny said confidently. "I've been on a roll since we got to town. Tomorrow, if I'm any judge, I'm due to start a new roll."

"Yeah?" said Sean.

"It's not your money, if that's what's bugging you."

"Well—no."

"Being pope pays well," observed Benny. He leaned forward and spoke to the handsome chauffeur. "Let's go pick up some girls." He turned to Sean and winked. "Once a missionary, always a missionary."

15

The Doctrine of Back-Up Truths

At the end of the pleasant Monte Carlo stay, Pope Benedict XVI and his entourage arrived back at the Vatican. His Holiness was delighted to find that his living quarters had been redecorated according to his exacting specifications and that his *faux*-Mediterranean swimming pool had been properly installed.

His Holiness was less delighted to find that his papacy was beginning to attract unfavorable reviews.

Questions were being asked by the media. Was the former Vatican staff's retirement involuntary? The media said Yes, quoting members of the former Vatican staff. Was the faithful former Vatican staff being replaced by the new pope's cronies? The media suspected Yes, quoting informed sources within the hierarchy. Should the papacy be more forthcoming and candid about this matter? The media urged Yes, quoting each other.

Esther Geld flew in from New York and called a meeting of the brain trust to discuss strategy. The pope proposed that they meet in the new swimming pool. The proposal was accepted. They convened in the Sicilian harbor directly beneath Mount Aetna.

"We have a problem," began Ms. Geld, who had chosen a black swimming suit that would do justice to her foxy voice and shape. She proceeded to present a detailed analysis of the problem.

"I have an idea," Benny announced when she was through. He had chosen a black pair of trunks that would do justice to his portly, papal physique.

"Let's hear it," said Esther Geld, "and please keep your hands to yourself."

Everyone wanted to hear Benny's idea. He was the pope, they nodded in unified agreement, and he had a right to his opinion. On the issue of his hand placement, however, they divided along gender lines.

"Let's come clean," advised Benny. "Let's remind them that the old staff couldn't speak English. I replaced them with a staff that could. What do you expect when you elect an English-speaking pope? An English-speaking staff. Besides, English is the number one language in the world."

"That's basic American logic," said Andrea, whose choice of a daring mauve suit had caught the pope's discerning eye, as it had been designed to do.

"Except that the number one language is Chinese," said Mike, whose cardinal-red trunks had drawn a rare favorable comment from Ms. Geld. Ron, who would be the next to speak, also wore a pair of trunks, which could only be described as nondescript. Which is to say, Ron continued to look like Ron.

"We kept one of the Chinese cooks," Ron reminded them all.

"There you go," said Benny. "We're number two, but we kept a number one cook. That's got to count for something."

"Damn it, Benny!" said Esther. "Keep your hands to yourself!"

"You are one helluva beautiful woman," said Benny, showing a smiling face.

"Thank you," she said sarcastically. "I hate it when you drink," she added with a disapproval that would have bordered on contempt if the object of her disapproval had not been the pope.

"How do we deal with the charge of cronyism?" she asked, moving on to the next subject.

"Tell 'em it was my way of saying Thank you. Tell 'em I was rewarding you for your good works. Isn't that basic Catholic doctrine? You do good works and you get a reward. The reward is heaven. This is heaven, right? I'm the pope, right? The pope is supposed to be a good Catholic. He's supposed to follow basic Catholic doctrine. I'm following basic Catholic doctrine. That means I'm a good Catholic, which means I'm a good pope. A good pope is supposed to have good friends. He's supposed to reward them. That doesn't make them cronies. This is basic Aristotelian logic. Andrea, are you taking notes?"

"Am I supposed to?" asked Andrea. "Do you find *me* attractive?"

"Am I supposed to?" countered Benny. In spite of her mauve suit, Andrea remained on the cusp between rather nice-looking and plain. But although she was a mere six, she was beginning to enjoy Benny's manual attention.

Laughter floated across the blue Mediterranean look-alike, attracting the attention of a flock of curious paparazzi.

"I love it when you drink," giggled Andrea. "It makes you funny."

"I am one helluva funny man," said Benny.

"Keep your hands to yourself!" said Ms. Geld.

"I don't mind," said Andrea, turning red and warm. "Really."

"What do we tell the press?" asked Ms. Geld, wriggling free from an attempted display of affection.

"Mike will think of something," predicted Benny. "Mike, think of something. That's your job. That's why we keep you around. You're good at thinking of things. You're my number one cardinal. For God's sake, think of something."

"I'm thinking," cried Mike as he floated toward the Aegean alongside Esther Geld, who was busy reminding him to keep his hands to himself.

"He's thinking," cried Benny as he floated toward Monte Carlo with red, warm Andrea in tow.

Ron climbed out of the pool and sprinted toward Gibraltar, where he awakened the Swiss Guard, who shooed the paparazzi off the Rock.

§

Next morning Mike Bacchus called a press conference to discuss the case, *The Former Vatican Staff* v. *The Pope's Cronies*, and as may arise.

"His Holiness refuses to dignify these charges with an answer," began Mike.

"His Holiness categorically denies these charges," added Mike.

"These charges are politically motivated," he went on. "Isn't that obvious?" He added a sentence including the phrase, "vast anti-American conspiracy."

"That was taken out of context," he remembered to reply on several occasions.

He pointed out numerous errors, real or perceived, in the published reports. He also cast aspersions on the characters of various members of the former Vatican staff, directing the press to a pro-American-pope home page for details.

The reporters soon lost interest in the case of the former Vatican staff. Their curiosity was now piqued by a set of tabloid photos, about which they asked many questions. These questions were put simultaneously and in accusatory voices.

"No more questions," said Mike, and he exited gracefully, his robe fluttering in the late autumn breeze.

§

"What should we say about those damned pictures?"

Esther Geld was referring to the tabloid photos of the recent swimming pool frolic involving the charter members of her brain trust. The pictures, according to the tabloids, were "compromising," though it was not clear from a casual glance who was being compromised. The brain trust was taking these pictures seriously. So seriously that it was not meeting in the swimming pool, and its members were dressed in their work clothes and were, for the most part, sober. They were again meeting in the Sistine Chapel, within eyeing distance of a Botticelli fresco that failed to do justice to the genius of that great master.

"Let's say they're fake," said Benny. "Let's say they've been doctored. Let's say our enemies broke into our private pool and performed actions we don't approve of. Let's say this one couldn't be me because I'm not wearing my pope costume. Let's say it was taken before I got converted. Let's say I was baptizing Andrea. Let's say she's my sister."

"We can't say that," said Andrea.

"Why not?"

"Because it can't all be true."

"Maybe not all at once," conceded Benny. "But if we take them one at a time, we'll be home free."

"Truth changes," Mike explained to Andrea. "You've just got to figure out the best order to present it in. For instance, you don't start out by saying you're Benny's sister. You start out by blaming our enemies. A few days later, you go to your first back-up truth, that the pictures are fakes. A couple more days and you go to your second back-up truth, that they've been doctored. After they bring in the photography experts, you raise doubts about whether that's really Benny because he's not wearing his pope outfit. After that, it's on to the idea that the pictures were taken before he got converted. If that doesn't wash, you float the thought that he was baptizing you. By the time you get to the sister bit, they're on to something else and it's a dead issue."

"You're probably right," said Andrea. She looked at Benny with inappropriate lust in her eye. "I didn't want to be his sister anyway."

§

The tactic worked. Several weeks later, the media were on to something else. The pope and his entourage were gathered for a strategy session, this time back in the swimming pool, dressed as before.

"What should we say about The Deadly Sins?"

Esther Geld was referring to the investigative report that the Catholic Church owned a Las Vegas resort, which, the reporter went on to say (accurately), was purchased by Michael Bacchus with the assent of then-Cardinal Gottlieb, and which, the reporter added (again accurately), included a casino and an escort service, the latter being a front, the reporter implied (a matter of semantics, the sticking point being the tense of the word *being*), for a prostitution ring.

"Tell 'em we bought it to further the aims of the Church," advised Pope Benedict XVI. "One of the aims of the Church is to teach the flock to resist temptation. How can they learn to resist temptation unless we give 'em a chance?"

"I agree with Benny," said Andrea. "When I was a little kid I used to always beg my dad for candy bars. He got so tired of this he bought me a whole box of the things and told me to eat away. Now I can't even *think* of candy bars without getting sick."

"Andrea should've been a theologian," observed Benny with admiration.

"What about cigars?" asked Ron.

"Have one," offered Benny, reaching up to the summit of Mt. Vesuvius to pluck one of the cigars that were stashed there for the pope's pleasure.

"I mean, can you think of *cigars* without getting sick?" said Ron.

"I do it every day," said Benny proudly, lighting up.

"What about sex?" asked Andrea.

"Later," said Benny.

"She means, can you think of *sex* without getting sick?" said Ron.

"She knows the answer to that."

"What's our back-up truth?" asked Mike.

"That the Church is making a substantial profit."

The brain trust conceded that this was a fine back-up truth. They were unhappy, however, that there was even a need for the creation of truths, back-up truths, etc. They would be happier, they agreed, if they could spend less time in strategy sessions and more time cruising the Mediterranean, performing the job the College of Cardinals had hired them to do.

"Where are all these rumors coming from?" was the question Esther Geld finally got around to asking.

"In cases like this," observed Ron, "there's usually a leak."

"Find the leak!" demanded Esther. "Benny, put Lucy on the case."

"Lucy's on vacation," said Benny. He and Lucy had had an unpleasant chat about the amount of quality time Benny had been spending with her in comparison with the amount of quality time he had been spending with others, whom she characterized (inaccurately, he insisted), sometimes as her "rivals," at other times as "those snob bitches." She had left. He didn't think it wise to share these particulars with his colleagues. He also didn't think it wise to mention that the twins wanted more money and had suggested that if they didn't get it, they would write a joint autobiography, tentatively entitled *Children of a Lesser Dad*, and that he was doing some profound thinking about his options, none of which he found appealing.

"Bring her back," said Esther, referring to Lucy.

"We're not paying her to take vacations," said Mike.

"We're paying her to gather intelligence," said Ron.

"We're paying her to find leaks," said Andrea.

"I'll see what I can do," said Benny, wondering what he could do.

§

One week later, the media were accusing His Holiness of entertaining women in his cell. The think tank was back in the Sistine Chapel, gathered around a fresco by Ghirlandaio, an Italian painter who had saved his best work for other venues.

"What should we say about the women in Benny's life?"

Esther Geld was referring to Arielle and her charges, who had figured prominently in a story about some of the personnel in the new Vatican. Being sensitive to Andrea's feelings, Ms. Geld was careful not to mention any names.

"Tell 'em Jesus had women in his life," said Benny.

This statement did not entirely meet with Andrea's approval. Being a wordsmith, she knew the difference between *women* (pl.) and *a woman* (sing.). "Don't forget that he had favorites," she reminded Benny.

"He had favorites," agreed Benny.

"One in particular," insisted Andrea.

"One in particular."

"That truth will last for half a day," predicted Mike.

"Point out that his relationships were Platonic," said Benny.

"What?" said Andrea.

No one knew how to interpret Andrea's question. Didn't she know about Platonic relationships, or was she taking issue with Benny's claim? So Mike introduced the subject of a back-up truth.

"Remind 'em God created woman," said Benny. "If God put His mind to something, He did it for a reason. That's all you have to say. They'll get the message."

"That's a one-week truth," observed Mike.

"God also created man," said Andrea.

Mike shook his head. "I don't think we want to go there."

§

The media shifted its attention from the private life of Pope Benedict XVI to the biggest issue yet. The gravity of this issue made the Sistine Chapel the natural choice for a strategy meeting. It also made Mike check the structure for bugs.

"What should we say about the nuns?" asked Esther Geld after Mike had given them the go-ahead.

Ms. Geld was referring to an investigative report about the miraculous transformation of convents into brothels, which, the media sleuth claimed, had been established by then-Archbishop Benedict Gottlieb back in Kirkland and was now being instituted on a worldwide basis.

"I'll tell 'em it's an old Catholic tradition going all the way back to the Middle Ages," said Mike. "It's in Boccaccio." Mike was well-educated. He knew about Boccaccio and his dirty stories about lust-ridden medieval nuns. He had picked up this information back in parochial school. Not from the nuns, who may or may not have known the stories, but from a self-guided independent study he had pursued, not for credit, but out of pure intellectual curiosity.

"Good thinking," said Benny. "Then tell 'em a high percentage of the nuns have achieved salvation," said Benny. "Tell 'em they've helped a high percentage of their clients achieve salvation. Explain salvation. Explain Christian Tantrism. Explain that it comes from India. Point out that if the Catholic Church was big enough to admit that Galileo was right, we should be big enough to admit that those guys back in ancient India were right."

"This will require an encyclical," said Mike.

"Andrea," said Benny, "write an encyclical."

"I've never written an encyclical," admitted Andrea.

"It's like a term paper," explained Mike. "You've written term papers, right?"

"Not on Christian Tantrism."

"You know about Christian Tantrism, right?"

Andrea glanced over at Benny and blushed. She looked away. "When is it due?"

§

Andrea produced an encyclical, with the help of Benny and certain English-speaking members of the Vatican staff.

Benny figured out which points to include, using his expert, Arielle, as a consultant. The chauffeur and author of *Religion for Dolts* put Benny's thoughts into basic English.

Andrea translated the chauffeur's prose into encyclical form after Mike showed her what a basic encyclical looks like.

Then she checked for spelling errors.

Esther Geld urged Ron to try out the encyclical on several focus groups for their reactions.

Ron did so.

The non-Catholics were very positive. The lapsed Catholics were ecstatic. The more devoted Catholics had qualms. Lucy was combining business with pleasure in Reno and could not be reached for comment.

On Epiphany morning, Mike passed out copies two minutes before a televised press conference.

The encyclical read:

CHASTITY IN AN AGE
OF RAMPANT PERMISSIVENESS

Encyclical Letter
of
His Holiness
Pope Benedict XVI

Venerable brothers and sisters and dear sons and daughters and faithful disciples, greetings and the apostolic blessing from the Successor of Peter.

1. In every age, the holy Catholic Church must restate its moral teachings.

2. One of the most fundamental moral teachings concerns chastity ("The Virtues," pp. 1-3).

3. The present age has become rampantly permissive.

4. Chastity must be restated, with one eye on the apostolic teachings and the other eye on the present age.

5. The restatement of chastity must start with a return to Christian Tantrism.

6. Tantrism was taught and practiced by the sages of ancient India, including, some would say, Buddha.

7. Tantrism held that salvation is achieved through chastity.

8. Tantrism defined chastity as sex without lust.

9. Christian Tantrism was taught and practiced by Jesus Christ (see the recently-discovered *The Gospel according to Mary Magdalene,* forthcoming from the Vatican Press).

10. Christian Tantrism defines chastity as Christian sex without lust.

11. Christian salvation is achieved through Christian sex.

12. Christian sex is required of all believing adults, whether married or single.

§

Pope Benedict XVI stood before a battery of microphones to answer any questions that might arise.

Q: Aren't encyclicals usually a lot longer?

A: To tell the truth, I haven't read that many. Maybe three or four. I don't even remember their names, which were in Latin. I'm not good with the dead languages. My father, who was a rabbi, didn't speak Hebrew at home, probably because my mother, who was a Baptist Sunday School teacher, insisted on English. Her thinking was that having us all speak English was a good way to keep the family together. My parents were pro-family. They would have made fine Catholics, if God had so willed, which of course He didn't. It would have deprived me of my conversion experience, because I would have been brought up Catholic and I probably wouldn't be standing before you today, by the grace of God, as His Holiness Pope Benedict XVI. I'm a firm believer in Divine Providence. I'm convinced that at the beginning of time God created a lightning bolt with my name on it and was just waiting for the opportunity to use it. I'm not sure, of course, but my guess would be that my parents practiced Tantrism, my father preferring the Jewish variety but my mother insisting on the Christian. Incidentally, she would not have been surprised by the recent discovery of *The Gospel according to Mary Magdalene*. She was an early feminist, God rest her ardent soul. She made my father do the dishes while she wrote letters to the editor on a variety of issues, such as the glass ceiling, which used to get her goat, to use the vernacular. But getting back to the question concerning the length of encyclicals. You may have noticed that the price of paper is going through the roof. We've been trying to live within our means down at the Vatican, which explains why we kept this encyclical to a minimum number of words. Also, our publishers are telling us that short encyclicals are more likely to be bought and read than those long old rambling things. Not that there isn't a lot of good spiritual meat in many of them, and I'd prefer not to mention which ones. Every good Catholic has his or her favorite, which is as it should be. We're all unique individuals. The only thing we really have in common is our need for salvation, which, as I believe the encyclical points out, is achieved through the practice of Tantrism, preferably of the Christian variety. Next question?

Q: Speaking of money. What's your response to the recent report that the Esther Geld Agency, Inc., has funneled off fifteen percent of the Church's holdings?

A: I refuse to dignify those charges with an answer. I categorically deny those charges, which are obviously politically motivated. The data were taken out of context. The reporter didn't get her facts right. She is being used by the enemies of Christ's Church. I'm not going to name names. I think we all know who they are. That's all I intend to say on this issue.

Q: What about—

A: No more questions. In three minutes I'm due at the maiden performance of the *Missa Papae Benedictus,* which is Latin for *Mass in Honor of His Holiness Pope Benedict XVI* and will be available on CDs sometime around Good Friday. Take care, and God bless.

Then, after making a vague but significant gesture, the pope disappeared from his balcony into his private living quarters, where he watered his begonias.

§

"What should we say about this one?"

Esther Geld was referring to the latest media speculation concerning her agency's sudden show of wealth and the simultaneous disappearance of a huge cache of stocks, bonds, and real estate holdings from the Vatican's financial books. Was this a coincidence? the media wondered.

The brain trust pondered its strategy carefully. They had learned to trust in Benny's ability to lead them through the valley of the shadow of scandals, but there was something different about this scandal. It involved substantial amounts of money. It would test his talent to the utmost. It was, according to Mike's conservative calculation, a ten-truth problem. They shook their heads slowly and sadly and looked to Benny.

Benny had an idea, perhaps inspired by one of the many frescoes with which they were surrounded.

The members of the brain trust glanced at each other and smiled. When all seemed lost, Benny always came up with an idea. It made their job much easier.

"Scripture tells us to be not of the world. 'The world' refers to money, which, according to Scripture, makes the world go round. We were following Scripture, which contains the clear commands of God. We were moving in the direction of following this particular command. We were divesting."

"If we say that," said Ron, "we fall into a trap. They'll want us to continue to divest."

"Not so fast," said Ms. Geld, who was the beneficiary of the initial divestiture.

"Aristotle teaches us to do all things in moderation," reminded Mike. "A good definition of moderation would be fifteen percent."

"Thank God for Aristotle," said Benny.

"That solves half the problem," said Mike. "What about the Esther Geld Agency, Inc.?"

"We'll say she was worth every damned penny," said Benny, this time with conviction.

Everyone agreed that Esther Geld had earned her fifteen percent. Everyone was receiving a modest portion of that fifteen percent. They were all experts in their fields and were, in their modest opinions, worth their slice of the pie.

"Let's go swimming," suggested Benny. He was already in his trunks. The lust was beginning to build.

Esther did not want to go swimming. She wanted to discuss the problem in more detail. She was worried. She began to imagine worst-case scenarios.

Benny was not worried. "If worse comes to worst, we'll change the subject."

They wanted to know what he had in mind.

He cast about his stately person for a cigar. "I'll just come up with a new revelation," he said, careful not to burn himself with the match.

16

A Major, Major Revelation

It was past midnight, and the Vatican was pervaded by a holy quietness. The inhabitants of the sacred center of the cosmos had finished performing the fresh new innovative rituals of the Faith and remained in bed, slumbering peacefully. Only one person, a pajama-clad white male in his late forties or early fifties, was up and stirring, unable to sleep. He had a sudden hunch. He reached for his bedside phone. He dialed a number and waited.

"Lucy here," said a voice. "I can't come to the phone right now, but at the tone just leave your message and I'll get back to you. Unless you're selling something."

"Damn," said His Holiness under his breath.

The tone sounded.

"Lucy. This is Pope Benedict XVI. You probably know me better as Benny. I can't sleep. I've been meditating on my various sins and shortcomings. Come back, Lucy. Pick a number between one and two, multiply by one, and you have the amount of quality hours I'll give you each and every day. I promise. I'm the pope. A pope is as good as his word. Therefore, I'm as good as my word. That's basic logic. Mike taught me all about logic in pope school. He was a fine teacher. I was a good student. He gave me a B+."

"Benny?" inquired a female voice.

"Lucy? I thought I might catch you back in Reno. What the hell are you doing?"

"Getting ready for bed."

Benny bet himself that she was telling the truth. He debated whether to try for more truth. He decided in favor, but the decision was not made without anxiety.

"Are you now married, or are you considering marriage?"

"Why would *you* care?"

She had not answered his question, but that was okay. No news was good news. Benny abandoned this line of questioning and moved on to another topic.

"Listen, Lucy. Things are happening. The media's giving us a hard time."

"I've noticed."

"We've got to get to the bottom of things. We suspect a leak. Who's been ratting on us? This is the question we've been discussing. We need an answer, and I was thinking, who better to give us that answer than Lucy Good, Director of the Vatican Intelligence Agency?"

"What about Andrea?"

"You think *she's* the one who's been ratting?"

"Mice do not rat."

"Then why did you bring up her name?"

"I was suggesting her as my replacement. Andrea Wordsmith, Director, Vatican Intelligence Agency. The pay's not great, but it matches her abilities."

Benny fumbled around in his pajama pocket for a fine cigar. "Come back, little Lucy," he pleaded. "I'll give you a raise."

"I have a well-paying job, and I enjoy my new work."

He fumbled for a match. "I'm afraid to ask."

"You should be."

He struck the match. Nothing happened. He put down the unlit cigar and finished off a potent potable. The words began to flow. "Last night I had a revelation. I think it was from God, but

197

I may be mistaken. I didn't catch the name. It was a male voice—sophisticated, mature, authoritative. 'That's God,' I said to myself. 'Doesn't that sound like God?' I asked Andrea. But she was asleep. Her mind, such as it is, was at peace with the world. This morning I told the other members of my brain trust about this revelation. They also thought it sounded like God. Mike recommended I go on TV and let the world in on this bombshell. At eleven tonight, your time, I'm scheduled to appear on 'Nightgrill.' I'd have preferred another evening with Maven Plum, but she's already booked. She's doing a séance with Charlie somebody. Chaplin, I think. We had to settle for Roe Gates. He asks difficult questions, but I figure I can handle anything he throws at me. God is still on my side. We've always made a great team. Lucy, are you still with me?"

"Sorry, Benny, I've gotta get to work. But thanks for the info."

"Thank you for your support, Lucy. Keep in touch."

The phone went dead.

Benny snuffed out his unlit cigar and said a brief but fervent prayer and went back to bed.

§

Roe Gates sat behind a desk in his television studio, dressed in his special prosecutor's suit. He was checking his notes and a list of questions.

"Ten seconds."

Gates put down the notes and placed his gin and tonic under the desk.

"Five, four, three, two, one," said a voice, and Gates flashed two rows of sharp, well-ordered teeth at the television camera.

"Hello," said Gates, "I'm Roe Gates, and this . . . is . . . 'Nightgrill.' Our guest tonight has been very much in the news lately. He's Pope Benedict XVI, who night before last had a revelation from God—or perhaps I should say, he *claims* he had a revelation from God. Did he or didn't he? That's the subject of our program tonight, the pope's new revelation. Is it the genuine article, or is it a fake? That's what we want to find out. But before we get to that question, we have to take time out for these important messages."

§

Pope Benedict XVI sat behind a desk in his resplendent office, dressed in his official pope uniform and checking a copy of his script.

"Ten seconds."

The pope put down the script and placed his whiskey sour under the desk.

"Five, four, three, two, one," said a voice, and the face of His Holiness took on a sudden beatific radiance.

"We're back," announced Gates, "and we were just getting ready to speak to Pope Benedict XVI. Your Holiness, are you there?"

"I'm here, Roe," said Benedict XVI, "and you can just call me Pope."

Roe Gates turned on his top-form professional frown. "Pope, before the break I was telling our audience about this so-called 'new revelation.' Could you just give us your story, and I emphasize the word *story*, of the circumstances surrounding your receiving this wisdom from On High? And spare us the details, if you please."

"I'd be happy to do that, Roe."

"We'd be much obliged."

"Well, last night I was in my cell, praying—"

"Hold it right there," interrupted an incredulous Gates. "You were praying? In this day and age? You still believe in the power of prayer?"

"Indeed we do. Prayer is a big part of our religion," said the pope confidently. "Buddhists meditate. Hindus levitate. We happen to pray."

"Muslims pray a lot too, if I'm not mistaken."

The pope nodded thoughtfully. "I'd have to look it up, but I believe you may be right."

"Anyway, go on. You were in your cell, praying."

"Right. I was in my cell, praying—we're expected to do that, us popes, two or three times a day, for oh, half an hour per stint at the minimum—they give us a time clock so we can punch in and punch out—it goes on our record for future reference—the historians of tomorrow will want to have records of those things—you know how they are, those bat-eyed historians, they spend hours and hours in the library poring over a bunch of what to the majority of us are nothing but trivial details—I suppose they'll want to know which pontiffs were really pious and which ones were frauds and rascals and rogues and con men—"

"Could you just get to the point," Gates interrupted in the impatient way that was his trademark.

"Good idea," said Benedict XVI. "I was in my cell praying, when suddenly there was a great light, and an angel of the Lord appeared unto me."

"Wait a minute. Are you sure it was an angel of the Lord? Are you sure it wasn't something you ate?"

"It couldn't have been anything I ate. I'm on a diet. That's another thing you're expected to do as a pope. During the Lenten season, you're supposed to diet. They monitor you very closely, the doctors of the Church do, as to your daily caloric intake. You're supposed to imbibe 750 calories *per diem*, which is Latin for 'per day.' That's the recommended dosage, 750 cals. It's all very scientific. They want you to clean out the system every year by holding it down to 750 cals for a prescribed period of time, usually from Ash Wednesday to Holy Saturday."

"Seven hundred and fifty calories in any form? Including strong drink?"

"In any form. Snails, caviar, B & B, whatever."

"Which leads me to my next question. There are certain rumors floating around concerning a problem you may or may not have. Had you been drinking at the time you received your so-called 'revelation'?"

"Perhaps we have a problem of definition here. 'Drinking'? 'At the time'?"

"I believe Webster's defines drinking as 'partaking of alcoholic beverages.'"

"That's one way to define it," admitted Benedict XVI.

"Do you have a better definition?"

The pope took a dictionary from atop his desk and began to look up the word.

"Let's see, 'drinking, drinking'—from the Old English, *drinkan*. Hmm. Webster's also defines drinking as, number one, 'ingesting liquid into the mouth—'"

"Just stick to the original definition," Gates demanded in the way that had become his trademark. "Had you been partaking of alcoholic beverages at the time you received your quote-unquote 'revelation'?"

"'At the time'? What are we talking about here, exactly at the time, nine seconds before, a minute before?" asked Benny, who would have made a good lawyer, had God so willed it.

"Let me put it this way. Were you drunk when this quote-unquote 'angel of the Lord' appeared in your cell?"

"You can't get drunk on just 750 calories of B & B."

"Oh?"

"Maybe *you* can. I can't."

"Are you telling us it's all relative? You, the pope?" Gates was back to his incredulous tone.

"I'm saying it depends on your basic body type: ectomorph, mesomorph, endomorph. You're probably, and this is just a guess, ectomorph."

"Mesomorph," corrected Gates, puffing out his chest.

"Well, I happen to be endomorph, that's how God made me, which means I was stone sober when suddenly there was a great light and this angel of the Lord suddenly appeared in my cell—"

"Just hold it there one moment, please. You still haven't convinced us it was an angel of the Lord. How do you know it wasn't a popular character from 'Sesame Street?' Or a misplaced mascot from some sports team? Or an escaped lunatic from LAX?"

"In Rome?"

"I beg your pardon, is that where you received your revelation? In Rome?"

"Actually, it was here in the Vatican, which is not in Rome *per se*, which is Latin for 'as such.'"

"Okay, for purposes of discussion, let's stipulate that the guy who appeared in your cell *was* an angel of the Lord." Roe Gates would also have made a good lawyer, if he had not already been disbarred.

"It wasn't a guy," said Benedict XVI. "It was a woman."

Roe Gates paused effectively. "Pardon me," he said, "but are popes allowed to have women in their cells?"

"The rules say you can have women in your cells only from dawn to curfew—unless of course they're there to help you pray. In which case they can stay all night."

"Just as long as they're on their knees it's okay, is that what you're saying?"

"It depends on what they're doing on their knees."

"In other words, they have to be praying."

"Either that, or scrubbing the floor. Also, they have to be modestly attired and over the age of sixteen."

"Which your angel was?"

"I'd say so, yes. She appeared to be approximately twenty-one years of age and was wearing an attractive grey herringbone business suit, a white cotton blouse, a blue-and-grey bow tie, white stockings, and a pair of Nike runners. Her jet-black hair was severely drawn back and cinched by a slight rubber band, which created a ponytail that made her seem younger than her actual years."

"I believe the word is *belied*. 'The ponytail belied her actual age.' And what did she say, this so-called 'angel'?"

"She asked me if I had any questions."

"And what did you tell her?"

"I said I'd always been curious about this one question, I must have been, oh, maybe three years old when it first hit me, I was precocious as a child, being blessed with exceptionally strong genes from both sides, the Jewish father and the Baptist mother, which explains the high degree of intellectual curiosity I exhibited even at that tender—"

"What's the question?"

"Question?" asked Benedict XVI.

"The question you said you were curious about as a kid," said Gates.

"Oh yes. Where did God come from. I mean originally? That's the great and profound question I pondered as a young, gifted child, wise beyond my years."

"And this revelation contains her answers?"

"It contains *God's* answers, as told to His trusted messenger. As soon as I asked her that question, she sat right down at my computer and typed it in. While she was waiting for the answer, she said a little prayer, which—"

"What were the words of that prayer? I'm sure our Catholic viewers would like to know."

"I didn't actually catch the words, but it *seemed* like a prayer. Which made her eligible for being in my room beyond curfew. After the prayer, she cupped her hand behind her ear, like so," and Benedict XVI demonstrated, "in order to hear the divine answer, then enter it on the hard disk. I mention this last point because it's important that she wasn't making up the answer on her own, she was getting it straight from the horse's mouth."

"And you call *this* a revelation? From God?"

"Of course. He answered the question that had stumped me from my earliest childhood. He could have dodged it, but He didn't. Also, there are no spelling errors in the entire document.

My angel went through the entire file on my WorkPerfect spell-check program and came up with zilch errors, which has to tell you something."

"On that note," said steely-voiced Gates, "we'll take time out for a message. Don't go away, we'll be right back."

§

"How'm I doing, Mike?" asked Benny.

Michael Cardinal Bacchus slowly removed his face from behind his hands.

"Did I say something wrong, Mike? Something illogical? Geez, I hope not. Be straight with me, Mike. Would Aristotle have been proud? How was my Latin?"

Mike shook his head slowly. "Holy Jesus," he muttered.

"Maybe I should cut down on the Latin. Think that would help? People don't like smart-ass scholars. How'm I coming across? Don't spare my feelings, Mike. I can take it. I've got callouses on my soul. That's from suffering. Suffering has played a major role in my life. I used to be married, you know. Plus the fact that I've been excommunicated from a couple of churches. Speak to me, Mike. Tell me I'm doing great. I've been canned from a job or two and don't want to blow this one."

Mike sighed. "You're doing just great," he said, patting his friend on the back of his chasuble. "Keep up the good work," he added, rolling his eyes heavenward and reaching for his flask.

"Thank you, Michael," said Benny, wiping his sweat-beaded forehead with his embroidered right sleeve. "Remind me to give you a promotion. What's the next step up from cardinal?"

"Ten seconds," said a voice. "Five, four, three, two, one. . . ."

§

"We're back," said Gates, "and we've been talking to Pope Benedict XVI. Your Holiness, are you still with us?"

Benedict XVI announced that he was still there. He also reminded Roe Gates to call him Pope.

"Pope," said Gates, "I'm sure our viewers are anxious to hear your so-called, and I can't emphasize that word enough, your so-called 'revelation' from God. Do you happen to have a copy of it with you?"

"I do, Roe. I'm equally anxious to read it to your viewers. It says—"

"Before you read it," interrupted Gates, "perhaps you could address a question some of our viewers may have on their minds."

"Happy to do that, Roe," said the pope.

"Whatever happened to that angel?"

"As soon as she—I'm speaking here of the angel of the Lord—as soon as she had finished typing in the answer to my question, in other words the revelation, as soon as she had the answer to my precocious question concerning the ultimate origin of God firmly embedded on my hard disk, she turned to me, and a great white light shone round about her, and she spake, saying, 'Know, Benedict XVI, that I who speak to thee, I, the angel Meredith, am—'"

"Get to the point," demanded Gates in his best prosecutorial manner. "What happened to her?"

"She left."

"Could you be more specific? *How* did she leave? The same way she came in? Through a secret passageway, through the back door, exactly how?"

"She ascended into heaven," said Benedict XVI. "I've got the revelation," he added testily. "Do you or don't you want me to read it?"

Gates assured His Holiness that the world was all ears.

Benedict XVI read the revelation that he had written with only the aid of his trusted chauffeur:

In the beginning, there was heaven. It wasn't much at the time. The northern half was like an expanse of ice in Greenland, and the southern half was like a corn field in the middle of Iowa. It would have been a complete bore, except for the man and the woman. Actually, they weren't really a man and a woman as you know them today. They were more like just a him and a her.

They weren't higher beings. They weren't lower beings, either. My point is, they were a couple of *tertium quids,* which is Latin for 'third somethings.' They were just hanging around taking care of the place, keeping it from going to pot. Neither of them held down a regular job, because as everybody knows, the chief reason for working outside the home is to make money, and if there's nothing to spend money on, what's the use of putting in all that time at a meaningless job? So they were a zero-salary couple.

They played a lot of solitaire. But this was only in the mornings and afternoons. In the evenings, he'd go out for a walk. He'd get tired of having her kibitz while he was playing solitaire, so he'd take a stroll around the corn fields and watch the girls go by. He'd—

"Hold it right there!" interrupted Gates. "Where did these girls come from?"

Benedict XVI inspected the document closely. "Huh," he said, shaking his head. "It doesn't say. All it says is that there were some girls."

"That may or may not be true, but doesn't your inquiring mind want to know where they came from?"

"No, not really."

Roe Gates was incredulous, as only Roe Gates could be. "You mean to tell us that back there at the age of three you were dying to know where God came from, but that now, at the age of, what, fifty? you have absolutely no curiosity as to why at the beginning of time as we know it a bunch of alluring females suddenly show up from nowhere and take over an Iowa corn field?"

Benedict XVI shrugged sheepishly, to use a Biblical allusion. "I'm just reading God's revelation, that's all. I don't question His insight and wisdom. When you're lucky enough to get a scoop like this revelation, you don't question it, you just take it on faith that that's the way things were back there in the beginning of the world, and if you don't mind, I'd like to finish reading this new revelation."

"Well, okay," agreed Roe, who by this time was ahead on points, "but just for purposes of discussion."

"Now, where was I?" asked His Holiness. "Oh yes, the guy was tired of the woman's kibitzing while he was playing solitaire," and he continued:

So he'd take a stroll around the corn fields and watch the girls go by. He'd never even touch them or anything like that. He'd just stand there on the corner with his mouth half-open and eyeball them for about half an hour at the most, maybe think a few lascivious thoughts, then go home and take a cold shower. It was just an innocent hobby, the kind of a thing nobody thinks anything about these days.

But she didn't approve of this pastime. Well, strictly speaking nobody actually knew whether or not she approved of these girl-watching habits, because she had no close friends to confide in about the problem, if it really was a problem. All anybody knew is that he had it figured out that if she happened to find out the part about the girls, she probably wouldn't approve. How else would you explain the fact that he told her stories? That's right, when they climbed into bed at night he told her stories about what he'd been doing. Stories, as in alibis.

This is where *I* get into the picture. I was the one he told stories about.

His Holiness looked up. "Keep in mind, this is God speaking." He went on:

She'd start the conversation off in her confrontational mode, saying something like, "And what were you doing this evening, darling?"

He'd come right back with, "Oh, nothing, sweetheart, I just took a walk and talked to God."

"God?" she'd say suspiciously. "Who's this God person? She wouldn't happen to be one of them types who walk the streets at night looking for disconsolate males and offering to listen to their problems, would she?"

"Oh no," he'd say indignantly. "God's a male, in fact a very high-minded male," and then he'd go on to describe Me. In fact, he'd describe Me in such detail that before you knew it, there I was, big as life, with lots of very complimentary attributes and a well-developed personality, as well as being extremely entertaining —the sort of a person you'd enjoy having as a bachelor uncle.

That's just an example, of course. He went out practically every evening, the guy did, so he needed lots of alibis. He couldn't very well use just Me, he had to think of other higher beings to put in his stories, as characters. There was Me, of course, and Zeus, and Jupiter—you get the picture. But I was the first one, I remember that distinctly. The first one, and the most interesting. I'm not bragging, you understand, in fact I'm being humble, because what I'm saying is, I'm not personally responsible for all those fine qualities, I got them involuntarily, the guy—the "he" —just started piling them on to Me as a way of making himself look good to his lady friend (did I mention they weren't married?) by telling her what a top-notch higher being he was associating with.

The end.

Gates was astounded. "And *that's* the revelation?" he asked.

"That's it, Roe," said His Holiness proudly. Then, a little apologetically, "Has kind of an abrupt ending, doesn't it."

"We're pressed for time," said Gates, shaking his head in disbelief. "We'll get to the phones, right after this message."

§

"Have you got them on the line?" asked studio-confined Roe Gates, turning to an able young female assistant.

"They're ready, willing, and able."

"How do you want us to do this?" he asked, sipping his drink.

"We'll start with the gal from Missouri, then hit him with our surprise."

"They know what to say?"

"Missouri is gonna wing it," said the woman. "Nevada's all set up."

"Ten seconds," said a voice.

Gates placed his Manhattan out of camera view and prepared his camera face.

He pressed a button on his desk.

"Shyleen from Missouri, you're on the air—Shyleen, are you there?"

"Yes," reported a Missouri voice. "I'd just like to say it sounds to me like he's an atheist."

"The pope? An atheist?" said Gates, affecting astonishment but secretly savoring the irony. "Did you hear that, Your Holiness? The lady from Missouri called you an atheist."

"I don't like to quibble," said His Holiness, "but I believe she was referring to God."

"God? Of course she was referring to God. What do you mean, you believe she was referring to God?"

"Let's look at what she said," said the pope. "She said, and correct me if I'm wrong, she said, 'It sounds to me like He's an atheist.' *He* referring to God."

"I see what you mean. But I also heard what she said, and I could swear she was referring to you in that statement. 'It sounds to me like he's an atheist.' *He* referring to you."

"I distinctly heard an upper case in her voice."

"It was your imagination. Her voice quite clearly purveyed the lower case."

It was former lawyer against amateur lawyer, a great show. Who was ahead on points? At this point only God knew.

"Perhaps we could settle this controversy by taking a telephone poll," suggested the pope. "All those who heard an upper case in Shyleen from Missouri's voice can call one 900 number, and all those who heard a lower case in her voice can call another 900 number. There will be a nominal charge for both options."

"Maybe we should just ask her," countered Gates.

"Stipulated," agreed the pope, who was enjoying this new role in his life. "Let's ask her."

"Ma'am," inquired Gates, "which one of us is correct, the pope or me?"

"I'm all confused," admitted Shyleen. "All I want to know is if the pope is an atheist."

"Was that your original question?" asked the pope.

"That's what I called to talk about," she said. "I wanted to know if you're an atheist, because it sure sounded to me like you are."

"You didn't want to know if God is an atheist?" asked the pope.

"The thought never crossed my mind."

"In that case I'm going to have to apologize," said His Holiness. "I could have sworn you were wanting to know if God is an atheist. But now I see I was mistaken. Even us popes make mistakes, except of course when we're speaking *ex cathedra*, which is Latin for 'from the chair,' in which case our observations are usually right on the button."

"So," persisted the Missouri woman, "are you or aren't you?"

"Am I or am I not what?"

"An atheist."

"I'm a little confused," confessed the pope. "Could you please repeat the question in its entirety?"

"Are you, or are you not, an atheist?"

"I'll take the second option. Not."

"Pardon me for saying so, but it sure sounds like it."

"How so?" inquired the pope.

"Well, take your new quote-unquote 'revelation,' for instance. It distinctly says God was simply made up as an alibi. Right?"

"Right," agreed the pope. "Where do you get atheism out of that?"

"What it amounts to is, God is a figment of our imagination. He's just a fictional character."

"I don't know if I like that word *just*. Of course He's a fictional character! But *just*? You make it sound like there's something wrong with being a fictional character, which there certainly is not. Take Huckleberry Finn, for example. Millions of Americans have gotten entertainment, pleasure, and large doses of wisdom from Huck Finn, a fictional character, but not *just* a fictional character."

"So you put God in the same category as Huckleberry Finn?" persisted the woman from Missouri.

"Oh, absolutely."

"In other words, God doesn't really exist."

"Let me ask you this, Shyleen from Missouri. Does Huck Finn exist?"

"Just as a fictional character."

"There you go with 'just' again!"

"Okay," agreed Shyleen, "as a fictional character."

"So Huck Finn exists as a fictional character."

"Right," conceded Shyleen with a sigh.

"So Huck Finn exists," said the pope.

"Right."

"Therefore, God exists."

"I guess so. But not really."

"What do you mean, not really? He has a *fundamentum in re*, doesn't he?"

"Which is Latin for—?"

"In the vernacular, it means 'foundation in reality.'"

"I'm sorry," interrupted Gates, "but we've got another caller on the line." He pressed a button on his desk. "Hello, Virginia from

Nevada, you're on the air. What's your question for His Holiness?"

Virginia from Nevada wanted to return to the subject of the angel.

"Yes?" said Gates. "Do you have a specific question?"

"I'd just like to have the pope describe her physical appearance."

"Pope, did you hear that? The lady from Nevada wants you to describe the physical appearance of your so-called 'angel of the Lord.'"

"Let's see," said the pope, looking thoughtful. "She was, oh, about five foot eight, a hundred and twenty-five pounds, statuesque—there's a word that fits her perfectly, *statuesque*—"

"Did she have a coquettish smile?" asked Virginia.

"Ah, yessss—," said the former Benny Gottlieb. Then he changed his mind. "No, not a coquettish smile, definitely not, not at all—and come to think of it, she was only about five foot two and weighed, oh, at least two hundred pounds, in fact, she was probably closer to three hundred—"

"What was the color of her hair?" inquired Virginia.

"Her hair. . . ," said the pope.

Gates attempted to help his guest along. "Pope," he said, "Virginia from Nevada wants to know the color of the angel's hair."

"The angel's hair. . . ," said the pope.

"Its color," prompted Gates with obvious delight.

"Its color. . . ," said the pope with obvious anxiety.

"Well?" said Gates. "We're waiting. . . . The world is waiting to hear the color of the angel's hair."

"White," said the pope. "That's right. White. It was white. Definitely white."

"White? She was twenty-one years old, and she had white hair?"

"What did it look like in the dark?" asked Virginia.

"Who said anything about the dark?" asked the pope.

Benedict XVI suddenly heard the sound of his own voice over the telephone. "'Come to think of it, in the dark she's usually brunette,'" he heard himself say. "'We spend a lot of time in the dark together, Arielle and I. Strolling along the river under the moon— holding hands—discussing the poetry of Allen Ginsberg—asking profound questions—that kind of a thing.'"

"Who—," said the Benedict of the present.

"'I'm not prepared—,'" said a recorded voice very much like that of Virginia from Nevada.

"'Shhh. Neither am I,'" he heard himself say.

"'I wouldn't want to get—,'" said the Virginia-like voice.

"'There's always abortion,'" he heard himself whisper.

"'What?'" said the Virginia-like voice.

"'There's always abortion,'" he heard himself say.

"'Could you speak up?'" said the familiar voice.

"'THERE'S ALWAYS ABORTION!'" he heard himself shout.

There was silence at the Vatican for what seemed to be half an hour. Then His Holiness quickly got up from his chair and left.

"Pope?" said Gates.

Silence at the Vatican.

"Benedict XVI?" said Gates.

The silence continued.

"I guess he's gone," reported Gates. "Let's go to a commercial."

"Nightgrill" went to a commercial.

"He's gone?" asked the woman in his studio.

"Gone," said Gates with a satisfied smile. "Thanks. You were a great help, Ms. Good."

17

Endgame

THAT NIGHT AMERICA DID NOT SLEEP WELL. What about the divine revelation His Holiness had received? it asked itself. Was it the genuine article, or was it, as Roe Gates hinted, a fraud? Was the pope an atheist, as Shyleen from Missouri seemed to suggest? Was God just a fictional character? If so, was there anything terribly wrong with being a fictional character?

Was that really the voice of His Holiness on the tape? Did he in fact support a woman's right to choose?

Were all those investigative reports—about the pope's having replaced the Vatican staff with his cronies, about the Catholic Church owning a Las Vegas resort with a casino and escort service, about the pope's active sex life, about the conversion of convents into brothels, about a New York agency skimming off fifteen percent of the Church's holdings—were all those reports true, after all, and not just part of a smear campaign orchestrated by the far right?

And if they were true, was this just a private matter between the pope, his agent, his mistresses, and his God?

Had Benedict XVI blown it as the first American pope?

The next day, the pope's "Nightgrill" appearance was the subject of every American talk show, many of which featured an appearance by Michael Cardinal Bacchus, who said what he could to mend the damage. The attack dogs, however, had the advantage. They were in the actual studio, usually seated across from the host; Bacchus was in the distant Vatican, usually appearing on a screen, floating around in virtual space. They were asking the disturbing questions that had kept America awake all night; he was trying to answer with the Gottlieb logic he had been learning from Benny.

Mike was, he himself thought, semi-successful. Toward the end of the longest day in history, he had thought up an answer to the question the critics were beginning to ask: why wasn't His Holiness curious to know the origin of the girls in the Iowa corn field? His answer: His Holiness was at that very moment in his cell, on his knees, praying for a new revelation that would rend the veil hiding that remaining mystery.

But the next morning, a spot *Today/Enquirer* poll reported that Pope Benedict's approval rating was showing slippage. The American public had been asked, "In general, do you approve or disapprove of the job Benedict XVI is doing as pope?"

Those who approved constituted 69% of those polled; those who registered disapproval rose to 21%, with 10% "other" (either not sure or withholding their judgment or "couldn't care less.")

Broken down according to religious preference:

Catholics: approving 45%; disapproving 39%; other, 16%.
Protestants: approving 46%; disapproving 50%; other 4%.
Jews: approving 4%; disapproving 3%; other 93%.
Muslims: approving 3%; disapproving 4%; other 93%.
Unaffiliated: approving 95%; disapproving 1%; other 4%.

Commentators could not, however, agree on the significance of the drop in His Excellency's popularity, which one short month ago had stood near the historic high of 92% set by Pope Peter I immediately after Christ had established the papacy. One anonymous source, thought to be close to Cardinal Geronti, attributed what he referred to as "this unprecedented plunge" to "the stench of moral turpitude emanating from the pope's advisors, indeed—and I fervently pray it were not so—from the pope himself." Another pundit, thought to be representing the view of Cardinal Bacchus, cited these poll results as "quite natural, indeed typical of the end of the traditional 'honeymoon' period every pope enjoys on assuming office."

§

Esther Geld flew in from New York, accompanied by two new scandals.

"What are we going to do about the Geronti thing?" she asked the brain trust. "And what's this COTWOD thing all about?"

Ms. Geld was referring to a further investigation of Virginia Sweet's now-infamous tape, which showed that, besides containing then-Cardinal Gottlieb's ill-considered suggestion that abortion was a viable option, also showed that then-Cardinal Gottlieb had apparently planned to capture the papacy by sandbagging still-Cardinal Geronti. She was also referring to the media report that an informed source within the Vatican was alleging that Benedict XVI was a front for the Church of the Wide Open Door (COTWOD).

"Benny!!" she said with God-like wrath. "How could you have been so stupid?!"

Benny looked at the ceiling. The brain trust followed his gaze. They were again meeting in the Sistine Chapel. The pope was looking at *The Fall of Man and the Expulsion from the Garden of Eden*, a painting by Michelangelo.

"Benny!" she continued in the some tone. "Come clean on COTWOD!"

Benny looked at the wall above the altar. "Nice picture," he said. He was referring to *The Last Judgment*, a painting by the same artist.

"This is not an art lesson!" screamed Ms. Geld. She was in Benny's face.

Benny looked at Mike. "Tell her about COTWOD," he sighed, feeling about his person for an expensive cigar.

Mike gave a brief account of the relation between Benny's relatively minor missionary activity with COTWOD and his papal responsibilities, emphasizing the anguish Benny felt because of his divided loyalties.

Esther Geld replied with a somewhat longer account of her opinion of this admittedly-awkward arrangement, emphasizing the anguish she felt because of being excluded from her fifteen percent of Benny's COTWOD salary.

Mike pointed out that this was all past history. The future, he said, was the thing that concerned him most.

Esther Geld pointed out that the future depended on their ability to locate the "informed source within the Vatican."

"I think he's a double agent," said Andrea.

"It could be a she," observed Ron. This time he was not consulting his watch.

Esther looked at Benny closely and in a prosecutorial manner. "Where's Lucy?"

"She's working on the case," said Benny.

"On which side?" inquired Esther.

Benny did not answer. He was again looking at the ceiling, more specifically at a detail of *The Fall of Man* depicting Eve and her special relation to a large, impressive serpent.

"Benny!" shrieked Esther.

"I have an idea," said Benny.

The brain trust showed an interest in hearing Benny's idea.

Mike expected to hear Benny suggest that they wait till the storm blew over. Andrea expected Benny to say he would come up with a divine revelation showing that Mary's grandmother had been born free from original sin by divine grace. Esther expected Benny to say almost anything. Ron had no expectations, being at that moment headed for the men's room.

Benny lit a Fuente Fuente OpusX. "I think," he said, "I should resign."

The brain trust looked at Benny in disbelief. They looked at each other. They were agape. Benny? Resign? The most creative, innovative pope of the modern era, giving it all up? They were incredulous. They could not believe this was happening. Their jobs were at stake. And they were fully invested.

"Here's what we do," said Benny, waving his cigar about in the grand manner. "We send Mike over to Geronti. Mike feels him out on the subject. Mike strikes a deal. We get the rest of South America. We keep our Vegas holdings. We retain fifty percent of the profits from the convents. We get the assurance of a papal pardon and a promise on the Bible that he'll pray for us sinners, now and at the hour of our death."

"What if *he* dies before *we* do?" asked Andrea.

"He'll be in heaven, for God's sake. People pray in heaven. Am I right, Mike?"

"I doubt it," said Mike.

"Really? Why?"

"The need is no longer there."

Benny thought about this. Then he said, "I see your point. But he can at least put in a good word for us."

"There you go," said Mike.

"What if he doesn't make it to heaven?" asked Andrea.

"A pope?" said Benny incredulously. "Not making it to heaven?"

"It's conceivable," said Ron, just back from the men's room.

Benny looked closely at *The Last Judgment*. He frowned. "You just might be right."

§

Pope Benedict XVI stood before a battery of microphones and cameras, preparing to read a statement that he and the author of *Religion for Dolts* had prepared the preceding night and that Andrea had edited that very morning. Ron and Mike had also had noteworthy input, a fact duly reported on their suddenly-significant resumés.

"This will be brief," he said. "I stand before you today as the second Jewish pope and, what is perhaps even more important, the first American pope. It is with great sadness that I announce that I am resigning the papacy, effective immediately, to spend more time with my family. I think I have been a good pope. I think I have been a ground-breaking pope. But I leave those judgments in the hands of the historians.

"I have given this matter long and prayerful consideration. My conclusion is that this action is in the best interests of the Church and of my career. It also happens to be God's will.

"In relinquishing the papacy, I am also relinquishing the name Benedict XVI. Hereafter I will revert to my original name, Benny Gottlieb."

Benedict XVI removed his papal regalia and stood before the media as Benny Gottlieb. He lit a cigar, a Swisher Sweet.

"I have time for several questions."

The media were stunned. None of them had ever seen a pope resign. None of them had ever seen a resigned pope light a cigar. The majority of them had never seen a pope, resigned or staying the course, in his underwear. But they quickly quit being stunned. They were professional in the best sense of the word. Being professionals, they began to put questions to the ex-pope. Benny answered these questions to the best of his ability.

Q: You spoke of a family. Who did you have in mind?

A: I was referring to my brothers and sisters.

Q: Why haven't we heard of them before?

A: Probably because they're deceased.

Q: How can you spend time with dead people?

A: You may think I'm a little old-fashioned, but I still believe in séances.

Q: You said you'll be going by the name of *Benny* Gottlieb. Wasn't your name originally *Benedict?*

A: You've got a point. But I always hated the name Benedict. Who names a kid Benedict anymore? It's like Greenleaf. A couple of centuries ago there was this American poet called John

Greenleaf Whittier. Americans still name their kids John, and there are probably still Whittiers in the world. But Greenleaf? Give me a break. I rest my case.

Q: Your resignation. Could it possibly have anything to do with all these scandals?

A: Scandals? Which scandals? I never read the newspapers. So to answer your question, madam, my resignation has nothing, I repeat nothing, absolutely nothing, to do with these so-called "scandals." Which, by the way, were blown out of proportion by the media.

Q: What are your plans for the future?

A: All I can say to that is that I've been approached by many people and that I'm weighing my options. I think of this step, not as the end of Benny Gottlieb's career as a public servant, but as a new opportunity.

Q: Do you plan to remain Catholic?

A: As I said, I'm weighing all options. Sorry, no more questions. Now if you'll excuse me, I've got to catch a plane.

§

Michael Cardinal Bacchus had indeed been able to strike a bargain with Cardinal Geronti, contingent of course on Geronti's being elected pope, which both parties agreed was a foregone conclusion, pending the just and efficient working of God's revised will. On the question of South America, Geronti had stood his ground; Mike had, however, been able to come away with Cuba, if and when it were ever to revert to its Catholic status. On the question of the Church's Vegas holdings, Mike prevailed, perhaps because Geronti was eager to rid himself of unpleasant memories of his experience there. On the question of retaining fifty percent of the profits from the convents, a compromise was reached: Benedict XVI would retain twenty-five percent, but only on the condition that the convents revert to their original purpose. On the question of the papal pardon and intercession before the divine throne, Geronti insisted instead on the excommunication of Benedict XVI as well as of his entire entourage. Mike held out for a promise that there be no public announcement of this action, sharing the secret that Benedict had already been excommunicated from two religions and pointing out that a third would amount to cruel and unusual punishment, which was unconstitutional. Cardinal Geronti, though not conversant with the American Constitution, graciously granted this request on general Christian principles.

America was more forgiving. On returning to the shores of the New World, Benny discovered that his popularity had soared overnight. According to a *Today/Enquirer* poll, his approval rating had skyrocketed. Eighty-three percent of the American public had been impressed with Benny's wanting to spend more time with his family. The remaining seventeen percent were less impressed, citing skepticism about séances.

The Esther Geld Agency, Inc., was able to procure for him a nationwide speaking tour, a multimillion dollar advance on a trilogy detailing the story of his life, and a movie deal based on the trilogy. The agency was also rumored to be dickering with fifteen cable networks over plans to revive "Religion Talk," with Benny Gottlieb as host.

"Life," observed Benny over drinks in the Las Vegas Bellagio only one week after his resignation from the highest spiritual office in the universe, "is good."

"What's next?" said Mike, flirting with a whiskey sour and a passing young woman.

"Higher things," said Benny, winking and igniting an expensive panatela and preparing to sign autographs by a mob of well-wishers that had just recognized him.

§

Several years later, Maven Plum and Benny Gottlieb were strolling down a path, her hand resting lightly on his arm. They were filming a special, "An Evening with Maven Plum."

She gazed around at her surroundings. "What a *lovely, lovely* garden," she said, extending her palms to the heavens.

"The finest in Palm Springs," he said proudly.

"I have to say, Benny, you've done very well for yourself. Very well indeed."

"Thank you, Maven," he said modestly.

"The book . . . the movie! Nine Academy Awards!"

"Best picture, best actor, best supporting actress, best director, best screenplay—"

"Best musical score, best cinematography . . . what were the other two?"

"I always lose track," Benny said with a modest chuckle.

"My! Very impressive indeed. You *have* done extremely well for yourself."

Benny plucked a mango from an available tree. "America," he observed, "is the land of opportunity."

At this point the cameraman slipped and fell. "Cut!" he cried.

He picked himself up. "Sorry," he said.

"Did you get the stuff about America and opportunity?" asked a slightly peeved Ms. Plum.

"Yeah," said the cameraman, dusting off his pants.

"Ready to proceed?" she asked.

"Yeah."

"Let's roll," she said curtly.

The cameraman began to shoot again, embarrassed that he had blown his bit role.

Ms. Plum turned to her guest, lifted her chin, and adopted a look of intense seriousness. "Let me ask you this, Benny. Why *did* you resign the papacy?"

"I knew that question was bound to come up."

"Well? Your many fans and admirers want to know."

They strolled along in silence.

"Was it the scandals?"

Benny reverted to an effective silence before continuing. "I guess what it comes down to is, I just got tired of being a role model."

"*A* role model? *The* role model!"

"Okay," the former pope agreed, "*the* role model, the *senior* role model to the youth of the world. It was the pressure more than anything else, waking up every morning in my cell—"

"Your *single* cell!"

"That's right, waking up in my single cell, knowing that the world was looking up to me for moral and spiritual guidance, mothers and fathers were always pointing me out to their children as an example to follow, they were always saying, 'Be like him, be like His Holiness,' that's what I mean by the pressure, the incredible pressure, plus the fact that my work was finished, the question that always used to be considered unanswerable, where did God come from, now has an answer, because of the revelation I've been able to procure for the Church, and those are the reasons I resigned, it had nothing, I repeat absolutely nothing, to do with those so-called 'scandals.'"

"The women in your life," said Maven Plum. "I hate to bring this up, but—"

"Oh, that's perfectly all right," sighed Benny, biting his lower lip.

"Your guru, Arielle; your agent, Esther Geld; your ex-wife, Lucy; the angel Meredith; some would say your ghostwriter, Andrea; not to speak of the women you kept caged in your Kansas basement—the list goes on and on. How in heaven's name do you answer your detractors on that score?"

"They always want to bring up those old rumors, don't they. And I refuse, I absolutely refuse, to dignify them with an answer. But I'd like to make one thing perfectly clear. My relation with my agent, Ms. Geld, has always been, and let me emphasize this, purely professional."

She looked up at him, her eyes shining with admiration. "I just wanted to give you a chance to set the record straight, Benny."

"I appreciate that, Maven," said Benny, touching her shoulder.

The cameraman, Benny, and Ms. Plum came to a bend in the path. All three negotiated it successfully.

"There's also the question of your past," continued Ms. Plum. "There are persistent reports—"

"I know, I know," said Benny with a sigh.

"Don't interrupt me, please, I have to say this, as a conscientious reporter, that there are persistent stories going around that Gottlieb isn't your real name; that you aren't really Jewish, you were an orphan, brought up by an elderly Amish rabbit farmer named Good who called you Bunny; that you were excommunicated from the Amish church and sent packing; that you were befriended by an elderly evangelist named Reverend Barnabas; that in return for his kindness you got his young wife pregnant and then ran off with her; that after she bore you twins you divorced her; that you are currently thirty years behind on child support payments; that you were never a Unitarian minister, you were a truck driver who was intimate with every waitress from Maine to California, and after that a radio talk show host who got fired for fooling around with the boss's wife; that at the insistence of your agent you later adopted the name Benedict Gottlieb as a ploy to advance your religious career, the idea being, what's sauce for Saint Paul, who changed his name from Saul, can be sauce for Benny Good; that meteorological evidence suggests that you weren't really hit by lightning on the road to Topeka but were just borrowing another page from Saint Paul's book; that for years you have been addicted to cigars, strong drink, and gambling, not to speak of sex; that you have consistently refused to seek professional help for your problems."

Benny maintained a stoic silence.

"And how do you answer those persistent reports?" she finally inquired.

"What can I say?" asked Benny, throwing up his hands. "I'm circumcised."

Ms. Plum touched Benny's elbow with her hand and looked up at him with adoring eyes. "Others may disagree, and that is their privilege," she said, "but that's good enough for me."

They strolled.

"I've always wanted to ask you this," she went on. "Do you consider yourself a martyr?"

"Oh no. Not at all. Well, maybe just a little. My treatment by the media was not a pleasant experience. They parked outside my home, the phones never stopped ringing, I was subject to vilification, even character assassination of the worst sort, they scourged me, once or twice they spat upon me, they delivered me unto my enemies, the worst of whom, incidentally, I wouldn't want to go through the unspeakable horrors I've had to endure from those publicity-seeking bloodhounds. But I've learned to put the past behind me, to forgive and forget."

"Do you consider yourself—"

"I know what you're going to ask," interrupted Benny. "No, I don't consider myself a hero. That's a tremendous concept. Hero. I can't in all candid honesty say I consider myself a hero. I merely consider myself an average American who was brought up in very humble circumstances, who, in spite of overwhelming negative odds, has made the most of what this wonderful country has to offer."

They continued to stroll, this time in silence.

"The presidency," she went on. "You've also been mentioned—prominently mentioned, I might add—as the last great hope of this nation; the man with the solution to the problems of Social Security and Medicare; the problem of the environment; the drug problem; the problem of a decaying infrastructure; of the rapid depletion of the ozone layer; of the loss of a moral center; and of course of the terrorist threat and dealing with the problem of weapons of mass destruction. May I ask you, Benny, what are your thoughts on this matter of the presidency?"

"Oh, I'm sure there are many many others with equally good ideas," Benny said modestly.

"Who would you have in mind?"

"I wouldn't want to get into the business of naming names."

Ms. Plum paused and gazed at her guest intensely. "Tell me, Benny," she said. "Would you accept a draft?"

Benny looked directly at the camera. "I suppose if enough red-blooded patriotic Americans wanted me, then. . . ."

"Then?"

"Then I might consider it."

"Otherwise?"

"Otherwise," said Benny, indicating his living quarters, "I'd be quite happy to spend the rest of my life in this modest mansion."

"And what a marvelous mansion it is!"

"Would you like a tour?"

"I'd *love* it."

And so after dismissing the cameraman, Benny Gottlieb proceeded to give Maven Plum a tour of his Palm Springs habitat, a splendid building modeled on the White House. It began with the marble-pillared entrance. It included the bowling alley and the servants' quarters. It ended in the master bedroom.

Epilogue

I GAVE THE PRECEDING CHAPTERS to a small but representative focus group and asked for their input about two issues: (1) the absence in my story of any reference to the priest-as-pedophile outrage in the American Catholic Church, and (2) the question whether I should reveal what ultimately happens to the hero of my tale.

Many of the members of this group had noticed that the novel makes no reference to pedophilic priests and their fondness for altar boys, to say nothing of cardinals and bishops and their fondness for confidentiality.

Several proposed that I should update the story. The simplest way to do this, advised one thoughtful young woman, would be to expand the reference to Benny's pedophile activities during his stint as a truck driver, making sure to point out that the waifs for whom his Peterbilt provided "a home away from home" were exclusively, or at least prominently, male. This prompted a warm discussion of whether the term "waif" refers exclusively to a female child or is gender-neutral. The argument was cut short by an astute observation that Benny is Benny, a born womanizer, and that to insert such extraneous material would destroy the consistency of his character.

An alternative resolution of this problem, remarked the young woman, would be to portray Mike Bacchus as a pedophile. He was already an alcoholic, she argued; why not take the further step of making him a sexual deviate? But several in the group pointed out—rightly, I believe—that following this route would give Bacchus too much prominence, which would threaten Benny's position as the story's protagonist. It's Benny's story, someone pointed out; let Mike Bacchus be satisfied with his supporting role, which is, after all, significantly larger than that of the unfortunate cameraman.

Why not, asked an older gentleman who admitted that he had once aspired to write the Great American Novel but had given up this hope after burning the seventy-sixth draft—why not rethink the entire novel and begin anew, with a new plot and new characters? No one else championed this idea. In fact, it was at this point that several turned to me and asked my opinion. I replied that I did not like to kill off my characters. Are you saying, someone asked, that where fiction is concerned, you allow sex but no violence? Yes, I said, provided that the sex is portrayed with both delicacy and taste and is combined with philosophical discussion.

What, then, should be done about the novel's avoidance of any mention of the pedophile scandal?

This stage of the discussion ended abruptly with a wise woman's observation that compared to the goings-on in *Benedict XVI*, the scandal of priests and altar boys and payoffs and cover-ups looks like copy for a slow-news day.

After that problem had been resolved, we turned to the question of possible endings. As the author of this novel, I told them, I had developed a strong attachment to my central character and was concerned about his ultimate fate. Or maybe I just couldn't decide what, if anything, to do with him. And so I thought the group might provide that bolt from the blue that I had been waiting for but that had not yet hit me.

A slight majority of my focus group voiced the strong opinion that Benny should go on to become president, a position, they all agreed, that matched his set of job skills. Someone raised the objection that Esther Geld was already the agent for both of the two leading candidates, Governor Snow (Democrat) and General Brewster (Republican). Several suggested that our Benny run as a third-party candidate, preferably the nominee of a party no one has yet heard of. Someone else raised the objection that in order to be a viable candidate, Benny should be married. Several others suggested that he get back together with Lucy, but not, of course, before giving her the child support payments he owed her. Both of these suggestions turned out to be popular. So did the further proposal that after assuming office, Benny should move the U. S. Government to Las Vegas.

The others in the group were divided on this question of an appropriate ending. One middle-aged man argued that in a last chapter, I should depict Benny as growing bored with Palm Springs and the Maven Plums of the world and going back to being a truck driver and renewing his acquaintances with the Dollys of the world. This gentleman was hooted down, however, the general consensus being that though this might be a happy ending, it was not quite believable.

Another man, somewhat younger, thought I should send Benny back to the mission field for COTWOD (the Church of the Wide Open Door), spreading the gospel of Christian Tantrism, preferably in Manhattan. The others frowned on this suggestion, some because they believed Tantrism was already entrenched on that grand island, though perhaps not in its Christian form and perhaps with a slight relaxation of the Tantric standards, others because of their concern for the message it would send about a major public health issue.

Several leaned toward the option of having Benny go back to being the host of "Religion Talk." Though we spent some time bandying this idea about, we concluded that this path would lead nowhere. If in the last thousands of years the entire human race has reached no conclusion about the great religious issues, why would we expect a radio talk show to? A novel needs a strong ending. Sending Benny back to "Religion Talk" would not provide it.

One woman had the original idea of having Benny repent, make good on his child support payments, and move to Sri Lanka to adopt the Buddhist lifestyle. If a 'sixties drop-out from North Dakota can do it, she argued, why couldn't the main character? I myself thought this was a good point, but soon found that the suggestion only led to a heated debate within the group between that woman and several practicing Christians.

Another person—I don't recall the gender—proposed an alternative. Benny, said this person, should certainly repent, but instead of converting to either Buddhism or evangelical Christianity, he should simply rejoin the Amish and become a rabbit farmer. We all agreed that this would be an excellent ending, from the viewpoint of literary structure, and that it would give the lie to the cliché that you can't go home again. Several, however, thought this solution might be interpreted as being insensitive to the Amish. I was forced to counter that (1) the first chapter could already be interpreted as being insensitive to the Amish and (2) the Amish wouldn't read the novel anyway. This reply got us off on a long discussion of the two unrelated issues of political correctness (for example, how does one define it? has it become too vague a concept?) and the Amish (for example, do the Amish really practice excommunication? do they baptize their young, and if so, at what age? was Bunny Good a typical example of an Amish youth? do the Amish raise rabbits?).

One of the women finally got us off this fruitless discussion by recommending that in the last chapter, Benny should end up finding his mother on her deathbed, dying of cancer. Another quickly agreed, but suggested that cancer be replaced by AIDS. A third agreed with the second, going on to suggest that this would provide an appropriate opportunity for Benny to repent. A fourth quickly developed the idea that the story should end with Benny himself on a deathbed, dying of AIDS and eager to repent.

I don't recall who threw the first punch. All I remember is leaving the focus group to settle the issue in its own fashion while I made my way home to ponder this problem of a proper and convincing ending.

After much consideration, I have decided not to add a final chapter. I am calling it quits. My thinking is that a final chapter would be redundant. A rags-to-riches tale of how unscrupulous but charming Benny Good, a.k.a. Benny Gottlieb, becomes President of the United States would only repeat this story describing how unscrupulous but charming Benny Good, a.k.a. Benedict Gottlieb, became Pope Benedict XVI.

B. S. Buller[1]
New York City

The reader might wish to read another of the author's books, *Religion for Dolts.*

About the Author

PAUL WIEBE grew up in the Idaho outback. Early on he found that the life of irrigating spuds, driving trucks, repairing fences, digging ditches, chasing mad steers across the open range, and castrating the occasional boar was not to his liking.

This discovery led him to the halls of higher education. Bethel College (Kansas) granted him a B.A.; the University of Chicago eventually presented him with a Ph.D. and sent him away to Wichita State University. There he taught religion and literature and performed the tasks of his chosen profession—translating and writing books on the theory of religion, composing footnotes for journal articles, and arriving late at the meetings of those committees he could recall having been assigned to.

But his mastery of the academic proprieties was never more than tenuous. Thus it came as no surprise to his colleagues and students when he resigned his tenured position and, in an attempt to recapture a vanishing sanity, took to writing comic novels, which, besides *Benedict XVI*, include *Dead White Male*, *The Church of the Comic Spirit*, and *Christian Bride, Muslim Mosque*, all published by Komos Books.

Wiebe now lives in Southern California with his wife and pet mockingbird.

www.ingramcontent.com/pod-product-compliance
Lightning Source LLC
Chambersburg PA
CBHW030921120626
46554CB00001B/220